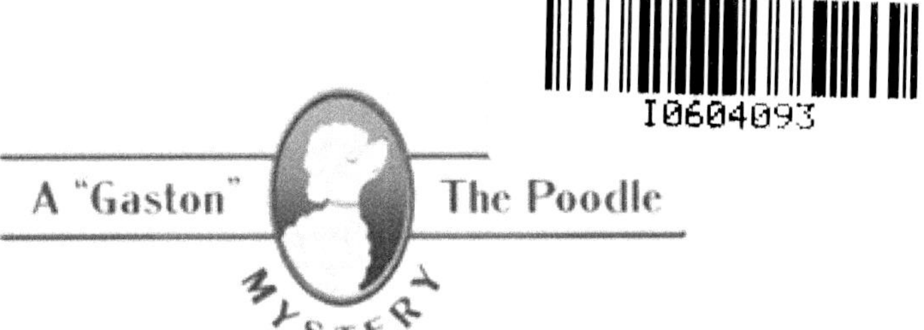

TO DIE FOR PICKLEBALL

JANICE DETRIE

To Die for Pickleball
Copyright © 2024 by Janice Detrie

ISBN: 978-0-9987342-3-1
All rights reserved
Printed in the United States of America

No part of this book may be used or reproduced in any manner whatsoever without the written permission of the author except in the case of brief quotations embodied in critical articles and reviews.

This is a work of fiction. Names, characters, places, and incidents are either a product of the author's imagination or are used fictitiously. Any resemblance to actual events, or persons or locales, living or dead, is purely coincidental.

Published by
Janice Detrie

Cover design by Eric Labacz
www.labaczdesign.com

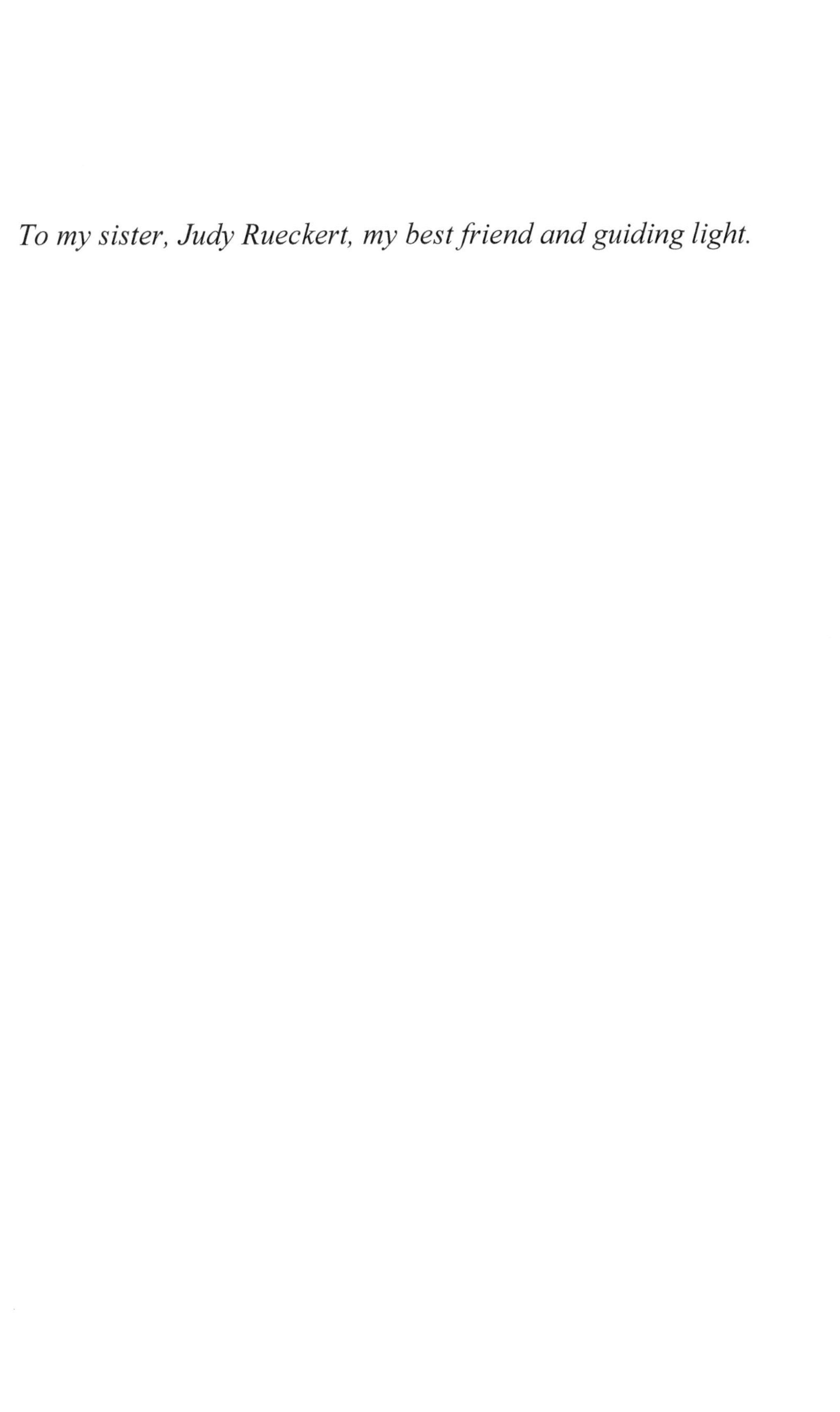

To my sister, Judy Rueckert, my best friend and guiding light.

CHAPTER ONE

Sandra Tooksbury didn't believe in fate or kismet, or some Karma God waiting to punish or reward your every action. But she did believe in love.

Sandra marched to the hair salon early in the morning and transformed herself from an eighty-year-old grey relic into a ravishing redhead, complete with teased tendrils and a glittery rhinestone barrette. Additionally, she wore her favorite jade green tunic and matching leggings, topped off with her new peacock boa. The exotic creation with bright turquoise and blue "eyes" nestled among the green feathers only cost $166 on eBay. Her Medic-Alert device was tucked discreetly inside her bodice.

As she perched on the hard metal bleachers in the drafty gymnasium with Gaston, her slightly overweight poodle, she felt like a Bird of Paradise in a chicken coop. The odor of stale sweat still lingered, despite the acrid smell of industrial floor cleaner and fresh polyurethane. A slight chill from the air conditioner prompted her to wrap her boa a bit tighter. She surveyed the nearly empty gym with its sagging basketball hoops and darkened scoreboard and marveled again that retired people actually rose before ten o'clock in the morning to come to such an inhospitable place.

Although Sandra wrestled for an hour with him, Gaston had finally submitted to donning the fake service dog harness, his familiar undercover disguise. He stopped trying to tear it off with his sharp little teeth. Were they investigating a new case, the famous dog detective and his advanced in years but worldly-wise owner? No, not this time.

Sandra Tooksbury was in love, a foolish notion for a woman approaching eighty-one years. But it undeniably was love in all its glory. She knew by the way her heart beat a bit faster when her new man drew near—once she reassured herself it wasn't her pacemaker acting up. Her stomach did little flip-flops even after she chomped on a double dose of extra strength antacid tablets. The sight of him in his athletic shorts made her breath quicken so much she kept a spare inhaler in her purse. So what if her beau was a tad younger than she was? Look at Ashton Kutcher and

Demi Moore. Better yet, Brigitte Macron and Emmanuel Macron; he was her high school student when they met. Age is only a meaningless number. Her new love, Arthur Ashenbrenner, possessed one claim to fame—his prowess at pickleball. Sandra reluctantly agreed to come to the gym to watch him play, although it was the last place where she wanted to spend her morning. Love will make you do strange things.

Her new man, Arthur, hummed an old Led Zeppelin tune while he set up a little net that looked like something toddlers would use for kiddie tennis. Resplendent in his crisp, white gym shorts and his lucky shirt, a green four-leaf clover formed with pickleball paddles on a black background, he looked every inch the Silver Fox. Another player was also busy setting up a little net, one of three stretched across the width of the gym.

A round-shouldered, white-haired man shuffled to the bleachers where she sat, moving so slowly Sandra feared he'd pass away standing up. Black knee braces seemed to hold him upright. He plopped a blue gym bag on the bench beside her and eased himself down on the seat.

"I'm Franklin Zuehlke. Are you joining us today?" Through thick horn-rimmed glasses, he eyed her from head to toe, stopping at her green strappy sandals. "I hope you have some gym shoes to change into. You won't last long in those flimsy things."

"My name is Sandra. No, I'm not playing pickleball. I'm just here to watch my gentleman friend play." She gestured to where Arthur was attaching the little net to a pole.

The old fellow blocked her view of Arthur bending over in his shorts, his still firm derriere looking good for someone over seventy.

Sandra tried not to let the disappointment show on her face as she politely replied, "I take it you play every Monday and Wednesday mornings, too?"

"I'm ninety. Never underestimate an old man with a pickleball paddle. But I'm no match for the Ashmeister. That man is a legend on the pickleball court. Not even a mind reader could predict where his spin serve will bounce. His volleys speed like a cruise missile and are just as deadly."

"Serves? Volleys? I remember hearing those words in tennis."

"Tennis? Hah! Pickleball requires more finesse. For instance, Arthur's dinks are as soft as baby kisses, just clearing the net and dropping straight to the floor."

"I have no idea what you're talking about, but it sounds

impressive." Sandra gave him an encouraging smile.

"It is. Everybody wants to be his partner and nobody wants to play against him. He's really out of our league." Franklin let out a wistful sigh.

"He plays in another more competitive league, but he enjoys this relaxed play just as much. That's why he's invited me to watch."

Her eyes followed Arthur as he took out an accordion pleated fence and stretched it across the floor, dividing the gym in half. This time Sandra could take in his graceful movements with no obstructions.

"He'd like me to join him in pickleball. But with my health issues, I'm not so sure. As you can see, my service dog comes wherever I go."

At the mention of the word dog, Gaston let out a little yip.

The old man reached out to pat him on the head, but Sandra warned, "He's a working dog so you can't touch him. Please just ignore him."

Gaston stared at the old man's hand like he'd like to give it a little nip.

"He can be a bit cantankerous. He doesn't like too much attention, especially from strangers."

Arthur sauntered over and whistled at Sandra's new hairdo. "I like your hair. You look prettier than Raquel Welch.

"Franklin, this is my new lady friend." He elbowed the older man. "Don't you think I'm a lucky guy?"

"She's a corker, all right. Looks like she could give you a run for your money." Franklin winked at her.

"I was a dancer in my younger years," Sandra said, failing to mention it was burlesque. Gaston's forefather was part of the act, pulling off pieces of her costume as she stripped and running off stage with them, much to the delight of the audience.

"She's still got some sexy dancing moves. Like I said, I'm very lucky." Arthur smiled at her, his brown eyes twinkling mischievously. "Meeting her was the best thing that happened since I moved here."

Arthur pulled a sweatband out of a red gym bag, adjusting it over his thick grey hair like a gladiator preparing for battle. Then he slid out a black racket with a fluorescent blue zigzag shape, like a ping pong paddle on steroids. He swished it through the air a few times and said, "When you see how much fun this game is, maybe you'll be willing to give it a shot."

More players filtered in, none of them younger than sixty years of age as far as Sandra could tell, and absolutely none of them as good looking in gym shorts as Arthur. A few women mingled with the men, chatting familiarly as they dug out rackets and orange or yellow balls from gym bags. An outburst of laughter exploded from one group clustered together. The dozen or so players started pairing up and drifting into positions on either side of the three nets.

Suddenly all talk stopped dead as a newcomer entered the court. He strutted in holding himself tall and erect, his clean-shaven face frozen into a perpetual sneer. His crew cut, perhaps a carryover from former service in the military, disguised an incipient bald spot. A green t-shirt proclaiming *Senior Softball Champions* was tucked into his belted golf shorts, with a cell phone encased in a holster. Even his spotless Nike shoes exuded an air of power and authority.

A muscular woman, the kind who'd been on the bottom of the cheerleading pyramid in high school, sidled up to him. She hesitated, fluffing her blonde hair with both hands before she greeted him with a smile. He ignored any pleasantries as he dropped his bag on the opposite side of the court. Yanking out his racket, he sliced it through the air a few times. His reptilian eyes settled on Arthur, and he muttered something to the woman. Following his stare, she nodded with a tight smile. The two strolled across the gym in their direction.

"Who's that?" Sandra asked in a hushed voice as she watched them stride over.

"The new guy, Jake." Franklin answered. "Only been coming a couple of weeks. Rumor is he got kicked out of his old league for unsportsmanlike conduct."

Jake stopped in front of Arthur and jeered, "You two old geezers ready to get your asses whipped?"

Sandra mentally nicknamed him "Jake the Snake."

"You want to be my partner for this first match?" Arthur said to Franklin. "Let's show this guy some class."

"Age before beauty," Jake said. "You can serve first."

The old man creakily got to his feet, racket in hand. He shuffled over to the empty court and stood at attention waiting for Arthur to join him. Jake and Blondie bounded over to the other side; both immediately positioned themselves in a semi-squat, ready for action.

Arthur gave her a friendly wave with his pickleball racket and crouched down in a businesslike stance. His muscular legs signaled power and movement, despite a slight paunch.

"You go first," he said to Franklin.

After the old man checked the safety strap on his thick glasses, he held the holey ball below his waist, shouting something that made no sense to Sandra. "Zero, zero, one."

Then he swung at the ball with an upward arc. A single bounce in their opponents' court and the rangy player returned it directly at Arthur. Sandra watched Arthur bat the little orange hole-filled ball back over the pint-sized net. She clung tightly to Gaston's harness as his bright eyes followed the bouncing ball. He gave a little whine as the ball whizzed past their vantage point on the bleachers, his front paws scrambling for the chase, but Sandra held fast. Jake the Snake instantly returned it.

After the ball bounced once, Arthur backhanded it at Jake, who moved close to the net and volleyed it back.

Arthur let it zoom past and shouted, "Hey, your foot was in the kitchen. That's a fault. We get a point."

"Are you blind? My foot was nowhere near the line. You lose. Take your second serve now." Even his crewcut bristled as he glared at Arthur, his mouth drawn into a menacing line. He moved even closer to the net.

"I saw your toe go over the line. Are you calling me a liar?" Arthur puffed out his chest and tightened his grip on the racket, also moving closer to the net.

Franklin picked up the ball, then walked slowly over and put his hand on Arthur's shoulder. "It's all right, Ashmeister. We'll get it back in no time. It's just a friendly game," he said as he handed him the ball.

Arthur shook his hand off and moved back to his side of the court, getting ready to serve. By the way he bit his lower lip, Sandra surmised he was fuming. Both angry men calmed down after a few serves and returns. Gaston grew bored with the regular bouncing back and forth and settled down at her feet for a little snooze. Sandra stifled a yawn and glanced around the gym. She gave up trying to follow three matches of pickleball at the same time. Players scuttled across the floor, rackets blazing, and called out numbers that still made no sense. Some occasionally cursed as balls whizzed by. Jake swore the loudest.

When his female partner missed a ball, he rebuked her. "You clumsy cow."

The woman quickly turned her reddening face away, but not

before Sandra noticed tears forming in her eyes.

The score between the two teams seesawed back and forth. They were always one point apart, and the game seemed to go on forever. Sandra's lower back started to ache from sitting on the uncomfortable metal bleachers. Arthur sped back and forth, covering at times for Franklin, who could not move with any speed. It was Jake's serve. They seemed to be ahead by one. Jake bounced it at Franklin, who managed a backhand return. Jake smashed at Franklin time after time, the old man valiantly trying to hit it back. Then Jake slammed it toward the outside, where Franklin couldn't reach. It bounced past the line.

"Out of bounds," Franklin shouted.

"Liar. It's in. We win," Jake argued.

"Franklin said it was out. And he should know," Arthur said, gripping his racket tightly. "He was closest to the ball."

"He doesn't know shit. He can barely see with those coke bottle glasses all fogged up. It's in, and we win. Quit being a sore loser." Jake started walking toward the bleachers.

"We don't like cheaters in this league," Arthur said. "We respect each other's calls."

"I don't know how you got such a hotshot reputation. You play like a girl. Susie here plays better." He nodded toward his partner. "And she's not even fast on her feet. The game's over. We won. Besides, I need to take a whizz."

A young woman with mousy brown hair pulled back into a tight ponytail wheeled a cart stuffed with cleaning supplies into the alcove between the men's and women's locker rooms. When she saw Jake heading in her direction, she stiffened straight up and grabbed the broom, holding it in front of her like a shield. He brushed past her and gave her a lecherous smile. She flinched and stepped back. Biting her lip, the woman swiftly headed for the women's locker room and put a yellow hazard sign in the doorway.

"What a jerk," Arthur said as he plopped down next to Sandra.

Gaston woke up, with a little yip and gave the man's hand a little lick.

"Thanks, boy. I needed that."

Franklin tottered over. "Sorry, Arthur. I should've had that one."

"It was out of bounds. But like you said, it's only a game."

A couple of players came up to Arthur.

The first one said, "You want to join us?"

Arthur answered, "No, I'll sit this one out with my lady friend. But Franklin here could have another go."

The foursome took their spots at the net in front of them, but before they could begin play, Jake came out of the men's room, cruised over to them, and said, "Hey, we're playing here.

"C'mon, Susie." He called to where the solidly built blonde was standing with another woman. "How's about a rematch? We'll take these dorks on now."

The blonde woman shook her head and held up her hand to say no, but wilted in front of his glare, lowering her hand. Her lips formed a smile that didn't reach her eyes. "Whatever you say, Jake." Susie picked up her racket and stood next to him.

Jake sneered at Franklin. "Doesn't an old geezer like you need to take a break? We'll take this set."

Franklin said to his new partner, "I could use a rest. Catch you next time." He trudged to the bleachers and slumped down.

The new game began fast and furious. Bounces and volleys, grunting and panting. Gaston sat up, alert and watchful, head jerking back and forth, eyes following the orange ball like a lion ready to pounce. Suddenly the ball took an unexpected rebound in front of him, and he darted after it, yanking his leash out of Sandra's grasp. He leapt down from the bleacher and caught it on the second bounce.

Jake had just swept over to backhand the return. But before he could pivot away, the little dog dashed in front of him, tripping him up. The man crashed into the net, bringing it down with him as he fell. The loud thunk as he hit the floor reverberated throughout the gym. Then the pole clattered down. The more he thrashed about to get up, the more tangled he got, like a flounder in a fisherman's net. Nearby games stopped as the players watched Jake struggle, barely able to hide their smiles. His curses filled the cavernous gym with spite.

"Damn that mutt. Little sunovabitch doesn't belong in a gym."

Meanwhile, Gaston did a lap around the gym, proudly carrying his "prey" in his jaw for all to see. When he was sure everyone was watching, he went over to Arthur and dropped it squarely on the floor in front of him. The poodle watched it roll under the bleachers, then went down on his haunches like he was taking a bow. Every one of the pickleball players applauded.

After staggering to his feet, Jake flung the pole aside and shook off the net. He lunged over and drew back his foot, ready to kick the little dog. Arthur jumped down and stepped in his way to block his move.

"Don't even think it," Arthur warned. "He's a harmless pooch. A service dog, for goodness' sake."

"He's a fat mongrel that needs a good ass kicking!" Jake raised his racket like a club and glowered at Gaston.

"You lay a hand on him and you'll live to regret it." Arthur balled his hands into fists.

"Oh, dear!" Sandra exclaimed. "He didn't mean to cause trouble. His hunter instincts just kicked in. Come here, Gaston."

She patted the bench and the little dog obediently hopped up beside her. "Sit."

He meekly sat.

"That's a love. You need to behave."

"He needs to be put down. He's no service dog. He's a menace," Jake snarled.

"Gaston is just high-spirited. He's totally harmless." Sandra clambered down from the bleachers. "You know, Arthur, Gaston and I really should go now. I'll call my handyman to come get us."

She rummaged through her purse for her cell phone to call Norm.

"No, Sandra. I'll take you home. Just let me pack up."

Arthur gathered his things together, carefully packing his racket and headband in his bag. He slowly straightened up and held out his arm. She gracefully took it, and they strolled through the gym, with Gaston pleasantly trotting along, smiling his doggy smile at the pickleball players. Jake watched them like a rattlesnake ready to strike. Sandra imagined fangs in place of his incisors.

Arthur was holding the car door open for her when Sandra noticed she'd left her boa behind.

"Oh, no. I must have dropped my boa underneath the bleachers in all the excitement."

"Would you like me to go back for it?" he asked, pausing with his hand on the door. "It's no trouble."

"No. No. Come back for it tomorrow. I've had enough of pickleball and the Center for Health and Wellness for one day. Let's do something unhealthy and go to the coffee shop for a latte, a cheese Danish, and a pup-a-chino for Gaston."

CHAPTER TWO

The loud clank of the garbage truck shattered the early morning stillness. Startled awake, Vlad Chomsky lay drenched in a cold sweat. A fragment of a dream lingered in his consciousness in which he was running down a dark hallway, some unnamed evil pursuing him. At the end of the hall, a strip of bright light shone underneath a door. Vlad turned the knob. It was locked. Suddenly a key materialized in his hand. Shaking badly, he tried to insert it into the lock, but he kept missing his target. Three, then four times he thrust the key forward. The shadow of the demon pursuing him loomed nearer. He dared not turn to look. He could feel the malice emanating toward him in a great wave and smell the stink of its hot breath. Fortunately, the truck's earsplitting grind ended the nightmare.

A few months ago he had stumbled upon Donna, the bookstore owner, lying in a pool of her own blood. The image of her lifeless eyes was etched upon his mind. When he turned out the lights at bedtime, her face, pale and bloated, reappeared. Vlad wished he could give his head a little shake like an etch-a-sketch to come up with a blank screen, but there was no way to unsee her. He started keeping a plug-in night light on when he slept alone. When he stayed at his fiancée Beatrice's house, he focused on the sound of her deep and even breathing next to him, and his anxiety disappeared.

After agreeing to be Sandra Tooksbury's guardian, Vlad juggled the responsibilities of attending her case manager's meetings along with shared custody of his three children and his job at the college When Beatrice accepted his marriage proposal at the end of a romantic Rhine River cruise, a vacation eventful not only for their betrothal but for the capture of two international jewel thieves, she turned his life around. The grey sameness of his burdensome days disappeared into her love's prismatic light. But she was out of town for a media conference. A wave of loneliness swept over him, the night terrors returned.

Insomnia plagued him in the darkest hour of three o'clock. He lay wide awake while the rest of the world was asleep, afraid to look at his alarm clock because if he did, the countdown would begin. *It's 3:15.*

I need to get up in three hours. It's 3:45, and I'm still awake. Now it's 4:30. This pillow is so lumpy. Five o'clock. The birds are chirping. Damn. Maybe if I take five deep relaxing breaths, I'll catch a few winks before the 6:30 alarm.

Vlad found it hard to forget that his yoga instructor, a sweet-faced ex-hippie, was really a ruthless killer. All the while Shar Frederick led them through the slow movements and the deep relaxations, she harbored murderous thoughts of revenge in her heart. A poison distilled in her kitchen, along with her herbal teas, killed her arch enemy. One death wasn't enough. Poor Donna, about to cast suspicion upon her, had to go, too. He and Beatrice would have been the next victims if Gaston hadn't tripped Shar while Vlad knocked the gun out of her hand. Even now he shuddered with the thought that he and Beatrice could have been another gun violence statistic if Shar had succeeded with her diabolical scheme. Thank God, Norm Clodfelder, Sandra's handyman and chauffeur, followed Gaston's lead and aided him in their rescue.

Vlad flung aside the covers and stumbled into his kitchenette to make some coffee. His alarm went off while he was shaving so he hurried back to his combination bedroom-living room to turn it off before it woke the neighbors. The walls of the efficiency were thin, the space limited, but the price was right, and the location was near his work and his guardianship obligation for Sandra, his landlady, and fellow sleuth with her bad-tempered dog, Gaston.

Since his instructor was now in jail awaiting trial, yoga was no longer an option for Vlad. He turned to the cardio room at the Center for Health and Wellness, otherwise known as CHAW, for exercise. His doctor told him vigorous physical activity would help with his sleep issues. Before he would write a prescription for sleep medication, his doctor recommended he try exercise or psychotherapy. Vlad chose the former.

When he left the house at 6:30, gym bag in hand, he was ready to start the day with his exercise routine, then do a quick change for work. Norm was already busy with a weed whacker trimming around the flower bed. Norm's grey ponytail, sticking out the back of a stained Green Bay Packers cap, swished as he swung the trimmer over the edges.

"Morning, Doc. You're up bright and early." He cheerfully greeted him with a friendly wave. He shut off the gadget and leaned on a nearby tree.

"So are you. You don't usually show your face around here until noon."

"Aw, I forgot to take the garbage bins to the street last night." Norm gave a sheepish grin. "Sandra reminded me when she took Gaston out for his morning potty break. She woke me up just in time to catch the truck. Ya don't want stinkin' garbage sitting around for two weeks."

"She seems to be quite taken with her new fellow, Mr. Wonderful. I've never seen her so enraptured. I half expect him to walk on water. Even Gaston tolerates him," Vlad commented with a hint of annoyance in his voice. "That dog still nips my ankle occasionally, after all we've been through together."

"He's just playing with ya, Doc. Likes to keep people guessing. You sometimes do the same, like when you're in your workout clothes on a weekday. Headin' to the gym?" Norm pointed to the duffle bag Vlad was toting.

"Trying to reclaim my body. Do you want to join me?" Vlad tipped his head toward the car in an invitation.

"Naw. I don't need buns of steel. I'm happier with buns of cinnamon. Besides, I went to the fitness center for a while. I worked out every day for a week on the stationary bike. But it wasn't getting me nowhere."

Vlad gave a pained smile before he spoke, "My doctor recommended a regular exercise program so I'm just following his advice."

"Ya should ease into it, Doc. Maybe just drive by the fitness center real slow, then go to the diner for a cuppa coffee and a donut. No need to rush into things."

"Thanks for the advice, but I think I'll stick to visiting the cardio room. It's helping with my sleep issues," Vlad lied.

"Seriously, Doc, maybe ya should try some natural sleep aids. I heard chamomile tea works for some people. Or try some over-the-counter stuff. When I take a decongestant for my allergies, it knocks me right out. Ya could try that."

"No. I'm doing all right with a workout program." Vlad pressed the remote to unlock his car and shoved his bag in the back.

"Are you sure, Doc? I seen your light on when I came home from the Thirsty Rhino after closing. That don't look all right to me," Norm observed.

"Occasionally, I fall asleep with the light on. No worries." Vlad waved away Norm's concern with a nonchalant gesture.

"If ya need someone to talk to, I'm your guy. I saw combat in 'Nam. It don't ever completely go away. You been through a lot lately," he said.

"Really, I'm fine. I better get going or I won't be able to fit in my cardio routine before my classes at the university."

"If you say so, Doc. Have a good one."

Norm turned the weed whacker back on, trimming the border near the front entry of the old three-story house, now converted into several rental units in addition to Vlad's. Sandra lived on the first floor while Norm inhabited the basement flat in exchange for doing the upkeep of the house and grounds.

Vlad raised an eyebrow when Sandra called Norm "her handyman." Eventually, he'd get the job done but sometimes needed a little help. Like when he put the battery in the smoke detector backwards in Vlad's efficiency. Or when he switched the hot and cold lines around after fixing the shower, and Vlad nearly got scalded when he went to turn it on. And he frequently left a rake or shovel where residents could trip over them. Little things like that. Norm was so ill-suited to his title; Vlad only called on him when the situation was desperate.

Vlad parked in the lot of the old high school, now converted into a fitness center when the new high school was built several years ago. The boxy, steel, and concrete structure with its lack of ornamentation screamed "institutional." The large double doors led past the office once used by the principal.

Instead of the school secretary, a perky woman in a page boy haircut and powder blue CHAW tee shirt greeted him at the counter with a wide smile. "Good morning, Dr. Chomsky," she said as he swiped his card past the electronic device that recorded his visit.

He walked down the hallway decorated with the poster of the 180 Club, an honor roll of members who attended 180 fitness classes the previous year. Other posters were hung honoring donors. A thermometer showed how close CHAW was to achieving its one-million-dollar fundraising goal. He slunk past the weight room, still reeling from the unpleasant memory of his first and only experience there.

A few weeks ago Vlad had ventured into the room under the delusion that strength training was a good balance to the recommended aerobics. Hit by the odor of unwashed socks, he paused in the doorway. The sight of muscles bulging from the tank tops of the early morning risers stopped him in his tracks. His cartoonish Bernie Brewers t-shirt and baggy gym shorts immediately identified him as the ninety-eight-pound weakling wearing sand on his face at the beach. Most ignored him as they heaved barbells over their heads or lifted weights on machines, grunting and sweating.

But one guy in a crew cut spotted him, curling his upper lip as he coldly eyed Vlad up and down. Then he said to a man sporting a tattoo of an eagle clutching a Harley banner.

"Wow. Looks like they let Peewee out of the Playhouse."

Both men laughed uproariously.

Another man with biceps as large as Vlad's thighs set down his weights and wandered over. "Would you like some help? I can show you how some of the machines work." He pointed to the contraptions with pulleys and benches and stacks of smaller weights.

Vlad murmured, "No, thank you," and quickly backed out of the room.

This morning Vlad continued up the stairway to the mezzanine overlooking the gym, where all the cardio machines were kept. An entire wall of glass meant one could monitor the Zumba classes or pickleball players or basketball enthusiasts using the gym. Vlad thought the glass wall was designed to distract equipment users from the pain of their exertions. Unfortunately, at this time in the morning, he surveyed a darkened basketball court, the usual bright lights missing. No distractions from his aches.

Only one other person, a slightly overweight bearded man perspiring in a track suit, was using the elliptical. Vlad watched him for a few seconds, his legs pumping up and down on the steps while his arms jerked back and forth on some handles. He had earbuds on, moving in rhythm to whatever music was playing. The machine required some coordination in addition to the fast movement so Vlad took a pass and settled on the treadmill. After placing his gym bag on the floor, he stepped on the machine, and considered his choices. No *5K Run* or *Rolling Hills* for him. He punched the manual setting with no incline, enjoying a pace of a brisk walk.

Walking was something he felt competent at doing. *I've been walking for forty-five years and haven't tripped too often.* He played some music in his head, the "Turkish March" by Mozart, imagining the lively piano music trickling over the keys. Soon he was sweating, too. After Mozart his mind moved to the Beatles, something bouncy and upbeat, with lyrics he could focus on instead of the slight ache in his calf muscle.

When Vlad glanced at his watch, he realized there was barely time to shower and dress for work. He hit *stop,* made a mental note of his progress to share with Beatrice, and scooped up his gym bag. As he hurried down the flight of stairs and into the dark gym, he noticed the eerie silence of a place normally teeming with lights and hubbub. The emergency exit lights cast off a strange glow. He quelled his rising anxiety by saying aloud, "Stop being so ridiculous."

He looked around for a light, observed a set of switches on the wall, and flicked them on. The fluorescent lights buzzed as brightness flooded the gym filling him with a sense of relief. As he rounded the dark tunnel to the men's locker room, still without any illumination, he noticed a thin strip of light from under the locker room door. The memory of his dream came flooding back, and he felt a vague uneasiness, the feeling of evil in pursuit, until he pushed open the swinging door. The row of empty toilet stalls, their doors hanging open, and the overpowering smell of disinfectant in the urinals brought him back into the world of the familiar and the mundane. A few deep breaths dispelled the dread. Vlad made quick use of the facilities before entering the shower room.

The noise of the running water greeted him, but he didn't hear any splashing or sounds of movement. One of the small locker doors was ajar, a large black bag rested on the wooden bench. A green t-shirt and black shorts were balled up on the floor under it.

A cell phone rang from somewhere in the pile of clothes, an unpleasant "ah-ooga" sound of an old Model T horn. Maybe its owner couldn't hear it above the sound of the rushing water.

Vlad stifled the urge to answer it. Instead, he called into the shower room, "Hey, your phone is ringing."

The only reply was the cascading water.

Vlad knew he should turn around and walk out, back into the bright lights of the gym, and retrace his steps to the front desk. Inform the spritely attendant that something was wrong in the men's locker room. But what if there wasn't? He'd look like a fool, dragging her down into the men's room. Suppose they encountered a surprised man getting dressed? Vlad would become the laughingstock of CHAW as the story of his cowardice made the rounds.

Stiffening his spine in with a sense of bravado, Vlad slowly crossed the tile floor, past the surrounding benches and grey metal lockers. He swallowed hard despite his dry mouth, moving past the tall standing scale with the arrow frozen at 170 pounds and the flickering fluorescent light above the mirrors. He caught a glimpse of himself, pale and ghostly, before he paused in front of the white towel hanging on a peg outside the shower room. He ordered his unwilling body to move.

The bare foot of a naked man lay like the compass of a needle pointing north, pointing to the soggy green boa wrapped around his neck. Legs sprawled out. Arms akimbo. Skull outlined by crew cut hair. All the more fragile in his nakedness. His eyes filled with the surprise of death invading his last private moments. An orange whiffle ball was stuck in his mouth.

Vlad jumped back a step, staring in disbelief. His heart pounded hard enough to burst through his chest. His ears filled with the loud roar of his blood. For an instant he felt out of control, unable to move, like he, too, was about to die. An inner explosion of terror wiped out any trace of thought. Before the darkness could pummel him into nothingness, he pivoted from the protruding tongue under the orange ball. He ran blindly from the locker room into safety.

The unknown evil of his dream finally formed into a recognizable human shape, strangled with an unusual feather boa. Only one person in Crawford flaunted a peacock boa. How on earth did Sandra's prized possession end up on a body in a men's locker room?

CHAPTER THREE

"Call the police!" Vlad sucked in short breaths as a cold shiver ran through him. "I found a dead man in the locker room. Lying in the shower."

The startled attendant grew wide-eyed with disbelief. "A dead man?" she repeated. "Are you sure he's dead?" She slid off the stool. "I've been trained in CPR. I should go check."

Vlad couldn't control himself as he spat out the words. "It's too late for that. I'm certain he's dead. Strangled with a scarf. Call the police now."

"The police?" She hesitated. "How bad was he?"

The words to describe the grotesque body with the orange ball in his mouth fled from his mind. He could only manage to say, "Real bad. Trust me. I've seen dead bodies before."

Vlad laid his head down on the counter and took a few deep breaths. Images of the dead man, lifeless limbs splayed, rose unbidden in his mind, mingled with the sightless eyes of the dead woman in the bookstore. The more he tried to erase them, the more they flashed wildly in his imagination. Vlad raised his head slowly as he opened his eyes and fixed them on the pale woman, her forehead knotted into a worried line. All her cheerfulness had leaked out like a defective balloon.

With trembling fingers she dialed the phone. "9-1-1. This is Debbie from CHAW. There's a dead man in the men's locker room. One of our members just found the body.... Yes, he's certain he's dead, strangled, he says. Send the police."

Vlad's knees no longer locked in place, causing him to sway dizzily. "Is there somewhere I could sit down? I-I don't feel well," he stammered as she hung up the phone.

"I'm sorry." Her worried eyes focused on him. "Come with me into the office. I just made a pot of coffee. You look like you could use a cup."

She led him into the windowless office. The familiar scent of freshly brewed coffee helped to dispel some of the horror. The spartan room held a metal desk and ancient wooden office chair, complete with rusty wheels that probably saw a lot of high school miscreants seated before it. Two grey utilitarian chairs completed the lineup. She gestured to the one closest to the desk. Vlad sank down on the cold metal chair with the well-worn padding. It wobbled and squeaked a bit under his weight. Not even a chair was stable in his life this morning. He watched as Debbie poured some black coffee into an enormous *5K Fun Run* cup and carefully carried it over to him.

"Thanks." He gratefully held the cup with both hands to keep from shaking. The hot liquid flooded his throat with welcome warmth.

"Are you all right?" She gazed at him sympathetically. "I probably would've run screaming in terror if I saw a dead man in the locker room. Or fainted dead away."

Vlad took another gulp before he answered. "I'm doing better, thank you. Starting to get over the shock."

"I can hardly believe it. A dead man! Did you recognize him?"

"It's hard to tell. His face was…was…" The image of the unseeing eyes and the blue tinted face loomed large in his mind. He shuddered. "Horrible. Like something out of a nightmare. Maybe I've seen him around the gym. I don't know his name. Death changes everything."

A woman in a hot pink warm-up jacket poked her head in the door. "Debbie, a squad car just pulled up with a couple of policemen. They're right behind me."

"I'll be right there." She hesitated at the door. "Take your time. Bradley doesn't come in until eight o'clock so his office is empty until then. It's just Kristin and me in the building this early."

"Kristin?" Vlad tried to remember who she was.

"The lady with the cleaning cart. Anyway, just yell if you need anything else." Debbie whisked out of the room.

Vlad heard her talking to the police. "One of our members just ran up. Said he found a dead body in the men's locker room."

A low masculine voice growled, "You didn't see it for yourself?"

"No. He didn't want me to try to administer CPR. Said it was too l-late for that," Debbie's voice cracked.

"We'll need to talk to the man who discovered the victim." The male voice grew strident.

"He's in the director's office. I gave him a cup of coffee to calm his nerves."

"Keep him there until I return," the policeman ordered.

"Do you know where the locker room is? On the west side of the gym?"

"Yeah. I went to high school here. I spent a lot of time in the locker room after sports practice. Have you informed your boss what's going on here?"

"Not yet. I'm on it next."

Then the policeman barked, "One of you men stand guard at the door. Don't let anyone leave until we get their statements. Who else is here?"

"Just a few early risers in the weight room. Someone in the cardio room and the man who found the body." She paused, then hurriedly said, "And Kristin, the custodian. She opens every morning."

"Roberts, you check out the other rooms and get names and addresses. Tell them we need a statement of anything they saw this morning. Until the medical examiner comes in to collect evidence and take a picture of the murder scene, this place is on lockdown. No one in or out. Is there another exit?"

Debbie said in a wavering voice, "There's emergency exits in the gym and the all-purpose room." She snapped her fingers. "Oh, and the old loading platform."

Vlad heard them tramp off.

The buzz of voices at the front desk grew louder. "A body in the men's locker room."

"Unbelievable! I thought Crawford was a sleepy, little out of the way town. Who knew we have big city problems?"

"Maybe it was an accident, a fall on slippery tiles. I almost took a tumble myself."

Debbie's voice interrupted the fuss. "I don't think you accidentally strangle yourself with a scarf."

Sandra's scarf! The shock of seeing the green feathery eyes winking at him from the neck of a corpse swept over him again. Vlad felt his heart explode in his chest. The stale air of the ill-ventilated room made it hard to catch his breath. The coffee cup slipped from his trembling fingers, landing on the tiles with a loud crash.

Debbie rushed into the room. "Are you all right, Dr. Chomsky?" She touched his shoulder, but he didn't look up at her.

"I'm so sorry." Vlad stared bleakly at the shards of glass and the brown liquid splattered over the floor. "I accidentally dropped the cup."

"No worries." Debbie grabbed some napkins and began gingerly picking up the pieces of glass. "I'll take care of it.'

She dumped the soggy mess into the garbage can and sopped up the remaining coffee with more napkins. After examining him anxiously, she asked. "Can I call someone to come for you after the policeman talks to you? You seem shaky."

"I'll be fine. Let me take a few deep breaths." Vlad inhaled to the count of four, focusing on the air traveling through his nostrils, down his throat, filling his chest, then he slowly exhaled. *Breath is life,* he thought. *I'm still alive, unlike that poor chap on the shower floor.* Two more breaths and his heart resumed its normal rhythm.

"More coffee?" Debbie asked.

Vlad shook his head, closed his eyes, and continued his slow breathing, gently waving her away. *If I can just keep breathing calmly, the panicky feeling will go away.*

"Do you mind if I call my boss from in here? I can probably still catch him at home. I'll tell him not to come in until that cop gives me the OK."

"Go ahead. Please make the call. Whatever you need to do."

Debbie swiftly dialed the number on the old black landline sitting on the desk, another leftover from the building's former life.

"Brad, you won't believe what happened this morning! A guy was murdered in the men's shower room. The police are here. Waiting on the medical examiner. It's just like on TV."

Vlad could hear the buzz of a voice on the other end but couldn't make out any words.

Debbie's voice grew shrill with excitement. "Dr. Chomsky. That's who found him. Nobody knows when he got killed, just that he was strangled with a scarf. CHAW is a crime scene."

Another buzz.

"No, you can't come in yet. I'll let you know when the cop gives the word to let people in."

The pink lady poked her head in again. "Debbie, there's a reporter from the *Daily Gazette* here. The cop won't let him through the door but he's asking for you. Said he heard about a dead body on the police scanner."

"Brad, there's a reporter here. No, I won't say a word. I'll try to get rid of him. Gotta go."

Debbie turned to Vlad. "Can I get you anything else? A glass of water?"

"No, thank you. You've been most kind."

Disjointed thoughts swirled about in Vlad's head like autumn leaves in an October wind. Vlad visualized his classroom with the whiteboard and the lectern, him standing before rows of students in his gym clothes. Would he have time to change before his first class? Should he just cancel today's lectures? What would the dean say when he heard the news? Vlad hoped the reporter kept his name out of it. The other professors in his department already gave him skeptical looks because his name appeared twice before in the *Daily Gazette*, once when he and Gaston captured a terrorist, a fire bomber wanted in several states, and an even bigger story when they brought down Shar Fredricks because of the two murders.

He checked his watch to see how much time had passed. Only fifteen minutes but it seemed like fifteen hours as he waited for the policeman to set him free. He closed his eyes again and just listened to the babble of voices in the lobby.

A gruff voice boomed above the cacophony. "Ladies, you need to sit down at the tables in the lobby and stop talking. Let the medical examiner through with his equipment. You reporters, Chief Roesch will make a statement at City Hall at two o'clock this afternoon. We're still interviewing witnesses. No one is authorized to speak to you. So clear out and let us do our job."

Vlad heard Debbie say, "I put a sign outside informing everyone that all morning classes are canceled. I called the instructors and told them not to come in."

"Good thinking. Roberts is nearly finished with the men upstairs. He'll get the names and addresses of these ladies. Then they all can go. I'll need to get your statement. Were you at this desk the whole time?"

"Except when I left for a minute to make coffee. No one came in or out except the early birds. You can double check the scanner for their card numbers."

"We'll do that. Thanks. The witness is still in the office?"

Before Debbie could answer the door was thrust open. Heavy footsteps tramped across the tiled floor. Through the slit of his half-closed eyes, Vlad saw a scuffed pair of brogans, below a trouser leg, that long ago lost its crease. As his eyes traveled up the rumpled brown suit, the paunchy overhang, the wrinkled almost white shirt and loosely knotted tie, he found himself staring into the hard face of a grizzled detective. The man's brooding brown eyes fixed on Vlad with such intensity he shivered in spite of the stuffiness of the room. The waves of resentment rolling off the man were palpable in the small room.

"Vlad Chomsky! Not you again. Do murder victims just happen to drop dead in your path?" The police detective spewed out the words, with his hands planted firmly on his hips and his lips drawn back in disdain.

Vlad met his sullen gaze. "Detective Johnson, I assure you, I wasn't looking for trouble this morning. Unfortunately, trouble found me."

CHAPTER FOUR

Intent on driving to the coffee shop, Arthur failed to notice the admiring glances sent his way by Sandra. She loved to watch him in profile, his straight patrician nose, his firmly chiseled chin, and the alluring way his silver hair dipped down over his forehead. She had to stop herself several times from reaching over to brush it out of his eyes. A man with hair! That alone was enough to send scintillating spasms of pleasure throughout her body as she imagined running her fingers through it. The physical aspects of their new relationship had yet to be explored beyond hand-holding and tender kissing. Sandra was more than ready to take the leap into free love, just like the 1960s. *Make love, not war!*

Gaston lay snoozing on her lap. The poor little fellow was exhausted after his harrowing experience at the gym. Chasing the pickleball roused all his predator instincts. He barked at a squirrel that he glimpsed from the car window as they sped to the coffee shop and scratched his front paws against the window in his attempt to cut to the chase.

"Gaston, behave yourself!"

Her sharp reprimand settled him down, and he drifted off with a gentle snore until Arthur parked the car in front of Literatus, the combination bookstore/coffee house now under new ownership since the former bookstore lady's untimely demise.

Then the poor little pooch nearly yanked her arm out of the socket when he tore after a pigeon perched on a nearby planter, barking furiously. The bird escaped in a flurry of feathers as Gaston honed in for the kill.

"What is wrong with your dog today? He's very excitable," Arthur commented as he grabbed the dog's harness and helped her rein the little fellow in.

After handing the leash to him, she rubbed her sore arm. If only she had her CBD oil in her purse!

"It's nothing a puppy treat from the coffee shop won't cure," Sandra replied with a smile.

Les, the new owner, glanced up from behind the glass case displaying delicious-looking bakery goods and smiled warmly. "It's so nice to see you again. Enjoy a pastry fresh from the oven," he said as he placed some scones on a tray.

"I love what you've done with the place," Sandra said.

Books now rose on shelves all the way to the ceiling. A sliding wooden ladder like in old movies gave the shop the air of an earl's manor house. The scent of new books mingled with the aroma of coffee beans. The glass jar full of dog treats in the shape of sandwich cookies was placed prominently on the counter.

Sandra ordered one for Gaston along with their lattes and cheese Danishes. Soon the poodle was happily munching his treat under the table while Arthur and Sandra sipped their coffee and nibbled on pastry.

"What did you think of the pickleball games?" Arthur asked.

"Everything moves so quickly; I had a hard time figuring it out. Finally, I just gave up on understanding the rules and just watched the people. The ladies seemed just as intent on winning as the men."

"The ladies love to play with the guys. That's why I thought you may like to join us. We'd make a hell of a team." He smiled encouragingly.

"I'm not as formidable as that big blonde woman who partnered with Jake the bully." Sandra ran her finger around the rim of her cup. "I'm afraid you'd be disappointed."

"I'd never be disappointed in you." He covered her hand with his, stopping the circular motion around the cup. "I'm so glad we met that day in the grocery store."

Sandra enjoyed the warmth of his touch, resting her hand on the table under his. "Me, too. Who'd imagine some oranges rolling across the store would bring us together?"

"Luckiest day of my life! When I looked up into your beautiful blue eyes to hand you an orange, I knew you were special. I could spend all day looking at you." He gave her hand a gentle squeeze.

"I'm sorry that bully ruined your morning. Of course, Gaston instigated some of that." She broke off a piece of her cheese Danish and popped it into her mouth. "He's normally so well-behaved."

"Dogs will be dogs. Too bad Jake doesn't have a sense of humor. He never likes to do anything to ruin his tough guy image. Always the macho man. People stay out of his way."

"I didn't realize you knew him from before?" She raised her

eyebrow with a quizzical glance.

"No, no. I just met him at the gym," Arthur said hastily. "But I know plenty of jerks like him. Ruthless. Win at any cost. I met plenty of them in my line of work."

"What did you do before you retired?" Sandra asked. "I told you about being a professional dancer, but you never mentioned what you did in your former life."

"I was an architectural engineer. A boring job. Nothing like your stint in show business. How did you get started?"

The words spilled out as she stared into his dark eyes. "My father was a traveling salesman, until he forgot to come back home when I was eleven. Mother worked nights cleaning offices to support my little sister and me. We were poor growing up."

Arthur grabbed her hand. "I'm sorry. Things must have been hard."

"My mother always said, 'When things get tough, the tough get going.' I got a job with a traveling burlesque show when I was fourteen. County fairs and such. Lied about my age. Sent money home until my sister got out of high school."

Arthur brought her hand to his lips and gently kissed it. "My strong, brave darling."

"What about you? How did you get into engineering?"

"When I was a teenager I went to work as a bellhop at a fancy hotel. I saw the rich people driving their expensive cars and thought, I'm going to own a car like that one day. I put myself through school on an engineering scholarship. Here I am today, living my dream. Still in demand as a part-time consultant."

Sandra sighed. "Dancing was my dream. It was hard work, but I had the time of my life."

"The photos of you in your sequined outfits and feather tiara were amazing. You were a knock-out. Still are." His eyes shown with admiration.

Sandra blushed and lowered her gaze. "Thank you. I miss those days. That's why I'm working on a new act, right, Gaston?"

At the mention of his name, the little poodle clambered out from under the table. He gave a gentle tug on his leash toward the door.

"He's telling us he's ready to go," Sandra giggled. "See how smart he is."

"Please allow me to get this, beautiful lady," Arthur said as he rose to his feet and reached into his pants pocket.

When he extracted his wallet out of his pocket, his keys caught on his pinkie finger. As he fumbled with both objects, the wallet fell to the floor. Gaston snatched the shiny leather wallet in his mouth and scurried under the table with it. When Arthur reached down to retrieve it, Gaston growled at him and inched farther away.

"Please give it back, boy," Arthur pleaded.

"Gaston Pierre Tooksbury! You bad boy!" Sandra scolded. "Arthur saved you from the mean man. Drop it this instant!"

Gaston gave the wallet a vigorous shake. He tucked it between his front paws and began chewing on it.

"He's ruining my wallet! It's handcrafted ostrich leather."

"That must be it," Sandra snapped her fingers, "His sharp sense of smell picked up on the wild bird scent. Remember how excited he got about the pigeon?"

"Wild bird or not, the wallet cost me a pretty penny."

Arthur scrunched under the table, grabbed the edge of the wallet, and yanked. Gaston held on for dear life and jerked back.

"Oh, no. He thinks you're playing tug-of-war," Sandra groaned. "It's his favorite game."

"Can't you get him under control?' Arthur gave up tugging and leaned back on his haunches, glaring at the dog under the table.

"I know." Sandra snapped her fingers "I still have a bit of cheese Danish. Gaston can't resist pastry." Sandra picked up the remaining chunk and held it under the table.

"Here, Lovey Puppy. It's cheese Danish," she cajoled. "Your favorite. You know how you adore creamy cheese."

Gaston sniffed at the morsel. He dropped the wallet and scurried out. Arthur snatched it up and started wiping it clean with a napkin. Gaston contentedly chewed the Danish at Sandra's feet, blissfully oblivious of Arthur's frustration and the drool he left on her shoe.

"Please let me do that for you." Sandra reached for the wallet.

"No, thank you. I'll take care of drying it myself. I need to pay anyway." Arthur held up the soggy wallet to more closely examine it, unable to keep from frowning.

"Look," Sandra exclaimed. "There's hardly any teeth marks. Those ostriches must be thick-skinned critters!"

As Arthur stalked off to the counter to pay, Sandra whispered to Gaston, "You were a naughty puppy. You need to apologize to Arthur *now*."

When Arthur returned Gaston gave a little whine, put his head down, and brushed up against his pant leg. Then he rolled over on his back, tummy up and four paws waving in a submissive pose.

"See, he's telling you how sorry he is. Aren't you, Gaston?" Sandra crooned. "He'll be a good boy all the way home. I know he will."

The little dog yipped softly and scrambled back on four paws.

"It's such a nice day. I was going to suggest going for a drive in the country this afternoon. Now that I've found you, I hate every minute we're apart," Arthur said as he held the coffee house door open for her. "Just the two of us. No Gaston."

"I'd love to, dearie, but I have plans for today. But we could go to the Rose Grotto tonight for supper. My treat."

"I couldn't let you do that. A gentleman always picks up the tab," Arthur insisted.

"Women's liberation, dearie. Equality means I pay in restaurants, too," Sandra argued. "Besides, my dog damaged your wallet. It's the least I can do."

Gaston trotted to the car quietly beside Sandra. He meekly hopped in the back seat and settled down without a sound. Arthur ignored his wide-eyed doggy look of innocence and started the car.

"So what are your plans for this afternoon?' Arthur asked as he smoothly pulled into traffic.

"I mentioned working on a new act. I'm hoping to take it to the Senior Center for a trial run next week. Then maybe I'll look for an agent. Or try to get on America's Got Talent."

"Are you planning on reviving your old act with the dancing? I bet you still look sexy in your sequins." He clicked his tongue like a teenage boy viewing the swimsuit edition of *Sports Illustrated.*

"Oh, no, dear man," she laughed. "No more hoochie-coochie for this gal. I'm featuring Gaston this time."

"What kind of an act? Do audiences outside of circuses still go for dog acts?"

"This isn't a circus act. Gaston has too much class for that. I'm training him for a grand performance, using his special abilities. Up until now he's used them to solve crimes. But he's more than a dog detective. He has extrasensory perception. I'm calling the act Gaston the Psychic Pooch."

Sandra thought she heard Arthur mutter, "More like Gaston the Psycho Pooch."

But her hearing wasn't that sharp. She often didn't hear correctly so she breezed on without a worry. "Catchy title, isn't it? I knew you'd be impressed."

CHAPTER FIVE

Sandra didn't waste any time getting to work with Gaston after Arthur dropped her off. If he was going to be a mind reading dog, the training needed to be subtle. A barely perceptible flick of her finger signaled him to bark in unison with the hand movement. Eventually, she'd need an assistant. One of Vlad's younger children would be perfect. Little blonde Kaitlyn would look adorable in a hot pink dress with a sequined bodice and crinoline underneath the satin skirt. She was only five years old; although she was bright, she didn't have the stamina and attention span for show biz. Sixteen-year-old Erin was pretty enough but, in Sandra's experiences, teenagers could be less cooperative than five-year-olds. That left Nicholas, very mature and intelligent at age eleven. With his Harry Potter glasses and charming smile, he'd be perfect in a magician's suit and bow tie. She already had hooked him when she asked to borrow his Uno cards for the trick.

"Why do you need my Uno cards?" he asked. "Won't a regular deck work?"

"Gaston won't know how to answer if it's a face card or an ace. He needs clear simple numbers," she explained.

"What's he going to do in the act?"

"He'll use his psychic abilities to reveal what card you're holding." Her eyes gleamed with the thought of Gaston entertaining an audience dressed in a midnight blue satin jacket emblazoned with question marks.

"Dogs can't be psychic. They don't have extrasensory perception." The boy gave her a skeptical look.

"Gaston isn't an ordinary dog. He's exceptionally intelligent, with a touch of ESP. I can train him using these." Sandra lifted the deck of Uno cards. "Give us a week to practice and you'll see."

"Will you show me how? I can help." The eagerness in his voice signaled his growing interest.

"The next time you stay with your father, you come to my apartment, and you can be my assistant." She grinned knowingly. "After all we're using your cards."

The boy's eyes widened along with his smile. Sandra knew Nicholas would be ready to perform once she had Gaston's mind reading trick perfected.

Sandra no sooner picked up the deck of Uno cards from the credenza when Arthur called.

"I'm sorry, lovely lady. I have to cancel for tonight. Something's come up with my consulting work. Can I take a rain check for tomorrow instead?"

"Of course, dearie. The offer still stands. My treat at the Rose Grotto. Come over at five for one of my famous martinis."

Sandra worked with Gaston throughout the afternoon, focusing on coordinating his barking with her cues. She rewarded him with so many treats he turned up his nose at his regular dog food until she spiced it up with a little beef broth and hamburger.

The night without Arthur stretched on interminably. She tried to console herself by thinking, *"A time of loneliness and isolation is when the caterpillar grows its wings."* The beautiful way she felt around Arthur, like a blue Morpho butterfly, just made her miss him all the more. Even a martini made with her special bottle of pricey gin—"it's hint of sweetness balanced by spicy notes of cinnamon and nutmeg"—didn't cheer her up. Gaston's reassuring paw on her pillow comforted her in the middle of the night when she woke up to pee. She fell back into a dreamless sleep until her alarm went off bright and early at ten a.m.

"Time to polish the act," she said as she flung back the covers. "First, your morning potty break, Gaston."

As she let the pooch back inside, she noted Norm had taken the garbage and recycle bins to the street, but his motorcycle was nowhere in sight. *He must have important business to be on the road before noon. I hope it isn't monkey business. You can never tell what notion he'll get in his head.*

"Gaston!" Sandra called after her morning coffee and toast. She wore her favorite coral shift dress with big pockets just right for hiding dog treats. "Gaston, come to Mom."

But he was nowhere in sight.

"You naughty boy! Are you hiding on me?"

She looked at the back of the hall closet. The little rascal often squirmed under the piles of old burlesque costumes from her former showgirl days. No Gaston concealed among the fripperies.

"I don't have time to go on a dog hunt for you!" Sandra scolded.

"I'm not getting any younger."

Sometimes she felt every minute of her eighty years weighing down on all her future accomplishments, like the hourglass of her life running out of sand.

Shuffling down the hallway in her fluffy pink slippers, Sandra paused at the laundry room. A basket of rumpled sheets was waiting to be folded and stashed in the linen closet. Sometimes the little poodle crawled on top for a cozy snooze. No doggy snores filled the room. After making certain he hadn't wormed his way underneath, she lifted up the pillowcase on top. Still no Gaston.

Back in the living room she opened the ziplock pouch of doggy treats from yesterday's session. Scritch! She took one out and waved it about, sweetly calling his name. Finally, Gaston crawled out from under the credenza and gave a hungry bark.

Holding a morsel in front of his nose, she commanded, "Lovey Puppy, *sit.*"

The little poodle immediately sat on his haunches and focused his eyes laser-like on her left hand holding the treat.

"Good boy."

She handed him the treat, and he gobbled it up while sitting obediently. Before she took another out of the pouch, she tapped the deck of Uno cards on the end table.

"Remember what we worked on yesterday?" She slipped a treat into the pocket of her loose-fitting dress carefully chosen for pockets generous enough to hold crumpled tissues or dog treats. "I'll pick a card out of the deck. Now watch my finger!"

She chose a card, a red three, closed her eyes, and held it to her forehead with her right hand. Her left hand remained in Gaston's line of vision.

"Oh, wondrous Gaston. From my mind to yours. I'm picturing this number, Think hard. I know you can see it. What number is on this card?" She twitched her left pointer finger down at her side three times, a motion so slight hopefully no one in the audience would see, but Gaston would.

Gaston barked three times, then eyed her expectantly. A thin trickle of saliva escaped from his mouth.

Sandra flourished the card to the invisible audience, her voice booming with excitement. "Look, ladies and gentlemen. Gaston the Psychic Pooch has read my mind! It's a red three."

She slipped him the treat, and he danced on his hind feet.

The two repeated the trick a few more times. Gaston performed flawlessly each time she pulled a differently numbered card.

"You're such a good boy!" Sandra chirruped as she scratched him in that special spot behind his ears, and he whined with pleasure. "Mom's so proud of you. You smart little pooch. Next, we'll figure out a way to do the different colors."

Their celebration was interrupted by a knock on the door. Gaston barked excitedly.

"Hush, Gaston! It's probably just the mailman. He wasn't too pleased the last time he brought a package to the door when you nipped his ankle! Please behave this time." She threw him a warning look as she flung open the door.

A shaggy-haired man in a wrinkled brown suit stood stolid as a grizzly bear in the entryway, his large frame looming over her. "Are you Sandra Tooksbury?" he asked.

'Yes, I am," she slowly answered.

The man clearly needed a date with a razor. He looked familiar, but she couldn't remember where she'd seen him before.

"How may I help you?"

He pulled out his wallet and flashed her a detective badge. "I'm Detective Johnson. May I come in?"

Detective Johnson! Now she remembered his daunting face from the newspaper photo.

"Yes, please. You'll have to excuse the way I'm dressed. I wasn't expecting company this early." She gestured at the pink fuzzy slippers and sateen housecoat.

The man glanced at his watch. "It's almost noon. I just have a few questions." He looked expectantly into her foyer.

"Oh dear, what's Norm done now?" She stepped back to let the policeman lumber past her. "I've told him to cut back on those visits to the Thirsty Rhino, especially when he rides his motorcycle. But will he listen to me?"

"I'm here concerning a different matter. There's been a murder," he rumbled on.

"A murder! Oh, my! You must be here for Gaston." Excitement crept into her voice. "I'm sure you read about his last case in the *Daily Gazette*. The headline was 'Poison Suspect Goes to the Dogs.' He's captured a terrorist and some jewel thieves, too. He'll be glad to help you track down the killer with his keen sense of smell. Gaston, show the policeman what you can do."

Sandra snapped her fingers and made a clicking sound with her tongue. Immediately Gaston assumed a bloodhound pose and began sniffing around the detective's shoe. He retraced the policeman's steps all the way to the door, then dropped to his haunches with a loud expectant bark.

"See how fast he can pick up a trail!" Sandra crowed.

The detective shot her a baleful look. The last time Sandra saw such an ominous stare she was peering at Samson, the gorilla at the Milwaukee Zoo, just before he went on a rampage, flinging fecal matter at the glass wall separating them.

"We have the medical examiner and skilled forensic investigators already on the case. We don't need any amateurs muddying the evidence. In fact, the evidence is why I'm here to talk to you."

"The evidence? I don't understand. What do I have to do with a murder?" Sandra wrung her hands, despite the twinge of arthritic pain.

She sank down on the loveseat. Gaston hopped beside her and licked her hand.

"An unusual scarf was found wrapped around the victim's neck. We believe it was used to strangle him. A peacock boa. You were last seen wearing it," Detective Johnson growled. He sat opposite in her recliner and fixed his stern gaze on her. "Several witnesses identified you as the owner."

"I was wearing it yesterday at the Center for Health and Wellness. I went to watch a pickleball game. But I dropped it under the bl-bleachers," she stammered, meeting his eyes. "I-we didn't go back for it."

The detective whipped a notepad out of his jacket pocket and perused it for a moment while Sandra broke out in a cold sweat. "Ah, the pickleball game. It seems there was a major altercation between the victim and a friend of yours, Arthur Ashenbrenner. Your dog caused the dispute. Then the victim, Jacob Bender, was found throttled in the men's locker room with your peacock boa around his throat and a pickleball with a dog's teeth marks jammed in his mouth."

"Surely you can't think I had anything to do with it. I'm an eighty-year-old woman," Sandra continued in a weak voice. "I'm not in the best of health. I frequently have seizures. My service dog will give an alert when he senses one is coming." She patted Gaston, who gave a sympathetic whine. "How could a frail old lady attack a fit and healthy man like Jacob Bender?"

"Foul play was definitely involved. We'll know more after the medical examiner has determined the cause of death. I'm here to inquire how well you know Mr. Ashenbrenner." His impassive stare chilled her to her core.

"We just started dating. I know he's a perfect gentleman. So polite and considerate. He would never harm anyone," Sandra said indignantly. She almost said, *He wouldn't be stupid enough to use my boa.* She never got any credit for all the things she managed not to say. "Anyone could have picked up my boa from the floor."

"Were you with Mr. Ashenbrenner all last night?" He stared at her; pen poised above the notepad.

"No, he brought me home yesterday afternoon. He broke our date for supper. Said he had an urgent matter for his consulting work to take care of." She fingered the dog treat in her pocket, then began shredding it with her nail.

"And you haven't seen him this morning at all?"

"No, I've been busy training my dog. He needs constant work to stay on top of his game." Sandra flicked away the treat crumbs in her pocket.

"You'll probably need to come down to the station so we can take down your statement."

Sandra met his gaze with her unflinching stare. "Of course. Anything to help the investigation. I have lots of experience in detective matters."

"Hmpf!" Detective Johnson snorted as he stood up." We're just beginning the investigation. I'll probably have more questions for you as we go along. Please don't get up. I can let myself out." The man tramped out the door.

Sandra dove for her cell phone and scrolled down her favorites searching for Vlad's number. Before she could punch his name, the phone rang. Vlad's name instantly popped up.

She stabbed the green phone icon and blurted out as Vlad echoed just as frantically, "We need to meet right away!"

CHAPTER SIX

"How the hell did Sandra's boa end up on a naked dead guy?" Beatrice's voice shot like a cannon over the phone.

Vlad's first impulse after the grilling by the detective was to call her, even though she was likely driving home from her media conference. Still in his gym clothes, he sat in the CHAW parking lot exhausted after reliving his encounter several times. He had to hand it to Detective Johnson. He shifted the questioning each time hoping to catch Vlad in some discrepancies, but Vlad's account never wavered. Telling the truth over and over mentally drained him. Thank goodness the detective didn't ask if he'd seen the boa before. He'd find out it was Sandra's soon enough. Anyone who saw her at CHAW would identify the flamboyant elderly lady with the peacock boa. If only he had walked away and pretended he'd never entered the locker room. Someone else would have discovered the body. He'd be at the university, free of the burden of the burly detective's relentless questioning.

"I have no idea." Vlad shook his head in disbelief. "Sandra's version of exercise is lifting the cocktail shaker. I can't imagine her in sweats at the gym."

"She does keep up with her dance moves for the Senior Center's beauty pageants. Last year the judges asked her not to wear her G-string and pasties for the swimsuit contest!"

"She doesn't just think outside the box, she denies a box even exists!" Vlad looked at his watch. "I need to cut this short. I have to get to my first lecture. Looks like I'll be changing clothes in my office."

"Maybe you should call in sick. Take a mental health day," Beatrice advised.

"Too early in the semester. I'm just learning all my students' names."

Over the phone Vlad heard the squeal of brakes and a long blow of the horn.

Beatrice cursed. "Damn! Some jerk just cut me off. I better pay attention to my driving. I still have ninety miles to go. I'll see you when I get home."

After she hung up Vlad followed a familiar route to Crawford University. The small private campus was planted in a woodland setting. Majestic oaks and colorful maples provided ample shade for the students scurrying to their first class of the fall day. The Humanities Building, one of the oldest on campus, stood boldly in the sunlight at the top of a tree-lined path. Featured on brochures enticing future students and their families, the three-story building of cream city brick had perfect symmetry—large arched center and matching wings. His office on the top floor was not as perfect, one of many small offices bunched together and accessible only by a small ancient elevator or a steep flight of stairs. Because Vlad chose the stairs, he was out of breath by the time he unlocked his office door. The department secretary greeted him, not bothering to look up from whatever game she was playing on her computer. He quickly changed into his dress pants and tailored oxford shirt. No time for a tie. He applied an extra swipe of deodorant to make up for the missing shower, slipped into his tweed jacket with the suede elbow patches, and headed to class.

Somehow Vlad made it through his morning lectures. Fortunately, the students who bothered to show up were apathetic and sleepy. World History, Part I, hadn't changed much in the thousand years of recorded time and neither had his notes. His attempt at making the material interesting was half-hearted but he soldiered on, even though his mind kept going back to the scene at CHAW, the feather boa moving like a snake tightening its grip on the dead man's neck. When his last class that morning filed out, he packed up his books and papers with shaking hands. He couldn't avoid talking to Sandra Tooksbury any longer. If she was involved, she needed his help.

Vlad scrolled down his FAVORITES for her phone number and jabbed his finger on her smiling face.

"We need to meet right away!" spilled out of her mouth the instant she picked up, mirroring his exact words. "A man was murdered at CHAW with my peacock boa!" Sandra exclaimed.

"I know. *I* found the body. It was horrible." He shuddered as a wave of revulsion washed over him.

"Oh, no. You poor man. Not again."

He heard the sympathy in her voice.

"That beastly detective just left. He thinks I may have something to do with it. Just because Gaston caused a little ruckus at the pickleball game yesterday."

"Pickleball! What the hell were you and Gaston doing at pickleball?"

"We went to watch Arthur play. My new man is quite athletic. A pickleball star. He wanted me to see how the game is played. Tried to convince me to join in. I told him I don't even own any gym clothes. Besides, Gaston and I are working on a new act. I have no time for games."

"What kind of a disturbance did Gaston cause?"

"He ran away with one of those silly little balls and accidentally tripped this ugly bully. The scoundrel had the nerve to try to kick my dog but Arthur stopped him. Unfortunately, that ball was found stuffed in Jake Bender's mouth with Gaston's teeth marks on it."

"Jake Bender's the name of the victim?"

"Yes, I called him Jake the Snake. The detective was asking questions about Arthur; he's probably looking to hang the rap on him and charge me as an accessory to the crime. We can't let that happen."

"I'm finished for today," Vlad said. "I'll cancel my office hours and head right over. Beatrice should be home from her conference by now. I'll pick her up on the way."

He headed back up the stairs to his office, unceremoniously dumping his books and papers on his desk and grabbing the gym bag.

"An emergency just came up so I'm canceling my office hours for today," Vlad told the department secretary on his way toward the stairs.

"Did one of the kids get hurt?" she asked.

"No, it's my guardianship, my landlady. She needs my help. Nothing major." He fled before she could ask any more questions.

His first stop was Beatrice's house. She answered the door in her blue jeans and a light teal sweater that made her grey eyes take on a delicate greenish hue. She greeted him with a warm embrace and kissed him fervently. The strength of her well-toned arms around his neck and the softness of her lips gave him a renewed sense of well-being, as if her love could dispel the evil that clung to him. He inhaled the sweet smell of verbena and an underlying scent that was hers alone. The intoxicating feeling of her closeness made him throw away all caution as he returned her eager kiss.

"My poor darling! How terrible to find that murdered man!" she said after they came up for air. "What can I do to help you get the image out of your mind?"

Vlad slid his hands down her back to draw her closer. He nuzzled her, brushing his lips against her neck as he spoke, "You're doing it right now."

He relaxed for the first time all day, until he felt something furry brush against his legs, then a stab of pain as sharp teeth sunk into his ankle.

"Yow!"

He backed away as Max, her newly acquired cat, pushed between them. The handsome tuxedo wound his body around Beatrice's ankles, purring loudly as he stared at Vlad with narrowed amber eyes, as though daring him to take a step closer.

"Did he nip at you?" she asked, reaching down to pet the cat. "He's been alone for two days, and he's starved for attention."

"Did you feed him? It felt like he wanted to take a chunk of my flesh to gnaw on."

Beatrice scooped the cat up in her arms, crooning, "You bad kitty. Now apologize to Vlad for biting him."

She waved one of the cat's paws at Vlad's arm in a conciliatory gesture. "See, he's sorry. He didn't mean any harm. He's just lonely."

Max pushed his head under her chin and rubbed his muzzle back and forth against her, a purr still vibrating in his throat.

"Please pet him to show him there are no hard feelings."

She thrust the cat at him. Vlad reluctantly patted the top of the little beast's head, then jerked his hand away as Max's teeth grazed his fingers. Beatrice kissed the cat on the top of his furry head and gently set him back down. Max scooted away toward the kitchen and his food bowl.

"Shall we continue what we started?" Beatrice asked, grabbing Vlad's hand and leading him toward her couch, her smile an open invitation.

Vlad felt tension building as he thought of Detective Johnson. It didn't take him long to discover who owned the boa. What would he find out next? The edginess that haunted him all day swiftly returned.

Vlad snatched his hand away and blurted, "I can't. We need to hustle over to Sandra's. I told her we'd be there as soon as possible."

"Let me get my jacket and we'll head out." She paused to get her light quilted jacket and fluff her short pixie cut hair with her fingers.

Vlad was already at the door, nervously smoothing his mustache as he waited for her to catch up.

WATCHING FROM HER PICTURE window, Sandra threw open the door before they had time to knock. "I'm so glad you both finally came. We need to get started. Norm's here already. There's no time to lose."

Gaston jumped up on Beatrice in a happy greeting, and she knelt to scratch behind his ears. The poodle whined in pleasure while Vlad looked on with a frown. The damn dog never greeted him like that.

Norm lifted a can of beer from his spot on the easy chair and said, "Hey! Bout time ya guys got here. Sandra's all in a tiz."

Sandra took Beatrice's jacket and hung it on the hall tree. After she turned to Vlad, he raised his hand to say no. The tweed jacket was his first purchase as a professor years ago. The familiar feel of the wool surrounded him like the arms of an old friend. He needed that comfort to get through the stressful day.

Vlad started questioning Sandra immediately. "When you were watching the pickleball game, did you notice anyone who was exhibiting any hostile behavior toward the victim?"

"It'd be easier to think of someone who wasn't hostile. Jake the Snake wasn't very likeable. He was a braggart and a bully and an animal abuser." Sandra took a big breath, spewing a litany of complaints as she paced back and forth. "He insulted this poor old man, Franklin, and mocked Arthur mercilessly. He sneered at—"

Vlad interrupted. "Sit down. Think hard. It's important."

He patted the love seat, and she meekly sat down. Gaston leapt up and curled up beside her, closing his eyes for a nap.

"You're a top-notch detective, and you have powerful observational skills. Anything seem out of the ordinary?"

"That blonde woman who was Jake's partner. He badmouthed her, yet she didn't bash him with her racquet. I know I would've if he called me 'a clumsy cow.'"

"Good. Keep thinking." He went to the top drawer of her credenza and pulled out a notebook and pen.

"Beatrice, can you start a list of suspects? Do you remember that woman's name?"

Sandra knotted her forehead with concentration. "Yes, now I remember. It was like in that song, *Wake Up, Little Susie*. I remember thinking Susie should wake up and smack him one."

Beatrice carefully wrote down Susie and said, "I've got it. Anyone else?"

"Maybe Franklin, the old man. He put up with a lot of crap from

Jake. Totally humiliating,"

Then Sandra snapped her fingers. "When Jake went to the men's room, he passed by this young woman with a cleaning cart. He said something to her, and she cringed."

"What did she look like?" Vlad asked.

"Kind of mousy, brown hair pulled back in a ponytail. Very thin. The CHAW t-shirt just hung on her like sackcloth." Sandra ticked each descriptor off on her fingers.

"Put down custodian. Possibly Kristin. Debbie said she was the only other staff member on duty in the early morning. Maybe she knows something or saw something."

"I know what she looks like. I can talk to her!' Sandra said excitedly.

"That's not such a good idea," Vlad shook his head. "You're already on the police radar. We don't need you to arouse any more suspicions. You need to lie low with Arthur."

"But I have Gaston. He has ESP when it comes to criminals. Look how he growled at that jewel thief when none of us suspected he was a phony," Sandra protested. "He'll ferret out the truth."

"No detective work for you and Gaston. He made a scene at the pickleball game. You both need to cool it for a while. You're too noticeable. The flashy way you dress and the way Gaston acts attract everyone's attention." Vlad gave her a firm stare. "Keep yourself busy. Do some fall cleaning. Work on Gaston's new act. Hang out with Arthur."

"What about me, Doc? What can I do?" Norm spoke up.

"Can you put some feelers out at the bar? See if anybody knows Jake or has heard any rumors."

'Good idea. Locals communicate in different avenues than the police," Beatrice said. "They gossip, hang out on social media, talk one on one in a bar. Norm is in a perfect place to pick up information the cops may have missed."

"Yeah, the grass is always greener at the bar. It's fertilized by bullshit." Norm gave Sandra a wink.

She smiled back weakly.

"Beatrice, we need you to go undercover. How do you feel about joining the pickleball group?"

"Pickleball? Me? I don't know anything about playing pickleball. When will I find time?" Beatrice shook the pen at Vlad.

"You'll pick it up quickly," Vlad reassured her. "You used to play tennis, right? It can't be that different. And you have flextime. Schedule yourself a late start one morning each week and join the pickleball players. Strike up a friendship with Susie. See if there's anybody who seems especially glad that Jake is dead."

"Besides anyone who ever knew him?" Sandra jumped in. "Probably his own mother didn't like him."

"I heard she threw him in the lion's cage at the zoo when he was little." Norm said. "She got ticketed by ASPCA for cruelty to animals."

Vlad paced the room, intent on finishing the list. "I'm going to hang around the weight room. I met a jerk there the first day I went in. Made fun of me—like I belonged in Pee Wee's Playhouse. From your description I'm pretty sure it was Jake. He had a friend. Maybe I can find out more from him."

"You lifting weights? Me playing pickleball? Heaven help us pull this investigation off!" Beatrice raised her hands skyward in mock supplication.

"You need more than heaven's help." Sandra stood up and jabbed her index finger at Vlad. "You need me and Gaston!"

At the mention of his name, the little dog woke up and barked at Vlad.

"Not this time! He's already done enough." Vlad glowered at the poodle until the barking stopped.

CHAPTER SEVEN

Clothes make the man. Sandra Tooksbury heard that old adage many times. Mark Twain said that "naked people had little or no influence on society." Being a former burlesque star, Sandra felt nearly naked people could have a big influence in show business. But she had to agree: People are judged on the basis of what they wear. If Vlad thought the way she dressed attracted too much attention, she'd change her appearance. Time to buy different clothes. The ladies at the Senior Center highly recommended St. Vinnie's for a good bargain on ladies' apparel.

After the team left she called Arthur and cancelled their date at the Rose Grotto. She wasn't certain she should tell him Gaston was on the case of the pickleball murder. Her new man acted a little miffed after the wallet incident, although his billfold was perfectly intact. The teeth marks gave it a distressed appearance—made it more vintage-looking. Obviously, he didn't know the retro look was very popular right now. He could probably sell that ostrich leather wallet on eBay for more than he paid for it.

Arthur's disappointment over the phone was palpable. "I was looking forward to seeing you all day," he mourned. "I really need a friendly face. Some policeman left a message. Jake Bender was murdered, and they want to speak to me ASAP. I put them off until tomorrow morning."

"Come to my place after your interview. We can commiserate about our experiences with the police. My peacock boa was found at the scene. A detective paid a visit to inform me of such."

"The boa you dropped?" Arthur exclaimed. "You should have let me go back for it."

"No matter. I'm innocent, and so are you. We'll talk tomorrow."

After she hung up she called Norm. "Are you busy? Could you drive me to the thrift store? I need to buy some clothes?"

"No prob-lay-mo. I know it's been tough shopping since Frederick's of Hollywood went belly up at the mall. But I never thought ya'd end up at the thrift store."

"I need a disguise. If Vlad thinks I'm going to sit around all day twiddling my thumbs and cleaning this house, he's sadly mistaken." Sandra's voice rose with indignation. "I'm going undercover, too. I need a disguise from St. Vinnie's."

"I'll be right there."

Sandra slipped into her trench coat, then surveyed her closet for a hat. She chose a black and white knit hat gathered in front like a turban that covered most of her red hair. When she glanced at her image in the hall mirror, she shook her head. She looked too much like a private eye. It would never do. Her old wool dog-walking hat looked better. She tucked her hair under the hat and pulled it down low.

When Gaston saw her put on her hat, he ran to where his leash hung. Standing on his hind legs, he grabbed the end in his mouth and gave it a tug. His bright eyes shone with joy. He emitted a few happy yips as he shook the leash in anticipation.

"Sorry, Lovey Puppy. You can't come with me today. I'm on a mission and don't need any distractions. And besides, you just were out and did your business fifteen minutes ago."

The little dog followed her to the door, eagerly trotting along her side.

When he pawed at her ankle, she nudged him back with her foot and said sharply, "Gaston, no!"

The poodle slunk away, with his head down and his tail limp. His sad puppy eyes gave a stinging reproach as she headed out the door.

"I decided on St. Vinnie's. Do you want to come in with me?" she asked Norm when she slid into the passenger's seat.

"No, thanks. I just bought a watch at the secondhand store. Now I'm saving up to buy the rest of it."

"At least it wasn't a secondhand smoke. That'd be bad for your health. Even worse than your jokes are for mine," Sandra shot back.

"You win," Norm said. "You can go Good Will Hunting on your own. I'll be back to pick you up in a half hour."

He dropped her off at the large, corrugated metal building, painted a dismal blue shade. The red neon sign in the display window flashed *open*. Sandra waved him off and pushed through the glass door, where she was greeted by several rows of shopping carts and a small statue of a balding man in an altar boy type robe. The words *Saint Vincent De Paul* were gilded on the pedestal base. His right hand was upraised in either a "hi-ya" gesture or a blessing. *The patron saint of thrift store shoppers*, Sandra thought. A large whiteboard on an easel had a handwritten sale: Yellow tags—50% off: All ladies shoes—$5.00.

A rack of women's coats stood behind the statue. A brown quilted car coat caught her eye. It had tarnished brass buttons, big front pockets, and an oversized collar. An old woman in a coat like that would be almost invisible. She checked the tag marked at twelve dollars. Her excitement grew because it was yellow. She grabbed an empty cart and tossed the coat in.

Next, Sandra searched the shelves of bargain shoes in her size. Most were strappy and high-heeled; she had several like that at home. These were probably worn once for a special occasion, then abandoned. There were flats in odd colors like fuschia or orange plaid and a few well-worn winter boots. Then she spotted a promising pair: black, tie-up, sensible, and orthopedic. Several ladies at the Senior Center, all much older than her, wore just such shoes. She could stalk a killer in those shoes through any rugged terrain. No twisted ankles or clumsy stumbles. They joined the coat in the cart.

Now for a long-sleeved knit shirt or sweater. There was an abundance of greys hanging among the size mediums. Perfect for blending into a wall. A ribbed turtleneck and a cowl-neck tunic drew her attention. Hallelujah! Both yellow tagged at four dollars.

Then she spotted her, thumbing through the skirts. The mousy girl from the Center for Health and Wellness. No ponytail today, her scraggly hair hung like a curtain covering her face. No slouching today. The baggy CHAW shirt couldn't hide her broad shoulders and well-defined biceps. She slid skirt after skirt along the rack with military like precision. Sandra couldn't let this opportunity slip away.

Sandra shrugged off the trench coat, wadded it up in the cart, and replaced it with the brown coat. She felt to make sure her hair was completely inside the hat, then casually pushed the cart over to the skirt aisle. Holding the two grey sweaters, she joined the young lady in checking out the skirts.

"Excuse me, dearie," Sandra said in her sweetest little old lady voice. "I'm hoping you could take a minute to give me a hand."

The girl turned toward her with eyes incredibly deep blue like the ocean on an overcast day. Sandra was so startled by the unexpected beauty of her eyes she forgot for a second she was hot on the case.

"Sure thing," the girl said pleasantly. "How can I help?"

"Uh, I'm…" Sandra had to think fast. "I'm going to a funeral this week, and I need something appropriate to wear. I look horrible in black so I was thinking grey would be just as respectful. I found these two. Which one would look better on me?" Sandra held up the two sweaters for the girl to see.

The girl studied them carefully before she answered. "The one with the cowl neck looks dressier, but don't you want to try them on? See which one fits you best."

"Of course. But first I need to find a skirt, or slacks, to wear with them. I think I probably wear a medium or size eight. It's been a while since I went clothes shopping. It's hard on a fixed income, you see." Sandra looked downcast. Her hands holding the garments shook a little.

"Let me help." The girl took the sweaters from Sandra and pushed her cart to the *medium* rack. "Most of these are too short. You don't want a miniskirt.' She moved past the front of the section filled with brightly colored garments, then paused and pulled out a longer A-line skirt. "Here's a purple one. It doesn't look too bad with the gray." She held up the sweaters with the skirt for Sandra to see.

"You're right. It looks good. I'll try them on." Sandra put the items in her cart, covering her trench coat with them. "I don't suppose you'd have time to come to the dressing room with me and give me your opinion? If my granddaughter were here, she'd tell me how they look." Sandra gave a heavy sigh. "I sure do miss her and my daughter. They moved away to Connecticut. I don't see much of them anymore."

"I have time. I take classes at the technical school but they don't start until four. Let me grab the skirt I was looking at. You can tell me if I should buy it." The girl brought out a black skirt with an uneven hem, trimmed in edging of lace. "My name's Kristin, by the way."

"My name is Sandra, but I wouldn't mind if you called me Grandma Sandy, like my granddaughter does," Sandra said with a smile. "You remind me of her. She's petite and fine featured, just like you with your pretty eyes."

Kristin blushed as she said. "Thank you. I didn't have time to put on makeup. I have to be to work at five in the morning."

"Dearie, you don't need it. You're fine just the way you are."

They arrived at the dressing rooms, and she continued, "I think I'll try on the cowl neck one first. You put on your skirt, and we can model for each other."

"It's going to look a little weird with my work shirt. I have a dark teal top I was planning on wearing it with," Kristin said. "I'm going to a funeral, too."

"Oh dear, I hope it wasn't anyone close to you."

Kristin's face looked grim as she mumbled, "Actually, I'm kind of glad he's dead. I probably shouldn't say that. My boss is making us go. The guy died where I work." She gave the black skirt a vigorous shake and scowled at it.

"Where is that, dearie?" Sandra acted clueless.

"I work at the Center for Health and Wellness." She pointed to the logo on her shirt. "One of our members was murdered this morning. Can you believe it?"

Sandra tsk-tsked. "How terrible!"

The young woman tossed the skirt into her cart and gave it a violent shove. "We all are being pressured to go to his funeral. To show the community we care. My mom told me not to speak ill of the dead, but he was an awful man." Then she added through a clenched jaw, "I hated him."

"Why is that, dear girl?"

"I can't talk about it. I've already said too much." Kristin abruptly turned away. "Let's try on our clothes."

SANDRA INSISTED KRISTIN ENTER her phone number in her cell phone before they left the thrift store. "I miss my granddaughter so much. Perhaps you wouldn't mind meeting me for coffee occasionally? Or I could take you out for a sundae at Collins' Dairy? It would mean so much to me."

"Sure. I'd be happy to. But I work very early in the morning, and I go to school."

"If you're off this time of day, we could meet for a quick bite at Collins' sometime. My treat."

"Sounds good. Give me a call next week."

As she watched the young lady walk away, Sandra thought, *Jake did something to you to make you so angry. I'm determined to find out.*

CHAPTER EIGHT

Gaston was still sulking when Sandra got home. He barely looked up from his comfy spot on the pink plush pillow.

When she said, "Lovey, I'm back," he gave a little woof, the dog equivalent of *Meh*, and closed his eyes.

Sandra unloaded her bag of clothes and headed for the laundry room. Stuffing her "new" used skirt and top into the washer, she set the dial on cold water delicate. She brainstormed ways to try out her new disguise at the CHAW, which had fitness classes just for older adults. Her Senior Center friends raved about them. Luckily, she had found a grey wig to cover her hair in the back room of St. Vinnie's where they had the medical equipment. Some poor chemo patients no longer needed it, she feared. Now it was hers.

Her phone rang. It was the activity director from Harmony Manor, the nearby nursing home.

"Hello, Mrs. Tooksbury. It's Allison, from Harmony, the place always in tune with your needs. Are you free tomorrow morning? It's our 'Rendezvous with Rover' day. The regular doggy visitor on this week's schedule had to cancel at the last minute. We were hoping you could bring your adorable poodle in his place. Our residents so look forward to interacting with the pooches."

Sandra considered several excuses for not appearing—a doctor's appointment, her car broke down, Gaston was going to the groomer's. Then she snapped her fingers. It'd be a perfect time to try out her new disguise.

"Of course we'll come, dearie. What time would you like us?"

"Could you please be here at nine? You'll be in the Memory Care wing."

"I'll see you tomorrow." She hung up with renewed enthusiasm.

Sandra grabbed a few Pork Chomps from the treat bag and walked over to Gaston. "Don't be mad, Lovey Puppy. Here's one of your favorites." She dangled a tidbit in front of his nose. "I need your help tomorrow. You won't have to wear your service dog harness. It will be my turn to wear a disguise. You'll do some tricks for the old people at

Harmony Manor."

Gaston hopped down from the couch and stood on his hind legs, his front paws resting on her knees. She gave him his treat, and he dropped down to gobble it up. His happy *arf* said all was forgiven.

AT NINE O'CLOCK SHARP Sandra entered the lobby of Harmony Manor, her poodle in tow, and pressed the buzzer. Wearing the grey cowl top and drab purple skirt, she felt anonymous without her makeup and usual splendiferous outfits. She smoothed the grey wig over her hair, slipped off the brown coat, and waited.

A disembodied voice spoke on the intercom. "May I help you?"

"It's Sandra Tooksbury and Gaston, here for Allison."

"I'll buzz you in. She's expecting you."

No matter how bright the yellow paint was, and how profuse the flowery paintings on the walls, they didn't hide the institutional appearance of the large room. A no-nonsense woman sat enthroned at the large metal desk next to a basket filled with plastic flowers. She asked Sandra to sign the registry book. Before she scribbled her name and the purpose of her visit, Allison appeared, dressed in bright red crops and a matching ruffled collar zip jacket, her long wavy hair corralled by a scrunchy. She blinked her eyes a few times and stared openmouthed at Sandra. Gaston yipped, breaking the silence.

"Mrs. Tooksbury?" she asked in an uncertain voice. Quickly recovering her poise, she thrust her hand toward Sandra and vigorously shook her hand. "We're so glad you could step in at the last minute. We appreciate your flexibility."

Allison led them down a long hallway, past the nurses' station, and into a wing with a Memory Care sign over the door. She punched in a code on the keypad to open the door and ushered them into the uncomfortably warm unit. Several of the residents were assembled in a central area. A circular hallway surrounded the gathering place, with individual rooms lining the halls. Large cheerful signs emblazoned with pumpkins and fall leaves, much like kindergarten name tags, identified the owner of each room. The smell of disinfectant didn't quite cover the faint odor of urine as they traveled past the residents' rooms. They entered the gathering area. Allison hung Sandra's brown coat on a hall tree and introduced her and Gaston.

The pup was on his best behavior. Sandra took him through his usual act, sitting up, playing dead, rolling over, shaking hands, dancing in a circle on his hind legs. His comical expressions and cheerful yips brought smiles to his captive audience. Then he moved from person to person, allowing them to pet him and shake his paw. He tolerated scratches behind his ears from an old man in mismatched shoes and licked the hand of a woman in a wheelchair holding a stuffed bunny on her lap, causing her to giggle with delight.

After all the elderly patients in the center area had a chance to interact with the little poodle, Allison led them in a round of applause amid the happy murmur of voices. She helped Sandra into her coat. But instead of heading directly back to the entrance to the unit, she paused in front of a room with the placard, Nancy Zuehlke.

"I have a favor to ask. Nancy is having a rough morning. We couldn't get her to come to breakfast. She's very agitated. Her husband can usually calm her down, but he's playing pickleball. It's his one respite from his wife's horrible disease," Allison explained. "Perhaps Gaston might distract her. But if you'd prefer to skip this little detour—"

"No, no," Sandra hastily said. "We're happy to help if we can."

Alison glided into the room lit only by a single lamp on an end table. A wall was filled with family photos. Sandra recognized a much younger Franklin with the woman and two children, a boy and a girl.

"I just met Nancy's husband," Sandra said. "My gentleman friend also plays pickleball."

She took a step closer to the wall. High school graduation pictures of the two offspring flanked the family photo. The young woman also smiled broadly from a framed snapshot with a mountain view in the background, her arms wrapped around a Golden Retriever. In another picture the son beamed at the camera with a family of his own—two children and wife.

A frail elderly lady sat in her recliner, her white hair tumbling wildly in her face as she rocked back and forth in jerky movements. She muttered nonstop as the television droned on.

"Nancy," Allison said in a cheerful voice. "I've brought you some special visitors."

Sandra followed her further into the room, with Gaston trotting obediently behind her.

The woman looked up with a guarded expression, like she was about to be interviewed by a police detective and didn't want to reveal any damaging information. Her expression turned sly. "It's not the kids. I don't know anything about where they went. They came the other day, those kids. What was their names? You got to take it because they're ahead of you. They're always two steps ahead of me. So it wasn't my fault."

"It's not anything like that," Allison soothed. "I brought a little dog to see you. The other day you were talking about your dog, Louie. How much you missed him. I thought you'd like to meet Gaston."

At the mention of his name, Gaston bounded forward to greet the woman. Nancy glanced at him.

"Is that your dog? He's so little. You can't count on him to keep away the burglars. Louie was just here this morning. He's all right, though. You can talk to him, and he'll do what you tell him."

She reached down to pat Gaston's head. Then she focused on the picture of the young woman.

"Is Melissa coming? Her teacher called me up from whatchamacallit school. To warn me about him. I can't think of his name. I got to think of his name."

"Melissa's not coming. But Franklin will be here soon," Allison said gently.

"She told me not to let her go with him," the old lady continued. "I'm not going to. It's so far away. But she never listens. Everything goes wrong sometimes."

Nancy gaped at Sandra. "Are you a friend of Melissa's? Maybe you know his name? It was Jack, John. Something like that."

Sandra looked questioningly at Allison, who answered for her,

"This is Sandra. The dog belongs to her. She brought him in for a little visit."

"I don't want to visit. I want to talk to Melissa. I've got to tell her to stay away from him. I just hope it goes right this time. Can you get me her phone number?" Her voice grew more frantic. "Someone needs to warn her."

Allison gently touched the woman's hand, "It's ok, Nancy. It'll be all right."

Nancy jerked her hand away from Allison's touch. "But I don't feel like anything's all right. It's all wrong. It's been wrong for a long time." She started to cry.

Sandra looked helplessly at the poor woman. Gaston nuzzled Nancy's hand, and she absentmindedly stroked his head, tears dropping on his fur.

"It's all wrong,' she repeated. "I can't find that letter. I can't find her boots. I can't find anything." Her face grew contorted with emotion.

"We'd better go," Sandra said. "I don't want to upset her anymore."

"I'll send the nurse in. She'll give her something to calm her down," Allison said reassuringly.

She spoke to a resident assistant at the nurses' station, then walked Sandra to the Memory Care door, speaking in a low voice.

"Her daughter, Melissa, died many years ago under mysterious circumstances on a trip to Las Vegas. There was a man involved but the police couldn't find any evidence of wrongdoing. Unfortunately, sometimes Nancy's mind gets stuck in that black hole."

They were at the door with the keypad again. Allison punched in the code.

"I'm sorry about Nancy. I really thought seeing your dog would lift her out of her funk. She talks about her dog, Louie, all the time when she's in a better frame of mind. I better go check on her again."

She disappeared down the hallway.

Sandra opened the heavy door, but before she stepped through it, she saw an attendant carrying a stack of laundry drop a rolled-up sock. Unfortunately, Gaston also saw it. He tugged on his leash, breaking free. He dashed away, nearly tripping her in his mad escape. Sandra lost her grip on the door. It slammed shut in her face, knocking her wig slightly askew. Fearing the havoc Gaston could create running freely in the care center, Sandra grabbed the door handle to follow him. Her action set off an earsplitting alarm, like a civil defense siren warning of incoming missiles. It reverberated throughout the unit. A young male attendant in navy blue scrubs and Crocs hustled over to enter the code shutting off the noise.

"Where do you think you're going?" he said as he clutched her arm, preventing her from opening the door. "You know you aren't allowed out. Please come with me back to your room."

"Young man, unhand me." Sandra struggled against his firm grasp. "My dog just ran out that door. I need to catch him before he gets in serious trouble."

"Dog? What dog?" He surveyed the hallway. "There's no dog here."

"But he was just here," Sandra stammered. "I told you he ran out the door."

"Residents aren't allowed out without permission. Those are the rules. Let me help you to the dining area. It's time for your morning snack.

Apple slices and caramel cream cheese dip. You won't want to miss it."

The young resident assistant firmly steered her down the hallway. She could see another aide wheeling a cart filled with glasses of juice and plates of apple slices toward the area they just left.

"I don't live here. I was visiting with my dog," Sandra argued. "We just put on a little show for the residents. Rendezvous with Rover."

"My supervisor said yesterday the show was cancelled. You'll have to do better than that." He continued steering her down the hall.

"Let me go this instant." Sandra pulled her arm free. "You're making a mistake, young man." She stopped and glared at him, hands on her hips.

"Do you miss your dog? I can find you a stuffie to cuddle instead," he cajoled. "Please come with me to the activity room."

"Yes. The activity room." Sandra's face brightened. "Allison, the director, was just here. She walked me to the door. You can check."

"After I get you back into your room," the young man stubbornly insisted.

"I don't have a room. I don't live here, I tell you. For God's sake!" her voice quivered with frustration.

Sandra remembered her cell phone in her coat pocket. She pulled it out and held it in front of the resident assistant's face. "Look. I have a cell phone." She scrolled down to the call history and found Allison's name. "Here's Allison's number. Shall I call her and we'll see if I'm telling the truth?"

The young man's face grew flushed. "That won't be necessary. I'm so sorry. You look like one of the patients." His eyes widened with the realization of how that sounded. "I mean, I'm new on the job. I don't know all the residents yet. I mistook you for another lady. But now I can tell you're not a Memory Care resident."

"If this fiasco is over, will you please let me out so I can find my dog?"

"Of course. I'll open the door right away."

The man nearly ran to the keypad and entered the code. He opened the door only to discover Gaston sitting on his haunches, panting loudly, with his tongue hanging out, patiently waiting for Sandra. "And here's your dog. I'm so sorry. I hope you won't mention this to Allison."

"Since you apologized I'll let it pass. You do have to be careful that no one wanders off, I suppose. Next time, check with your supervisor before you jump to conclusions. Good day, young man."

Sandra scowled as she watched the door close. Her unhappy gaze lit on Gaston.

"Gaston, you naughty puppy," she scolded. "You were a bad boy, running away like that. No more Pork Chomps for you."

She bent down and picked up his leash. As she straightened up, she gloated, "At least we know my undercover disguise is a huge success."

CHAPTER NINE

"Can I come over? I could really use a friendly face," Arthur sounded distraught on the phone. "That detective treated me like Satan's hit man. I feel like I'm the number one suspect. I need to find a good lawyer."

"Please come right away. We'll put our heads together and figure out your next step."

Sandra shed her frumpy disguise like a snake shedding its skin. She flitted into a red silk tunic and matching pants. A shake of her head and a teasing comb took care of her flattened hair. She quickly patted on a minimum layer of foundation. She applied an extra coat of mascara and hoped Arthur was too upset to notice she wasn't her usual glamorous self. She barely had time to dab on some blush before he knocked.

As she glided to the door, she warned Gaston, "You need to be a good boy. None of your shenanigans. Especially after that stunt you pulled this morning. If you can't behave, you'll get a time-out in the kennel."

Stored in the laundry room, the kennel loomed ominously over the piles of unwashed clothes. Her threat to imprison the misbehaving poodle there was as empty as the laundry basket that stood beside it. Gaston ambled to his pink pillow bed, ignoring the knock at the door, and turned a few circles before settling down.

"You poor darling!" Sandra swooped into Arthur's arms the second she opened the door.

He clutched her to his chest like he was a drowning man tossed out of a plane and she was the life preserver under the seat.

"The interview was awful." Arthur's usually meticulous hair was clumped in strands on his forehead, shiny with perspiration. His voice rumbled with indignation "That detective makes Dr. Evil seem like Mr. Rogers. He stares at you like you've just murdered his sweet old granny. Then he starts firing question after question, hoping to catch you in a lie. I'm drenched in sweat after that dreadful inquisition."

She brushed his silver hair gently back from his forehead and kissed him sweetly. "How awful. You look like you've been through the wringer. I met that terrible man yesterday. He insinuated Gaston was a troublemaker. Come and sit on the couch. I know it's early in the day, but you look like you could use a martini."

Ignoring the wet stains under the armpits of his cashmere shirt, Sandra hung up his leather jacket on the hall tree, grasped his hand, and led him to the couch. A cocktail shaker glinted from the coffee table. As Arthur sank into the cushions, she poured the contents of the shaker into two empty martini glasses before she nestled beside him.

"It's the peacock boa," Arthur blurted out. "The medical examiner said Jake was strangled with the boa. He was surprised how strong the thing was. Strong enough to be used as a murder weapon." He shook his head. "Unbelievable."

"When I ordered it from eBay, the seller guaranteed it was all natural and heavyweight. I paid a lot for it. I thought it would last forever it was so well-made." Sandra's eyebrows knitted together, snarled in a puzzling thought. "I should have asked that detective what happens to it after the trial. I hope I get it back. That is assuming they catch the killer."

"From the way Detective Johnson interrogated me, I'm pretty sure he thinks *I'm* the killer. The questions came at me like a verbal assault rifle. How long have I known Jake? Were there any other fights or disagreements? Can I think of anyone else who had a motive to kill him? Where was I between the hours of five and seven a.m.?" Arthur pounded on the arm rest with his fist. "For Christ's sake, I was home in bed like any sensible retired person would be!"

"Did he say the medical examiner determined the time of death?" Sandra asked pointedly. "He didn't have that information when he questioned me yesterday."

"The brute didn't say—only asked me if anyone could verify my whereabouts. I told him I live alone." Arthur picked up the martini glass and swallowed a swig.

She sighed loudly. "If only we had spent the night together. I'd be your alibi."

"We've only been seeing each other for a few weeks. I didn't get the feeling you were ready for that kind of commitment. Are you?" Uncertainty colored his voice.

Her words came out in a rush. "Dear man, I'm more than ready. I didn't want to scare you off. You just moved to Crawford; I want to be more than a fling."

"Beautiful lady, you could never be just a fling. Any man would be lucky to hold you in his arms. You're so exciting and intelligent. Brains and beauty." He set down the glass and slid his arms around her. "I love talking to you. I haven't felt this close to anyone in a very long time."

Sandra snuggled closer. "I feel the same. I had a terrible experience with a big phony just a few months ago. We were on a romantic river cruise. The man cozied up to me, pretended to be smitten with me. He turned out to be a thief, an international criminal. Wanted in several countries. I fell for his act. I was such a fool. Now I'm more cautious."

"I'm so sorry to hear that. I've had my share of bad romances, too. So many false promises. Ladies who only say what they think you want to hear. It's been hard. But you're different from the others."

"I tell it like it is. It's who I am. Take it or leave it."

"Nothing phony about you. You're the real thing. I'd never leave you. I'm falling in love with you." Arthur raised his hand to her face, then gently lifted her hand to his. "In fact, I'd like to take you with me the next time I travel to Italy on my consulting job. I'd show you the beautiful Italian Riviera. White sandy beaches. Perfect place for a honeymoon."

Sandra sighed. "I'd love that. I've never traveled to Italy or the Mediterranean."

"Picturesque villas nestled into the side of a cliff overlooking the sea. One's a fancy hotel with incredible wine and the most delicious food. The blue Mediterranean sparkles just like your eyes."

"You make everything sound so special."

"Not as special as you, my lovely lady. I can tell we have a spark."

He drew her lips near to his. Sandra smelled the pleasant musk of his aftershave, closed her eyes, and felt the warmth of his mouth on hers. The spark was starting to ignite a long-lost flame inside her.

Suddenly a squeal of brakes came from outside. Then a loud metallic crash. A horn blasted through the still, fall air. Both of them jerked apart as Gaston jumped off his pillow and started barking.

"What was that?"

Arthur stood up and dashed to the window overlooking the street, with Sandra close behind. "What the hell?"

A beat-up grey Buick stopped at the point of contact with the back bumper of his shiny black Ford Thunderbird. A scruffy figure in a

Green Bay Packers cap slowly emerged from the Buick, scratching his head. He studied the dented fender of the Buick and stepped back to scrutinize the sports car. Then Norm slowly made his way up the driveway to Sandra's door.

"Oh dear," Sandra moaned. "That's my handyman, Norm. He drives my car. It looks like he's had a little fender bender."

"With my pristine Thunderbird!"

Arthur sprinted out the door in a flash, not even stopping to put on his jacket. Gaston rushed out in front of him and barked a greeting to Norm.

"Hiya, little buddy," Norm said as he patted his head.

Arthur pushed past them and went to examine his car. As his eyes swept over the damage, his face contorted with rage.

"Look what you did to my car!" He fired out the words like bullets from an assault rifle.

"I know, dude. I'm sorry. There's a scratch above your bumper." Norm pointed to the thin white line. "I can go down to Auto Express and buy a can of paint to match your car. I'll buff it out and fix 'er up like new."

"I'm not allowing an oaf like you to work on my expensive car. I'll take it to the Ford dealer and have it fixed properly." Arthur stood wide-legged, fists planted firmly on his hips.

"Suit yourself, man. Just trying to help."

Then Norm turned to Sandra and said, "Your car is way worse. Look at the front fender. I'm really sorry. But I'll get it repaired. My pal at the auto body shop owes me a favor."

"I'm sure you'll take care of it, dearie," Sandra said reassuringly. "It's not as bad as it looks. Is it still drivable?"

"Yeah, I can back 'er up and put it in the garage. No prob-lay-mo."

"What the hell happened?" Arthur asked.

"I'd like to blame it on the lazy mechanic at the shop," Norm answered. "He was working on my car. He musta took a brake. Get it. B-R-A-K-E."

Arthur's face turned red and his voice grew frosty. "I fail to see any humor in the situation."

Sandra jumped in. "I have insurance. I'll go in the house and call my agent. He'll see to the proper repairs. But I need to tell him what happened, Norm."

Norm appeared sheepish as he answered. "I looked down for a second to change the radio station. When I looked up, that big black Thunderbird was right there. Like it jumped in front of me. I couldn't slam on the brakes quick enough. I feel awful. Not a good way to meet the fella that Sandra has been raving about. 'He's so handsome. So smart. Such a good pickleball player.'

"I'm Norm, her handyman. I take care of the place for her." Norm held out his callused hand with an uncertain smile, which Arthur pointedly ignored. He dropped his arm back to his side as he belatedly added, "And we solve cases together."

"Solve cases?" Arthur repeated with a confused look.

"Never mind, dearie. I'll explain later. Let's go back inside so I can make the call." Sandra gently rested her hand on the man's forearm. A gust of cold air ruffled her flowing tunic, making her shiver. "Besides, it's a little chilly out here without my coat."

"I'm so sorry, beautiful. How thoughtless of me. I can see you're shaking in the cold air. Let me put my arm around you to warm you up." Arthur draped his arm over her and guided her back along the driveway, whispering in her ear, "We can take up where we left off."

Norm raised his arm in a friendly wave and called to their retreating backs. "It was nice meeting ya, Arthur." Under his breath he said, "Not."

He noticed Gaston still hovering by the Thunderbird. "Ya better catch up with them and get back inside, little fella. It's getting cold out here."

The dog sniffed the ground around the Thunderbird's wheel, pausing to watch the wind blow some fallen leaves under the car's body. Gaston gave a sharp yip, raised his back leg, and sent a gush of warm urine on Arthur's sleek whitewall tires. After another happy *arf*, he trotted up the driveway with a satisfied expression on his doggy face.

CHAPTER TEN

Whenever the first voice Vlad heard in the morning was Maria's, his ex-wife, he knew it was going to be a bad day. Her shrill pitch sent shivers down his spine, worse than his grade schoolteacher's fingernails scraping on a blackboard. Alice's Red Queen could go toe to toe with her and come out of the battle in shreds. Whatever tenderness Maria possessed was lavished on Gordy, Vlad's replacement, and the leftover crumbs doled out to their three kids. Most of their conversations after the divorce were amicable, for the sake of the children, but occasionally Maria relapsed into the Untamed Shrew, like this morning.

"I need you to pick up the kids early on Saturday morning. Gordy and I are attending the Chicago Build Expo this weekend, and we need an early start."

After a fitful night's sleep, Vlad's brain felt groggy. He answered slowly, "How early do you want to leave?"

"Be here at five. We want to get to McCormick Place by eight. Can't miss the first speaker. She's talking about a digital marketing strategy that withstands the elements. Gordy thinks we need to embrace technology and build sustainability more."

Gordy owned the real estate office where Maria worked so she viewed his words as the gospel according to Gordy. Vlad learned not to cast any aspersions on Gordy's pronouncements except when it came to child rearing, since Gordy had not been blessed with children in his previous two marriages. "I can be there before five, if you need me."

"That would be fine. I should warn you, Erin will probably ask you to take her driving. She's in Driver's Ed Behind the Wheel, and she's always whining that she never gets enough practice. I'm not too sure I want her to get a driver's license yet. We'd have to share the car, and I need to be ready to show a house at the drop of a hat."

"If Nicholas can watch Kaitlyn for a little while, I can take her out." Vlad got out of bed and turned on the drip coffee maker he'd set up the night before. The comforting sound of coffee splashing in the pot and the wafting smell of hazelnut made talking to Maria almost bearable.

"Nicholas has an Odyssey of the Mind practice at Alex's house at one so if you're going to cave in to Erin's demands, do it in the morning. You'll need to drop him off and pick him up at four."

"No problem. Anything else?" Vlad stifled a yawn as he rubbed some crud from his eyes.

Maria droned on, "I forgot to mention. Gordy and I are staying overnight in Chicago. Can you stay in the house with the kids tomorrow night? There's no room in your cracker box closet for all three. I don't want them staying at your fiancé's place either. She has that nasty cat. You know I'm extremely allergic. They come home with cat hair all over their clothes, and I sneeze all night."

"I'll pack an overnight bag. What about Kaitlyn? Does she have anything on Saturday?"

"Not really, but I promised you'd take her to the library. They just changed the play center to a fall harvest theme. She didn't have time to pick apples last time and had a major meltdown."

A dull ache radiated from his stomach as he listened to Maria's litany of complaints. How had he once found her voice mellifluous and appealing? Now he managed to interject, "I'll take her while Nick's at OM."

"You miss the joys of Kaitlyn's tantrums. She never acts up when she's with you," Maria sniped.

Vlad thought, *There's a good reason for that. She's stubborn like you, and you two butt heads at times.*

Instead he said, "Don't worry. I've got this. Just go and learn about digital marketing in real estate."

Vlad sat wearily at the kitchen table while he waited for the coffee maker to sputter loudly then stop, signaling he could pour a cup. He looked around his combination bedroom, living room, and kitchen and sighed. He knew he should make up the Murphy bed and push it back into the wall. A few months ago Norm finally got the mechanism fixed so it properly sprang into the wall position. Yesterday's clothes were scattered on the love seat, and dirty dishes were piled in the sink from several days ago. Students' quiz papers were stacked on the table ready to be shoved in his briefcase with his laptop. The new athletic wear he bought at the SuperSaver was still in the bag on his dresser. There was too much to do before he took a shower. It was so overwhelming that that the dull ache sharpened into a knife-like pain in his guts. He willed himself to rise up off the chair and move. It was his morning to go undercover at the weight room, hence the new t-shirt and shorts. He hadn't been back to CHAW since discovering the body. But today his part of the investigation would begin in earnest. If only he felt up to the job.

Vlad's first impulse when signaling the turn into the CHAW's parking lot was to drive on past. The theory that exercise improves mental health seemed like a bunch of malarkey. Couldn't prove it by his experience. Just the opposite. Being ridiculed in the weight room and finding a dead body in the locker room didn't seem conducive for emotional wellness.

He told himself. *I'm doing this for Sandra, not for myself.* She lent him her car to find Erin when his daughter had been swept away by the terrorist plot. The discount rent on the apartment helped keep him from sinking into debt when Maria asked him to move out. She was a surrogate grandmother to his kids. They loved their Auntie Sandra so much and even loved Gaston, although he couldn't fathom why. Images of her, pale and fragile in her bandages suffering from a third-degree burn, popped up in his mind. He had visited her daily in rehab while she recuperated for months after a mishap with Gaston's burning hoop trick set her kitchen ablaze. To prevent a stranger from becoming her court appointed guardian, Vlad stepped in to assume the role himself. He sighed and resignedly picked up his gym bag.

The weight room was packed with early morning enthusiasts. Vlad knew the bully had gone to his reward. He hoped his buddy would be there—the guy with the Harley eagle tattoo who laughed at his jokes. Vlad made sure there'd be no reason to make fun of his gym clothes. He bought a copy of *Men's Health* at the drugstore to guide him in his purchase of appropriate garb and didn't shave for a week. His incipient beard was as scruffy as any criminal's on TV cop shows, and he didn't bother combing his bed head hair.

There was the sidekick, working out on a seated machine pushing a large sledge with legs that looked like giant redwoods. Arm muscles bulged from his white sleeveless undershirt; the eagle tat pulsed with the exertion. The guy's body was drenched with so much sweat it pooled into a puddle under him. Luckily, the leg press next to him was vacant. Vlad took a deep cleansing breath to brace his nostrils for the stench that emanated from Tattoo Guy and marched over to the equipment. Unsure of how much weight his legs could push, he just went with what was left on the machine. Too much. It took all his concentration to drive them forward. Soon he was grunting in unison with Tat Guy, unsure of how much longer he could keep his legs moving. Already they felt like they were molded from gelatin.

During a short break when Tat Guy paused to wipe the sweat from his forehead with a grimy towel, Vlad casually commented, "Hard to believe someone got murdered in the locker room. Did you know the man?"

Tat Guy's face darkened as he twisted his lips into a snarl "Yeah, I knew him. He was a good buddy of mine. I hope the cops catch the bastard who offed him."

Then he mashed the towel into a ball and flung it to the floor by the free-standing weights. He slowly got to his feet, eyes following the trajectory of the towel.

Vlad quickly spoke, "I never met him. What was he like?"

"He was a hell of a guy. Nobody messed with him. A big hit with the ladies, too." Tat Guy moved over to the free weights and knelt to construct a bar bell.

Grateful for the break from the machine, Vlad followed on rubbery legs, determined to continue the conversation. He grabbed a bar and dropped it down, putting some twenty pounders on the ends. A twinge of pain in his back caused him to reconsider. Vlad spotted a set of dumb bells and removed some of the weights, hoping the Leviathan didn't notice his shift to lighter weights.

"I take it he wasn't married?" he asked still kneeling.

Tat Guy stood up and began a bicep curl. "Naw, why settle for hamburger when you can have steak every night?"

Vlad felt a bigger tug in his lower back as he rose from his knees and hefted the dumb bells, lifting as high as his chest. He ignored the warning stab of pain and kept on talking.

"Did you hang around any place special?"

"Mostly the Thirsty Rhino. Lots of chicks there. Sometimes Hogs and Honeys." Tat Guy hefted the bar bell over his head and grunted, "Why you wanna know?"

"Just wondering. Seemed like a bad way to go for a good guy, like you're telling me he was." Vlad set his weights down and brushed away the trickle of sweat from his eyes. His legs were still quivering. He leaned against the wall, not trusting himself to walk yet.

Tat Guy set the bar bell down, too, and said, "Maybe some of the punks in the bars didn't think he was so great. But Jake never gave a damn what anybody thought. He liked to give the nerds around here some shit, too. We'd have a good laugh about it."

Just then, Brad, the CHAW director, entered the room, heartily greeting some of the men using the equipment, "Hey, Tom, good to see you taking advantage of the early morning hours. I always say, 'The early bird catches the burn.'"

He stopped by a patron on the bench press. "You, too, Mike. Getting in shape for the Fall Fun Run?"

The man answered, "You betcha. I'm going to beat last year's time."

Brad drifted over to the machine Vlad had just vacated. "I like to get a good workout in before I start the day, too. Gets the old heart pumping and the blood flowing."

Before he adjusted the weights, he noticed Vlad propped up against the wall.

"Dr. Chomsky, how are you doing?" A look of concern clouded his face as Brad veered in his direction. "What a terrible thing to have happened. I can't even imagine finding a body in the men's locker room. If there's anything CHAW can do to help deal with it, please let us know." He placed a sympathetic hand on Vlad's shoulder.

Tat Gut set down the bar bell and stared at Vlad with narrowed eyes. "What the hell is he talking about?"

"Don't you know? Vlad found Jake's body in the shower," Brad said. "He alerted Debbie, and she called the police. Stayed around to help the detective with the investigation." His eyes shone as he praised Vlad. "You're kind of a hero. We appreciate your courage." He grabbed Vlad's hand and shook it vigorously.

Clenching his beefy hands into fists, the tattooed man exploded, "What kind of a game are you playing, asking me all those questions and acting dumb? Are you some kind of freak? Some kind of sick bastard who gets off on other people's pain?"

"I'm sure there's some kind of mistake." Brad's face grew flushed. "Dr. Chomsky's a professor at Crawford University. He's a respectable man, even been in the newspapers a few times for helping the police solve crimes. He's one of the good guys." He took a tentative step toward the angry man.

Tat Guy raised one of his fists, then paused it midair. Turning toward Vlad, he growled, "The only mistake is that you messed with the wrong guy. *Me.* You asshole!"

After dropping his fist he advanced so near that Vlad could feel his hot breath on his cheeks and smell the garlicky sausage he had for breakfast.

"Stay out of my way. I'll flatten you if you ever get in my face again."

Tat Guy gave him a hard shove, then stormed out of the weight room. Not even the wall could keep Vlad upright. As he pitched sideways, he thought of Icarus plunging to the earth. Time slowed down as his sweaty fingers slipped along the concrete block but he could find no purchase. His back contorted in a piercing spasm as he landed in an awkward heap. Between his spongy legs and dubious lower back, Vlad wondered if he would he ever walk normally again.

Instead of the hard floor, a smelly wadded-up towel cushioned Vlad's descent.

One of God's tender mercies.

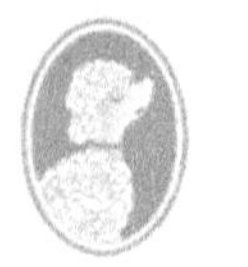

CHAPTER ELEVEN

"I'm so sorry, Doctor Chomsky." Brad grasped Vlad's forearm to haul him to his feet. "I can't imagine why Marco reacted that way. Whatever you said certainly didn't warrant such a violent response. I'll follow up with him. He's under a lot of stress since the murder. Jake Bender was his best friend."

Vlad gratefully accepted the director's helping hand. When he tried to stand upright, his lower back screamed in pain. He clung to Brad's arm like a barnacle to the side of a ship. Unable to do much more than sway unsteadily on his feet, he managed to say, "Just a misunderstanding. I didn't realize how close he was to the victim when I started chatting with him about the tragedy."

"Are you OK? Were you injured when you fell? You seem a bit wobbly." The director's face reflected his growing alarm.

"It's an old sports injury. It flares up once in a while." Vlad neglected to share the sport was boudoir gymnastics with a twenty-year-old coed during his wild oats phase. His face grew red with the memory of his attempts at Marlboro Man sex. Thank God Beatrice saved him from such foolishness.

"Try taking a few steps. Work out the kinks." Brad continued to offer his arm as ballast as Vlad took a few tentative steps. "That's it. You're doing great. Try a few more."

Vlad's legs were no longer quivering, but his back throbbed with each small movement. The pain was bearable; it had to be bearable. He had classes to teach on Friday morning. Two big lectures. Then he was done for the week. Could he show a video? The students wouldn't mind. Half of them were hungover from Thursday's early start on the weekend partying. He bit his lip to keep from groaning as he took a few more tentative steps.

"Shall I escort you to the locker room to change?" Brad asked solicitously.

Vlad let out an emphatic, "Hell, no! I never want to set foot in that place again."

Vlad's outburst startled the director. "I'm so sorry. How

thoughtless of me. You obviously aren't ready to return to the scene of the crime."

"I'm still having nightmares about the poor man." Vlad gestured to where he dropped his bag. "I'll need my gym bag to dress for work. I hope I have some pain relief tablets in there."

"I have some over-the-counter tablets in my office. How about changing in the men's room on this floor? While you're dressing I'll get you some medication and a glass of water."

Brad assisted him to the men's room, plunked his duffle on the counter, and scooted out.

Fortunately, the restroom was in the middle of the hallway. Vlad grasped the side of the sink and gritted his teeth. He kicked off his shoes without untying them and slipped out of his gym shorts. To hell with modesty. He didn't care if anyone saw him in his skivvies. He just wanted to get his shirt and pants on and flee.

It was slow-going. Bending down to pull up his khakis was pure torture. He let go of the sink and muddled through zipping and snapping them. Getting out of the snug t-shirt was a bit harder. He didn't have the body for an athletic fit. He grasped the bottom hem and tried to pull it over his head, but that involved some tugging and twisting. It hurt like hell. He gave up and put his long-sleeved polo shirt over the tee. Good thing he'd applied extra cologne today. After splashing some cold water on his face, he was ready to slide into his penny loafers. His white socks peeked out from the trouser leg.

Brad entered with two blue tablets and a glass of cold water. "I always take two at first. You need to get on top of the pain. Then it's one every twelve hours. I brought you what's left in the bottle. That's the least I can do."

Vlad gulped the two down with a tip of the glass. He shoved his shorts and gym shoes in the bag and hobbled out of the building.

By the time he pulled into the parking lot at school, the pain medication was starting to kick in. He grabbed his briefcase with his laptop and went straight to the lecture hall. In his Medieval Europe class he was going to speak about the rise of Islam and the crusades of Europe's knights. Luckily, he'd downloaded a video about Islamic culture and could show the beginning of the conflict. World Civilization was more challenging. He'd have to tough it through his lecture on Mesopotamia, maybe let them get into study groups and review for the upcoming test.

Standing up front at the lectern, Vlad heard an earring laden young man snicker when he noticed the red stripe of Vlad's white crew socks above his loafers, The student elbowed the long-haired coed next to him, and they both hid their laugh behind their hands. A quote flashed in his mind: "Old age and treachery will always beat youth and exuberance." Sandra was living proof of that maxim. He wanted to warn the young man not to be so cocky. Instead, he shuffled his notes and launched into his talk.

After his classes the elevator jerked and moaned as Vlad rode it to the top of the Humanities Building. He limped past the secretary, pain etched on his face. He bit the inside of his cheek to keep from groaning.

"What on earth happened to you?" she exclaimed.

"Just a fall off the bike." He attempted nonchalance. "No big deal."

Once in the sanctuary of his office, he lay down on the floor and closed his eyes. The hard surface felt better on his back. He imagined himself sinking into the floor, softening all his muscles as he slowly inhaled and exhaled. Staff left early on Fridays. Only three more hours. He conjured up Beatrice's sweet smile, her sexy dark eyes, her gentle touch, her tube of lidocaine. They could order a pizza and discuss where to go next on the case.

Suddenly his office door was thrust open. A male voice interrupted his reverie.

"Vlad, there's an urgent matter we need to discuss."

The clomp of footsteps, then a panicked shout, "On my God, are you all right? Answer me, man. Do I need to call 9-1-1?"

He opened his eyes to discover Chuck Robbins, the department head, looming over him like a Macy's Thanksgiving Day balloon, his face as white as the Pillsbury Doughboy's.

A groan escaped his lips. "I'm ok."

"You don't look ok. Flat on your back. You're not having a heart attack," Chuck squealed. "That's how I found Jerome when he had his big coronary! Holy Mother of God, I don't want another colleague almost dying on my watch."

Chuck dashed over to the landline on Vlad's desk. "Let me call for help."

He picked up the receiver and hit a button. "Hello. 9-1-1."

"NO! Stop! Please don't," Vlad cried. "Tell them it's a mistake. I'm fine. I had a fall earlier this morning and wrenched my back, that's all. It feels better when I lie down."

Chuck blathered into the phone. "Never mind. He says he's all right. But I'm not so sure about that. He seems a little incoherent. I'll stay on the line until he gets up off the floor."

Vlad pushed himself up to a sitting posture. "Put the phone down. It isn't necessary. I can get up. It just takes me a little longer."

To prove it he slowly shifted to his right side, distributed his weight on his outstretched arms, and thrust his body into an upright position. After standing defiantly, he declared, "See, I'm not in any danger of dying."

Chuck cradled the phone to his chest, reluctant to give up control of the situation, "You look like hell. The EMTs can be here in minutes."

"No. Please hang up."

Vlad glared at the man until he apologized to the dispatcher and rang off.

"Thank you. Now can you tell me why you're in my office?"

Chuck's ears tinged red as he said, "I'd like to take a sabbatical next semester. I've been offered a fellowship at the University of Cape Town to study the current political climate. It'd give my Modern Africa class a real jolt."

"Congratulations! But what does this have to do with me?"

"There's only money in the budget for a part-time replacement. I was hoping you'd pick up one of my classes for the spring semester."

"Let me consider it. I can't think clearly at this moment," Vlad replied.

"Sure thing. Why don't you take the rest of the day off? I'll cover for you if an emergency comes up," Chuck offered with an expansive wave of his hand.

"Your kindness is much appreciated."

Vlad ushered him out of his office and turned out the lights. His briefcase filled with student papers could wait until Sunday night.

INSTEAD OF GOING TO HIS APARTMENT, Vlad drove to Beatrice's house. She'd be home soon. Until then he could resume his supine position on her living room floor in peace. He put his key in the lock, *click,* and the door opened to a dimly lit interior, uninhabited except by him. The carpeted floor in her living room beckoned alluringly. Descending into its soft embrace, Vlad heaved a sigh of pure contentment as he closed his eyes. Alone at last his mind drifted to a place where pain finally existed on the periphery. His breathing became so deep and regular it was transformed into a gentle snore.

Thousands of tiny sharp knives penetrated his skin as the furry assassin landed on his chest and emitted a bloodcurdling *mrow*. Vlad's eyes flew open to discover two searing yellow orbs scrutinizing him menacingly. The demon cat! Vlad felt Max's switching tail hitting his stomach like an overseer's whip. Sharp fangs drew near to his exposed throat. For the second time that day, the breath of his attacker was so close he could smell the fishy cat food. His survival instincts took over. He thrust the cat off his defenseless body and leapt to his feet, ignoring the loud protests of his lower back.

With his heart beating wildly and his breath coming in gasps, Vlad fled to the shelter of the utility closet with the demon cat hot on his heels. He knew he could find a source of protection there. The cat's earsplitting yowls echoed throughout the empty house. Just as claws grazed his exposed ankle, he made it through the door and slammed it in the beast's face.

Vlad froze for a moment, trying to quiet his nerves as the cat's yowls quieted to a few hisses, then silence. He took more calming breaths despite the overpowering scent of ammonia and lemon furniture polish until his heart slowed to its normal pace. He fumbled in the dark for the light and flicked it on. The overhead bare bulb illuminated the crowded space, and he found the weapon he needed hanging on a hook.

Clutching Beatrice's heavy-duty straw broom to his chest, Vlad cautiously opened the door. The cat skulked on his haunches in the hallway, closely watching his every move, ears drawn back, tail twitching, eyes glinting ominously. The instant Vlad tiptoed out of the sanctuary Max turned into a spitting, hissing tornado.

He hurtled himself at Vlad, claws slicing the air like a Texas chainsaw massacre in a cat's body. His fur stood on end so he appeared twice as vicious. Vlad bore the brunt of the attack, fending him off with the broom, the bristles thwarting the deadly claws.

"Get back, you devil!" Vlad shouted.

The cat hissed in reply.

Vlad thrust the broom in the cat's face. Max fell back grudgingly. Pieces of straw littered the hallway. Step by step Vlad painstakingly made his way back to the living room. Each movement forward was accompanied by a swat of the cat's paw. Max's deep throated growls signaled a stalemate as he stalked his prey. Vlad sighted his goal,

Beatrice's Lazy Girl recliner. Never taking his eyes off the enemy, Vlad backed into the chair and sat down. He gave the broom an occasional warning shake. Max retreated to the arm of the couch where he kept Vlad under surveillance. Vlad slowly raised the footrest under the watchful eyes of the cat, easing the pressure on his lower back.

A few hours later Beatrice found the two of them in a truce. Vlad was dozing in the recliner, with the broom resting on his chest. Max was curled up nearby on the couch, also sleeping soundly. Neither moved a muscle as she crept into the room.

When she turned on the lamp, she clapped her hands in delight. "I'm so glad to see the two of you are beginning to become friends."

# CHAPTER TWELVE

When Sandra saw Jacob Bender's obituary in the *Daily Gazette*, she knew it was time to go snooping through his home. Should she attempt a break-in when most of his friends were at his funeral, like burglars robbing the deceased's empty house? At least she hoped it was empty. But even if he had a roommate, she had the perfect cover story to maneuver her way inside if someone was there.

After thumbing through the phone book without much success, she said to Gaston, "Lovey Puppy, we've got to find out where Jake Bender lived so we can do a thorough search."

At the sound of her voice, the dog clambered out of his new sheepskin dog bed, a present from Arthur, and ambled over to her. He sniffed her hand, but when he found there wasn't a dog treat in it, he went back to his comfy bed and closed his eyes.

Sandra snapped her fingers. "I know. We can try Juanita's daughter again. She was a big help with the Alexandria Adams case."

Sandra dialed her friend. After a few minutes of conversation, she asked, "How's your daughter doing at the police station?"

Juanita couldn't keep the pride out of her voice. "Rosalie's the evening dispatcher. She's already got a commendation for quick thinking involving a drug overdose. Saved a kid's life."

"I knew a girl as sharp as your daughter would go far. I'm wondering if she could give me a little hand with our current investigation. You know, my peacock feather boa was found at the murder scene."

"Found at the scene? Hell, it was wrapped around the naked guy's neck. It wasn't a quickie gone bad, was it?" Juanita giggled.

"Get serious. That hulk of a detective came to question me. My new man is his number one suspect, just because they had a little spat the day before. I've got to find out who really had a motive to bump the guy off."

"Why don't you lend your dog to the cops? He has a nose for ferreting out criminals."

"I tried, but that detective doesn't take Gaston seriously. That's why I've taken it upon myself to find the guilty party."

"What do you need Rosalie for? She's only a dispatcher."

"She can get me the address of the victim, that's all."

"I'll text her right away. She liked sneaking the autopsy report to you from the last case. She gets a little bored handling noise complaints and lost dog calls. She felt like an undercover informant. Got her blood pumping."

As soon as Sandra received Jake Bender's address on her phone, she called Norm. "Can you come up right away? I've got a job for you."

In the meantime she wiped off all her makeup and dressed in her thrift store clothes. She was just finishing tucking her hair in the grey bobbed wig when Norm came in. Gaston greeted him at the door with a happy yip.

When Norm saw her, he whistled. "I hardly recognize you. Are you going undercover? Just like the alligator wearing a vest?"

"What are you talking about?"

"He was an investigator. Good thing you put on your sneakers. If I was a medieval spy, I'd be called Sir Veillance."

"Enough already. Can you drive us over to the apartment complex at this address, 568 Cole Street? I'll fill you in on my plan on the drive over. Come on, Gaston. Let's get to work."

The little dog tolerated putting on the service dog harness without a growl or a whine. He trotted to the dented Buick and hopped in the back seat, pressing his wet nose to the rear window. He seemed to listen intently while Sandra explained her scheme to get into Jake's apartment.

When they arrived the apartment manager, a large pear-shaped woman in a faded gold and green jogging suit and brown clog slippers the size of canoes, answered Sandra's knock on the rental office door. The office doubled as her apartment. A television blared in the next room with the angry voices of arguing guests on a tabloid talk show. The woman brushed her uncombed salt and pepper hair away from her face, but her eyes drifted to the open door where the voices rose to a fever pitch, much to the delight of the cheering audience. Sandra cleared her throat with a loud *ahem* before she launched into her spiel.

"May I ask a favor of you?" she began.

The woman eyed Gaston warily and said, "We don't allow no dogs or cats in the apartments. Landlord's orders."

"I'm not looking for a place to rent. I'm in town for my nephew's funeral tomorrow. My nephew is—was—Jacob Bender. Poor unfortunate lad. Struck down in the prime of his life." Sandra drew a handkerchief out of her brown coat pocket and dabbed at her eyes. "I'm just devastated."

Suddenly the woman shifted her attention to Sandra. "We never had no one who lived here get murdered before. It was a shock to everyone in the building."

"What a tragedy. Jacob was only sixty. He had his whole life ahead of him. He left us too soon." Sandra bit her lip, trying to hold back the tears.

"Yeah, it was a damn shame. He always paid his rent on time. Kept the noise down when he entertained his lady friends. Lent me a beer a time or two. Never smoked in his apartment. We don't get many tenants like him." She sighed loudly. "I'll miss him. My condolences. He never mentioned no relatives."

"My sister and our parents had a falling-out when Jake was born. We were brought up Catholic, and Angie, Jake's mother, took up with a Jewish fellow. Broke Mother's heart when she refused to have him baptized. They stopped speaking, then Angie and Ezra moved away."

"Geez, Jake never mentioned he was part Jewish." The manager shook her head.

"My sister wasn't very religious so it wouldn't have been important. We lost touch for many years. I didn't even know when she passed until I saw it in the newspaper obituary. Angela Bender, nee Orlowski. Ezra's deceased, too." Sandra's voice cracked "The obituary didn't even mention me, his last living relative."

"Too bad," the manager clucked sympathetically.

"I was wondering if I could look around his place. Maybe find a picture of my sister. I know it's a lot to ask, but it would mean so much to me. I only have her high school photo."

The manager screwed up her face with indecision. "I'm not sure the cops would like it. They came and got his computer. Searched his apartment for hours. His buddy's supposed to clear out the rest of his stuff."

"Please. It would mean so much to me. No one will ever know. I'll be in and out quick as can be. Angie was my only sister." Sandra clasped her hands together in supplication.

"I guess so. As long as that dog don't cause no trouble." She glared at Gaston. "I'll get the keys."

The woman trudged over to a hook on the wall that held a giant ring filled with a dozen keys.

"Let's go. The apartment's upstairs."

Sandra slowly followed the woman up the stairs, thanking her profusely all the way. She could barely contain her excitement at the prospect of searching Jacob Bender's apartment like a true detective. She reached down and gave Gaston a little warning pat. She needed his psychic abilities now more than ever.

The manager opened the door and stood aside while Sandra and Gaston entered the room, scanning the man's apartment. Sliding doors to a coat closet hung open, jammed full with leather jackets and various sport team hoodies. A black leather pit group surrounded the biggest flat-screen television Sandra had ever seen. Empty beer bottles and pizza boxes littered the fake stone coffee table. A computer desk with papers stuffed into every compartment screamed to be thoroughly searched. A single abstract painting on the wall displayed bright patches of reds and blues that barely concealed a nude woman.

"Not many family pictures in here," the manager commented as she scrutinized Sandra and Gaston's move toward the desk. "Don't know what you're gonna find in the bedroom." She stared pointedly at the painting.

Suddenly a voice called from downstairs. "Hey there. Anybody around to show me an apartment?"

The manager drifted to the top of the stairs and shouted, "I'm up here. Be with you in a minute."

Sandra heard footsteps on the stairs but was too busy shuffling through bar tabs and grocery receipts to look at the source.

The top of a Green Bay Packers hat appeared at the foot of the staircase.

"Ya mind if I come up?" Norm didn't wait for an answer as he loped up the stairs. He whistled when he saw the manager.

"Wow, green and gold. Ya must be a Packer fan, too. I never miss a game. How about you?"

"They barely won last week. The defense kept them in the game. I can't believe how many passes were dropped." The woman's face lit up when she started to talk about the Packers. "The new defense coach seems to know his stuff."

"The team just needs some time to gel," Norm said. "I heard there's a vacant apartment here. That true?"

"We actually will have two openings. This one here." The

woman jerked her head toward the open door. "There's one downstairs, too."

"Could ya show me the downstairs one? I'm not too crazy about climbing stairs after a hard night's work."

"Sure. Just a minute."

The manager called into Jake's apartment. "I'll be right back. I need to show this fellow around."

"No worries." Sandra waved her away. "I'm almost done here."

She heard Norm ask the woman, "What does a Minnesota Vikings fan do when their team wins the Superbowl?"

"I don't know. Faint?"

"Nah, they turn off the PlayStation Four."

The manager laughed all the way down the stairs.

"Quick, Gaston. We haven't got much time. Norm's only got so many football jokes."

Sandra rifled through another compartment scattering bills and advertisements for credit cards and electronics. Nothing stood out as a reason for murder. She opened the drawer at the side to find a tangle of charger cords and empty CD cases.

"Nothing here. The police probably took away all the good clues," she said.

Gaston let out a little wuff and trotted toward the next room, with Sandra close behind. She pushed open the door to the kitchen. The little dog stood on his hind legs and scratched at the counter with his front paws.

"Sorry, love, but you won't find any Pork Chomps or Pup-a-ronis in here."

Sandra checked out the refrigerator. Pickles, catsup, and Gatorade were lined up in the door's shelf. A half-eaten Chinese take-out congealed in a cardboard carton on the top shelf. A gallon jug containing some foul-looking liquid stood next to it. The bottom shelf held the remainder of a twelve-pack of beer.

"Ugh! How can anyone live like this?" Sandra said as she sniffed at the pile of dirty dishes in the sink.

She started opening cabinets and saw pots and pans, a large cast iron skillet, beer glasses emblazoned with names of multiple breweries, and some stoneware plates. Something red and white caught her eye. She picked it up. An old Betty Crocker's Picture Cookbook with a pattern of white curlicues on the red cover. Gaston barked twice. She flipped opened the cover. In a spidery handwriting she read: To Mr. and Mrs. Ezra Bender, Feb. 10, 1962, from Mr. and Mrs. Eugene Harris.

"Funny. Jake Bender didn't seem like the sentimental type to hang on to his dead mother's cookbook. His kitchen doesn't look like he did any cleaning, much less cooking, does it, Gaston?"

The dog barked again when he heard his name. Sandra thumbed through the book's well-worn pages, splotched with food stains and penciled-in notations like *Add more sugar* and *Skip the fennel*. Tucked between the "Baking at High Altitudes" page and the stiff endpaper, she found several bank checking statements addressed to Eugene Harris at this apartment's address. She unfolded the top one, dated just two weeks ago, and scanned the deposits and withdrawals. Four cash deposits of nine thousand and five hundred dollars each leapt off the page at her. Dumbfounded, she stared at the numbers.

"What on earth was Jake the Snake doing to earn this much cash in a month?" Sandra muttered. "This account has over forty thousand dollars in it."

Gaston gave a warning bark. Voices could be heard in the next room. With fingers trembling with excitement, Sandra stuffed the bank statements in her coat pocket. She slammed the cookbook shut and hastily replaced it on the shelf. Her heart was beating like Buddy Rich doing a drum solo.

Then the woman called through the door, "Are you about done in here? Did you find what you were looking for?"

Sandra took a deep breath to calm her shaky nerves before she answered. "No such luck. But you were a dear to let me look." She hoped her downcast eyes and quivering lip would convince the manager of her sorrow due to the fruitless search.

"Did you hear about the football player who was going blind?" She heard Norm say. "They made him a ref."

The manager was laughing heartily as Sandra entered the room. Gaston led the way, his head down and tail dragging. Sandra lifted a crumpled tissue to her eyes and dabbed away at a fake tear. The two shuffled past the two Packers fans.

Still chuckling, the manager elbowed Norm and declared, "I'm looking forward to you moving in here. You're a hoot!"

Sandra choked back a sob. "I'll have to remember my sister as she was in her youth. Poor girl! Left Jake all alone. Like the song says, 'Only the good die young.'"

"In that case, I guess you and me don't need to worry about kicking the bucket anytime soon." Norm elbowed the manager back, sending her off into another round of laughter.

Sandra gave him a subtle thumbs-up as she stumbled past. He gave her an equally subtle nod. He watched the two detectives start down the stairs before he returned to his conversation with the manager.

"Did ya hear the one about the guy who found a used football at the secondhand store?"

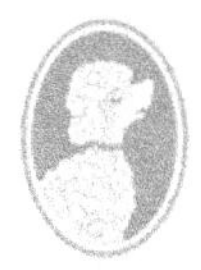

CHAPTER THIRTEEN

"Look what I found in an old cookbook!" Sandra waved the bank statements at Norm when he arrived at the car ten minutes later. "A savings account statement under a different name but with Jake Bender's address. He's been making regular cash deposits of about forty thousand every month. Where did he get that kind of money?"

Gaston pawed at the back of Norm's seat and yipped in his ear.

"I bet not doing anything legal. Was he selling drugs? Fencing stolen goods? Money laundering? Some sort of internet scam? Gambling? I can think of a dozen ways Jake could be dealing in that kind of dough." Norm tapped his finger on the steering wheel before he reached for the keys to start the Buick. "Maybe we should get the gang together." He pulled into the street.

"It's four thirty on a Friday afternoon. Vlad is bound to be home by this time."

"Maybe we should check Beezy's place first. He might be in the mood for a little afternoon delight." Norm arched his eyebrow. "He's been working overtime. Lights on half the night. Something's getting to him. He looks like hell in the morning."

"I've been so wrapped up with Arthur I haven't even noticed."

"Have ya told your fella Gaston's on the Jake Bender case?"

"Not yet. Ever since Lovey Puppy chewed on his fancy wallet he acts cranky whenever I mention Gaston's talents. He blames him for the fight with Jake, which put him on the police detective's radar. I decided not to push the matter until the situation calms down."

"Prob'ly for the best. Ya don't want to scare him off before things get hot between you two."

"They're starting to heat up. He's talking about a trip to the Italian Riviera. He wants to take me to a fancy hotel overlooking the sea. Raves about the wine and the food. Says it's a great place for a honeymoon," Sandra said with a faraway look in her eyes.

"Honeymoon? Isn't that rushing things? You've only been going out a few months." Norm's voice rose. "You barely know the guy."

"I know all I need. At my age I haven't got a lot of time left. And

I've never seen the Mediterranean Sea. He says the sea is as blue and sparkling as my eyes." She sighed, then snapped her fingers. "But first we have to solve this case so there isn't a cloud hanging over him. I need every bit of Gaston's intuition."

"And the Doc's brains and Beezy's tech skills. Maybe she can figure out how to hack into Jake's account." He slowed the car down as they approached Beatrice's house. "The Doc's car is in her driveway. I bet they're both here."

Norm pressed the doorbell several times. "I better give them fair warning to get themselves together. Nothing worse than coitus interruptus."

Sandra handed Gaston's leash to him. "Would you mind holding on to the pooch? He and Beatrice's new cat don't get along that well."

Beatrice answered the door fully clothed. She narrowed her eyes when she saw Sandra's outfit, then gave her head a little shake. "Please come in. Vlad's in the living room, and I shut the cat up in my bedroom so Gaston won't need to be leashed."

As Sandra brushed past Beatrice said, "Is that a new look for you? I hardly recognize you, especially with your hair tucked in that wig. I didn't know brown was your color."

"It's not, dearie. I went snooping undercover today."

"Wait 'til you see what she found," Norm said. "Jake the Snake was up to something."

Vlad gave them a weak wave from his spot on the recliner. Sandra could see the tip of an ice pack behind his back.

"Are you all right?" she asked.

'No, I'm not. I had a minor incident at CHAW and took a spill. Aggravated my back problems again. But Beatrice is taking good care of me."

He smiled at her, and she smiled sweetly back.

"Sorry to hear you're laid up. I'm sure it's only temporary. Can't keep a good man down," Sandra said. "I did a little sleuthing today in Jake Bender's apartment, and here's what I found."

She handed Vlad the bank statements.

He winced as he reached for the papers. "What do you have here?" He studied them for a few minutes, then exhaled with a loud whoosh. "I don't believe it. How the hell did you get your hands on these?"

"When I read Jake's obituary, I came up with a plan." Sandra related the events at the apartment building. "Norm distracted the building manager, and Gaston led me to the kitchen."

"Was he looking for a cheese Danish?" Vlad said.

'No, he was using his keen sense of detection. He pointed straight to the suspicious cookbook."

Sandra patted Gaston on the head. "Right, lovey?"

Gaston yipped, then headed for the couch. He hopped up and stretched out, knocking off one of the small pillows and resting his head on the other. Soon he was napping.

"A bank account with a hundred thousand dollars could be a good motive for murder." Beatrice clutched the bank papers. "We need to find out where this money came from."

"Can you hack into the bank's records, Beezy?' Norm arched his eyebrows toward her. 'You're a computer whiz."

"I'm not that much of a whiz," Beatrice said hastily.

"You should turn this over to the police." Vlad looked worried. "You could get in trouble for obtaining evidence under false pretenses or trespassing with intent to commit fraud. I'm no lawyer, but I'm sure you broke some laws by taking this. Detective Johnson won't take too kindly if you hinder his investigation."

"Not yet. I'm not giving that fat detective my hot lead." Sandra folded her arms across her chest. "I want to see if I can find anything out on my own first."

"Gaston needs more time."

Nodding at the dog, Norm held out his hand for the bank papers. Beatrice reluctantly handed them over.

"He's just getting started."

"From the sound of his obituary, I'm pretty sure Jake didn't inherit it. His parents died some time ago, and these deposits are current." Sandra tapped the side of her cheek. "The manager said something about a good buddy who was going to clear out the apartment."

"That would be Marco, his best friend, according to Brad at CHAW. He's the guy who pushed me down just because I was asking too many questions about Jake," Vlad said.

"What are we gonna do next?" Norm asked.

"The newspaper said the funeral's tomorrow. One of us should go." Sandra looked around the room at each one.

Vlad gripped the arms of the recliner tightly. "It can't be me. Marco would recognize me. No telling what he'd do. He has a big problem with anger management."

"But he wouldn't hurt a decrepit old lady, Jake's long-lost aunt." Sandra pulled the wig down firmly and gave each one a vacant, open-mouthed stare. "I'll do it!"

"What if there's some pickleball players? Won't they recognize you and Gaston?" Beatrice folded her arms across her chest. "That dog's unforgettable."

"I'm going solo. No makeup. I'll wear the grey wig. Nobody pays attention to old people. They figure we're taking up space on our way out, that our biggest achievement is not having to wear diapers. I'll be invisible. Don't worry."

JAKE BENDER'S FINAL SEND-OFF was sparsely attended. Sandra recognized the apartment manager and Susie, the blonde from pickleball, seated in the row of chairs. A few ragtag mourners in casual dress gathered at the back of the room sharing stories in hushed tones. Sandra stumbled over a small tear in the threadbare carpet as she paid her respects to the sole greeter, a muscle-bound man dressed in a black polo shirt. The inked eagle's talons on his upper lower arm convinced her that he must be Marco. A framed photo of Jake smiling proudly in front of a bright red Camaro stood next to a brass urn on a wooden altar covered with a purple table runner. A large gold cross hung on the wall was illuminated with a floodlight. The three floral arrangements sent from well-wishers gave off a cloyingly sweet scent.

"My condolences," she mumbled.

The man barely acknowledged her with a nod. His eyes were focused on the sobbing Susie, whose tear-streaked face seemed genuinely distraught. Sandra drifted slowly to a seat in the last row where she could observe all the action without notice. She clutched Jake's memorial card in her hand. It repeated the information from the newspaper. Nothing new to learn about the deceased.

A small group of better dressed mourners entered. Sandra remembered the friendly receptionist leading the group, now dressed in a black tweed jacket with a gold chain and black tailored pants instead of the obligatory CHAW shirt. The elderly Franklin shuffled behind her. Then an authoritative man with broad shoulders and trim waist strutted in while the rest of the CHAW staff straggled behind. He wore a concerned look on his face and stopped to console Marco, resting his hand on the larger man's shoulder as he uttered platitudes of condolences. One woman in the group made the sign of the cross on her chest as she bowed her head before the altar, but most of them filed by with bored expressions.

Kristin brought up the rear, dressed in the lace trimmed black skirt from the thrift shop and a dark teal sweater, which made her look even more pale. Her hair was damp, like she just stepped out of the shower. Her face was scrubbed clean and makeup free, not even lipstick. Sandra swore the girl looked at the picture of Jake with pure hatred before she cast down her eyes and stumbled past Marco with only a nod of her head. As she passed the altar with her hands folded modestly in front, Sandra saw her flash her middle finger at the urn before she took her place in the chairs with the rest of the staff.

Sandra wished Gaston were with her with his infallible judgment of people. She could always depend on him to expose the deceitful as well as the trustworthy just by his yip or his growl. She felt like she was swimming in a muddy river without him. But Beatrice was right. He would blow her cover if he showed up at Jake's funeral. She imagined him biting Marco on the ankle.

The funeral director's service was blessedly short. He read the usual Twenty-Third Psalm, said a few words about what a good life Jake led. *After all,* Sandra thought, *he hadn't blown up any government offices or murdered multiple victims, at least to the funeral director's knowledge.*

Then Marco stood up and announced, "We're continuing the celebration of Jake's life at the Thirsty Rhino. First round of drinks is on me."

He grabbed the urn and picture off the altar. "C'mon, Buddy. You can't miss this. You're the guest of honor." He tucked the urn under his arm and led the motley crew out of the funeral home.

Sandra texted Norm. *Funeral crowd heading to Thirsty Rhino. Your chance to investigate.*

Then Sandra hurried to catch up with Kristin, who trudged behind her coworkers. She shook her head when one of them asked, "Are you coming with us?"

"Hello, dear girl," she said in a lowered voice. "I was so surprised to see you here. Is this the funeral your boss insisted you attend?"

Kristin hung her head. "Yes. I showed up at the visitation, but I'm done. I'm finished with Jake Bender. If I'd known he was a friend of yours, I wouldn't have bad-mouthed him in the store."

"He's not a friend of mine. I just live in his apartment building. I was curious to see who his friends really were." Sandra sniffed. "He wasn't a very likeable man, I'm afraid."

"Not likeable is an understatement. He won't be missed much at CHAW," Kristin said.

She quickened her step as they left the building.

Sandra struggled to keep up. Even in her orthopedic shoes, she was no match for the younger woman. Kristin was getting away before she could ask her more questions. Then Sandra let her purse slip off her wrist. The clasp flew open when it hit the ground, and all the contents spilled onto the sidewalk.

"Oh, no! I lost my grip. Could you please help me, Kristin? I have trouble bending down."

"Sure thing." The young woman hastened back and began scooping items back into the handbag. After she gathered everything, she stood up, handing the purse back to Sandra. "Here you go, ma'am."

"Please remember to call me Grandma Sandy. Let's go for a coffee. We can share bad stories about Jake Bender and commiserate."

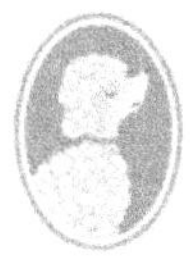

CHAPTER FOURTEEN

Norm pulled up to the curb with Gaston peering out the passenger side window. Sandra noticed the dog pawing at the window when he saw her. After quickly turning away she grabbed Kristin's arm and diverted her attention to the funeral home parking lot.

"Did you bring a car, dearie? Or should I call us a cab?"

Sandra gave her head a little shake at Norm, and he drove away. "My car's over here."

Kristen led her to an older, boxy-looking model. The back seat was piled high with boxes, a twelve-pack of diet cola, and a backpack so stuffed the zipper wouldn't close. Magazines and books covered the floor.

Kristen caught Sandra's perplexed look. "I found a good rummage sale yesterday. The books were only ten cents. I got a set of pots and pans real cheap. Even had the lids. The lady threw in an old slow cooker. Ever since my mom moved to Tennessee two years ago, I've been on my own, making do with just a skillet and a saucepan."

"I've been on my own since my daughter moved, too. She keeps asking me to visit, but Connecticut seems so far away," Sandra said as she slid into her seat.

"My mom seems to have fallen off the face of the earth. She calls me at Christmas and on my birthday. That's about it. She's too busy with her new boyfriend, I guess. My big brother joined the army. He's in South Korea and never calls either." Kristin's eyes were fixed on the road, but her mouth looked like she had just eaten a bitter wasabi pea.

"I'm sorry to hear that, dearie. Sometimes our lives just get in the way of our good intentions." She tucked the memorial card with Jake's picture on it in her purse.

"I hope you don't mind if we go to Frank's Diner for coffee," Kristin said. "I like to sit in the booth in the back. Nobody bothers you there."

"You're the driver. I'm fine wherever you want to go."

The waitress, an apple-shaped woman, greeted Kristin heartily when they walked into the diner. The buttons on her Pepto-Bismol pink uniform painfully stretched over her substantial breasts.

"Where you been, sweetie? You haven't come in for the lunch special lately," she said as she brought two glasses of water and their menus.

The lunch special, written on a chalkboard, was two breaded pork chops, mashed potatoes, and a choice of soup or salad. The smell of greasy bacon lingered like a cloud of smog. Every table in the restaurant was occupied except for the booth nearest the restroom. When Sandra caught a whiff of the flatulent odor, she understood why.

"I've been very busy. A lot going on at work," Kristin said as she picked up her menu, avoiding the woman's gaze.

"I bet. Everybody's been talking about that guy that was murdered in the men's locker room. Some crazy peacock thing wrapped around his neck and a pickleball stuffed in his mouth. You didn't see nothing, did you? Ain't you got the early morning shift?"

"I don't want to talk about it." Kristin slammed the menu on the table. "It's bad enough at work with cops swarming all over the place, asking the same questions over and over. I came here to grab a cup of coffee, not rehash all that crap."

"I'm sorry I brought it up. I'll get you those coffees." The waitress scooted away.

"Having a rough time of it at CHAW?" Sandra asked. She turned the pages of the thick menu, watching Kristin's reaction out of the corner of her eye.

"There's a detective that's in everybody's face. Looks like a grizzly bear. Acts like one, too." Scowling, she pushed the menu away. "He made me walk through what I did that morning again and again. I told him I was moving the freestanding punching bags out of the old kickboxing room into the new bigger room. Then I had to mop the floor of the old room before I could move the yoga mats in. I wasn't anywhere near the locker rooms."

"You moved that equipment all by yourself?" Sandra asked incredulously.

The girl's bony wrists stuck out of the sleeves of her teal top.

"Didn't any of the male staff help you?"

"Didn't need their help," she snorted. "I'm used to working by myself. I get more done without a man trying to tell me the right way to do it."

"You must be stronger than you look." Sandra's eyes moved to the girl's biceps.

"My mom used to say I'm wiry but strong. She told my brother to watch out and don't get me mad. When I lose my temper things can get ugly."

The waitress's face matched the pink of her uniform as she set the coffees down. "I hope you know I didn't mean nothing. I was just repeating gossip. I didn't mean to tick you off. Not much happens in Crawford. Gotta make the most of when something big happens." She took out her pad, pencil poised to write. "You want to order anything else?"

Kristin looked first at Sandra who shook her head before she said, "No, thanks. Sorry for dumping on you."

"It's ok. I know how hard you work, sweetie. Getting up at the crack of dawn, scrubbing floors and such. Then going to technical school. You're entitled to be out of sorts now and then."

After tucking the pad back in her apron pocket, the woman looked relieved as she walked to the next table.

Sandra poured a packet of creamer into her coffee and stirred it. When she was sure the waitress was out of earshot, she said in a low voice, "That Jake Bender was a piece of work. I was glad I didn't live on the same floor as him. What with his drinking and bringing in different women."

"He was a piece of shit, more like it," Kristin hissed. "I tried to avoid him as much as I could."

"I could never figure out where he got his money. He seemed too young to collect Social Security. Yet he never was late with his rent. Could afford a CHAW membership. Do you think he had a good pension or a big inheritance?"

"If his folks were rich he must have been the black sheep with a blacker heart. He liked to play pickleball just to harass the other players. Piss them off. He had a mean streak. Even liked to embarrass poor Mr. Franklin, a ninety-year-old man. Yelled 'dead man walking' sometimes when he went past."

Kristen stopped talking as an unshaven man in a flannel shirt and grubby jeans walked past their table. The smell of deodorant cakes and stale urine wafted past them when he opened the door to the men's room. Sandra held her breath until the door closed behind him and it was safe to breathe again.

The girl leaned in nearer to Sandra. "Then he started in on me.

Stood too close to me at first. Creeped me out."

"I could see him pushing your boundaries," Sandra said. "I nicknamed him Jake the Snake. Never told anyone else. Just thought it."

Kristen nodded. "You understand how he was. He'd talk dirty to me, say gross things that he was going to do to me when he saw me alone."

"What did he say?" Sandra kept her eyes on the girl's face and waited.

Kristin's wrinkled up her nose. "It's too gross to repeat. But he'd whisper, 'I can tell you like it rough. You don't fool me with your Goody Two Shoes act.' Then flash his evil grin."

"What a horrible man! I can see why you wanted to avoid him."

"It got worse." Her voice dropped so low Sandra strained to hear. "He would brush up against me in the hallway. Grabbed my butt or my boobs when no one else was around. Especially when no one else was around."

Kristin squeezed her eyes shut. "Once he tried to make me touch him." Her fingers tightened around the coffee mug's handle. "Touch him down there."

"That's terrible, my poor girl." Sandra reached across the table to touch her clenched fist.

The girl's fingers were cold as the ice in her water glass.

"Didn't you report him to your director?"

She raised her eyes to Sandra's. "I finally worked up enough courage to tell Brad some of the stuff Jake said, but I don't think he believed me. He said he'd have to think about how to proceed. I was too embarrassed to tell him the rest. I was ready to quit my job when… when…" Her voice trailed off and broke down for a few heartbeats as her eyes started to water.

She wiped her eyes and continued. "I don't need to worry. Jake is never going to torment me or anyone else again."

Sandra gently squeezed the girl's hand. "No wonder you don't want to talk about it. But maybe you should find someone professional who can help you process what happened."

Just then the man came out, pulling up his zipper, oblivious to the two of them sitting nearby. He wiped his hands on his grubby pant legs as he walked back to his spot at the counter.

Kristin immediately pulled her hand away. "Men are so gross!"

She scowled at the departing man. Then her face hardened as she shook her head. "Therapists cost money. I'm barely making ends meet now. Anyway, it's over. I've got to move on."

She drained her mug and looked expectantly at Sandra. "Are you ready to go? I can give you a lift home."

"I have a few errands to run. Would you mind giving me a lift to the pharmacy? I can call a cab from there when I'm done shopping." Sandra opened the side pocket on her purse and rummaged for change. "Let me get this, dearie."

"No, I'll pay Phyllis at the cash register. My treat, uh Grandma Sandy." The last words came out awkwardly. "Thank you for listening to me. I never told anybody everything that happened with Jake Bender. My mom taught me to fight my own battles. But with him I felt like I was losing."

"It took courage to talk to your boss. You'll keep finding that courage as you go along. Remember, a diamond can't be polished without friction. You can't develop grit without having troubles to overcome."

CHAPTER FIFTEEN

Norm reread Sandra's text: *Funeral crowd heading to Thirsty Rhino. Your chance to investigate.*

He looked at the bright-eyed poodle peering out the passenger side window at the mourners exiting the funeral home. Gaston let out a little whine in anticipation of Sandra rejoining them.

"Sorry, Little Buddy, it's time for you to go home. I travel solo at the bar."

Sandra gave them a slight shake of her head as she joined the throng swarming the parking lot. She clung to a young woman's arm. Norm guessed it was Kristin, the CHAW custodian she met at the thrift store. Sandra's plan to find out more details about the morning of Jake's murder was getting results. The memorial celebrating Jake's life being held at his hang out, The Thirsty Rhino, was a stroke of good luck. No one would question his presence.

But people would notice him with a dog. So his next stop was Sandra's place. When he opened the car door to let Gaston out, the pooch flopped down on the car seat and refused to budge. He even gave a warning growl when Norm yanked on his leash.

"Cut that out. I can't take you with me. Dogs aren't welcome at funerals."

Gaston responded with a loud *ruff.*

"I know it's rough, but you can't come with me."

Norm ignored the pleading eyes as he reached for Gaston. Finally, he resorted to carrying the recalcitrant pooch into the house. He dumped him in Sandra's entry and slammed the door shut. As he drove away he could hear the howls of protest.

The wake was in full swing by the time Norm got there. He could hear the hum of voices even before he pushed open the back door into the bar. Stevie, the frazzled bartender, was setting up beer after beer on the bar top. She brushed her bangs off her sweaty brow and gave Norm a quick smile.

"You want your usual?" she asked, heading to the draft nozzle.

"You got it, Stevie. Kinda big crowd for lunch hour, ain't it?"

Norm glanced around at all the revelers. *Born to Be Wild* was blaring out from the jukebox. Stale beer mixed with the odor of cheap cologne and barbequed meat. At a large table near the wall mural of the cartoonish rhino, someone had set up a slow cooker filled with Sloppy Joes. A pyramid of buns was stacked next to the paper plates and plastic forks. A white container of store-bought potato salad, a jar of dill pickles, and party bags of assorted chips completed the funeral dinner.

A skinny brunette wearing ripped jeans and cracked leather vest announced, "I brung Jake's favorite dessert." Then she unloaded a grocery bag filled with a cornucopia of different flavored Oreos.

"It's Jake Bender's funeral," Stevie answered. "His friend Marco asked George, the owner, if he could have Jake's celebration of life here since he's one of the faces painted on the mural." She jerked her head to the wall painting that depicted various patrons of the bar enjoying a drink with the rhino.

Norm found Jake's picture at the end of the bar, along with his and some of the other regulars.

"He's the guy who got killed at CHAW, right? I never noticed him here that much."

"He got into some tiff with Brett, the other bartender, and started hanging out more at Hogs and Honeys. But George let bygones be bygones and said yes to Marco's request."

Just then the muscular tattooed guy raised a glass of beer and shouted over the din, "Shut up, everybody. Let's raise a glass to Jake, the best damn friend a guy like me ever had. May he rest in peace."

Most of the crowd held up their beers and chimed in, "To Jake!"

The Tat Guy drained his glass, slammed the empty on the bar, and said to Stevie, "Hit me with another."

"Sure thing, Marco."

Norm knew he was looking at the guy who pushed Vlad down in the weight room. His biceps made the Incredible Hulk's look like fence posts. He was trying to figure out how to ask questions without getting a beer glass shoved down one of his body openings when some guy started talking.

"Remember how Jake loved to play poker? He even played it on the slots at the casino. He always laughed and said, 'I got more than an ace up my sleeve.' What a dude!"

"I never could catch him cheating," added another. "He was

either damn lucky or damn good."

"I remember when he won the walleye fishing contest," Marco said. "The judges couldn't figure out how his fish looked the same size as the runners-up yet weighed so much more. Even made him pass a lie detector test before they gave him the ten-thousand-dollar prize."

The skinny brunette twirled a lock of hair around her finger. "Wish I'd had one of those lie detector things when we were dating! I never did know if he was telling the truth when he said he had to work late."

Marco winked at Stevie when she brought him the beer. "Good thing they didn't cut the thing open. They would've found the lead weights in its gullet."

"He bought the first round at Hogs and Honeys that night. Jake was a great guy," the poker player sighed.

Norm noticed the apartment manager slowly making her way through the crowd to Marco. He took off his Green Bay Packers hat and undid his ponytail. Slouching over his beer glass, he masked his face with the veil of grey hair. He was glad he'd worn his best denim shirt instead of any Packers tees.

"Ya got any idea when you're getting Jake's stuff out of the apartment?" the woman asked Marco. "No rush—he's paid up for the month. I can give you all the time you need."

"Me and the gang will get at it this weekend. We gotta figure out what to do with his furniture and the rest of his belongings."

The manager glanced around the bar. "I'm surprised his aunt isn't here. I saw her at the funeral home."

"His aunt?" Marco said with a puzzled look. "Jake never mentioned no aunt."

"It was that little old lady in the brown coat. She talked to you at the visitation."

"The scrawny old bag that showed up at the beginning?" Marco's eyes widened with surprise. "That was his aunt?"

"So she claimed."

"Well, he didn't mention her in his will. Left everything to me except a few things for Susie. So the old bat better not try to pull a fast one."

He gestured to where a red-eyed blond was sniffling into a soggy tissue at a table with some CHAW regulars. "Susie's taking it pretty hard. She doesn't know Jake had a few other babes on the string. We won't go there today."

The apartment manager did a double take when she saw the back of Norm's head. She moved in for a closer look. "Is that you—Norm? I been waiting for you to come back with your application for the apartment. I can't hold it much longer. A couple of other people are interested."

Marco turned his steely eyes toward Norm. "You wanna rent Jake's apartment?"

"No, he's interested in the downstairs unit. He didn't even look upstairs."

"I'm thinking of moving to a bigger place." Norm tapped the side of his glass in a staccato beat. "I'm living in a one-room basement flat right now."

"He's a funny guy," the manager said. "He tells jokes a mile a minute. He's got a whole shitload of stories. I bet he's even got one about a funeral."

"'I don't think I should joke when it's such a sad occasion. That woman sitting over there is barely keeping it together." He directed their attention to Susie. "I don't want to send her off the deep end."

"I want to hear one of your jokes, I could use a good laugh." Marco frowned as he narrowed his eyes at Norm. "Don't mind her. She'll get over it." He threw a scornful look at the crying woman.

"C'mon. Tell us one. Just a little one." The apartment manager punched him playfully in the arm.

"All right. I got one about my Uncle Bud and Aunt Viv. They were getting up there in years and were trying to decide what epitaphs to put on their gravestones. Uncle Bud suggested Aunt Viv's headstone should read, *Silent at last*. Aunt Viv argued, 'Then yours should say, *Stiff at last*."

"That's pretty good. You got any more?" Marco asked.

The whole bar started listening.

"Tell us another one," someone shouted.

Norm heard murmurs of approval from almost everyone except the blond sniveling by herself in the corner.

"If you insist," Norm said. "I got one more."

He took a swig of beer before he started. "This guy Joe returned from a doctor's visit all bummed out. He just got told he only had twenty-four hours to live. So he told his wife, Hazel, and she started to cry. After wiping away her tears, Joe asked her to make love to him. Of course, she said yes, and they made passionate love.

"Six hours later Joe went to her again and said, 'Honey, now I only have eighteen hours left. Maybe we could get it on again.' Hazel agreed, and they went at it again.

"Later Joe was getting into bed and realized he only had eight hours of life left."

"I can see where this is going." The manager rolled her eyes.

"Shut up," said Marco. "Let the man finish his joke."

Norm continued. "Joe touched her shoulder and said, 'Honey, please just one more time before I die.' She agreed and afterwards she fell asleep. But Joe tossed and turned. He heard the clock ticking in his head, and it was down to only four hours. He tapped his wife on the shoulder and said, "I only have four hours left to go. Do you think we could—?'

"His wife sat up and said, 'For God's sake, Joe. Have a heart. I have to get up in the morning for your funeral, and you can just stay in bed!'"

Marco slapped him on the shoulder. "Good one, buddy. Hey, Stevie, Give this man another beer. Jake would've loved that one. You should hang around with us some more."

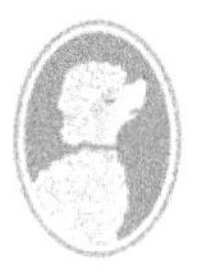

CHAPTER SIXTEEN

As the drinking in the Thirsty Rhino continued, Norm sipped the warm beer in his glass while pretending to keep pace with the funeral crowd. He hoped with enough alcohol tongues would loosen and he'd discover some useful information to help with the investigation. He figured drinking doesn't turn a person into someone they're not. It just makes them forget to hide themselves. Norm found himself nudged away from Marco as other friends of Jake's drifted over to lament the loss of their drinking buddy.

A squat guy built like an apartment-sized mini-fridge with a volleyball head recalled, "Jake could really raise hell on a snowmobile. Remember that time I dared him to go riding on Beaver Lake? The ice was getting a little slushy but he didn't care. He wasn't a pussy. He barely made it across the lake when we heard a loud crack. The ice caved right after he rode over that spot. Any other dude would be pissing his pants, but Jake just laughed."

"He'd tell the devil himself to shove off," a man wearing a Guns and Roses t-shirt added. "I don't get how he let somebody get the drop on him. He's the last dude you'd expect to get bumped off."

"Cops said he took a blow to the back of the head first. Some chickenshit snuck up on him, I figure, and strangled him when he was unconscious. Otherwise, Jake would've put up a hell of a fight," Mini-Fridge said. "The other guy would've ended up on the locker room floor."

Marco snarled. "The cops better find the bastard before I do. I'll tear him apart with my bare hands."

"Did he have any enemies? Who the hell'd want to off him?" Norm slipped his question in the chatter as he took a gulp of warm beer, watching Marco for his reaction.

Marco glowered at the empty beer mug. as if he'd like to crush it to slivers of glass. "Nobody, man. He didn't take crap from nobody, maybe dished it out once in a while. But dudes just laughed it off."

"Like when I got drunk at his place and passed out. He saran wrapped my hands all the way to my elbows. Took me an hour to get it off when I woke up with a hangover." This came from Mini-Fridge.

"That's nothing. He drew a penis on my face with permanent maker, like it was sticking in my mouth. Then took a picture and put it on Instagram," the Guns and Roses guy chimed in.

"We all laughed our asses off at that. But you weren't mad, were you?" Marco said.

"Hell no. Nobody held a grudge You didn't want to be the next target of one of Jake's pranks. If he thought he got under your skin, he'd keep it up. You're better off letting shit go. The next time we'd be at the bar all would be forgotten." Guns and Roses drained his glass and pointed to the empty for a refill.

"See, no enemies here. It's gotta be something else.' Marco scratched his head, staring at the bottles of booze lining the shelves.

"Any money problems?" Norm suggested. "Maybe he owed money to the wrong guy."

"You're barking up the wrong tree. Jake didn't have no money problems. He always had plenty of scratch." Mini-Fridge jerked his head toward the picture of Jake and his car resting on the bar beside the urn. "Enough for some hot wheels and memberships at the health club and the Moose Lodge."

"He usually had a wad of C-notes." The skinny woman in leather sauntered up to the bar. "One night he told me he had a live one on the hook. Dug up some dirt but he wouldn't say what. Said the jerk paid plenty to keep it quiet."

"Shut your trap. You don't know what you're talking about." Marco slammed his fist on the bar and glared at her. "He would never tell some bimbo his business. Jake ain't here to warn you to keep your goddam mouth closed. So I'm telling you. Shut the fuck up."

The poor woman bit her lip as she flushed red to the part in her hair. Her eyes welled with tears. "I'm sorry, Marco. I probably didn't hear him right." She slunk back to the food table and slouched down in her chair. Resting her forehead in her hands, she hid her face behind the pile of unopened cookie packages and started to cry.

Norm wondered what Marco knew about Jake's "business." Did it have something to do with the deposits in the bank account he'd set up with the fake identity? He was sure Sandra had found a big clue stuck in the old cookbook. Too bad Vlad was making her turn it in to the gorilla, Detective Johnson.

"Let's stop talking about Jake and have a drink to his memory.

Set us up with some shots, Stevie." Marco put a pile of cash on the bar and shoved it toward the bartender.

She obliged by grabbing a bottle of tequila and pouring in into the row of shot glasses lined neatly up. Revelers floated up to the bar to grab the small glasses. Marco joined them. After he tossed it down, he noticed Norm still perched a few bar stools away.

"Tell us a joke, funny boy." He shifted his piercing stare to Norm.

Norm threw out, "Ya know, tequila can't fix your life. But it's worth a shot."

"Don't you got anything better than that?'

"How do ya know yer too drunk to drive? When ya swerve to avoid hitting a tree and find out it's just yer air freshener."

A few chuckles came from the crowd, but Marco turned to scowl at the offenders.

Marco took a step closer to Norm. "I want another story like one about the dying guy and his wife. Before you have a shot." He pointed to an empty glass and the bottle still on the bar. "Oblige the jokester."

Stevie set the shot glass in front of Norm and filled it. He pushed it to the side and began to rattle off the next joke.

"A guy walks into a bar and sees his friend sitting beside a twelve-inch pianist with a toy piano.

"The guy says, 'That's amazing. Where did he come from?' So his friend pulls out an old lamp and says, "The genie inside this lamp will give you one wish.' The guy rubs the lamp and, to his surprise, a puff of purple smoke shoots out and slowly forms into a genie.

"The genie says in a booming voice, 'I can only grant you one wish.' The guy thinks for a moment and says, 'I wish for a million bucks.' Suddenly the bar is filled with ducks on top of ducks, bursting from the windows and doors, standing on the tables, dunking their heads into people's drinks. 'What the hell just happened?' the guy asks.

"His friend answers, 'Yeah, I know. Do you really think I wanted a twelve-inch pianist?'"

"Let's drink to that!" Marco thumped his glass on the bar for Stevie to refill, then tipped it back and gulped the contents in one motion.

Norm tried to follow suit with his untouched shot, but the tequila ended up flowing against his ear instead, soaking his shirt collar.

"When I can't hit my mouth, it's time for me to call it a night," Norm said. "I'll see ya around."

Before Marco could issue another order, Norm exited the bar, avoiding any eye contact with the remaining mourners. After he got the hell out, he thought, *Alcohol may not be the answer. But in Marco's case I hope it helps him forget the question. Tomorrow I call a meeting of the gang. We need to figure where to go next.*

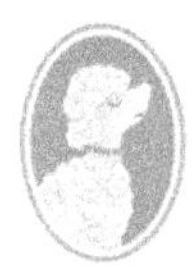

CHAPTER SEVENTEEN

"Have you ever played pickleball before?" The tall man loomed over her, a shabby headband holding his thinning grey hair firmly in place. The slogan emblazoned on his shirt said it all: *I'm a big dill on the pickleball court.*

Beatrice shifted the borrowed racquet in her sweaty hand before she answered. "No, this is my first time. My friend told me how much fun it is so I've been dying to try it. In fact, she lent me her racquet."

She held up the well-used orange paddle, Sandra's thrift store find. After Norm came home from Jake's funeral with a tale of possible extortion, the gang decided Beatrice had the best cover to investigate if the pickleball crowd knew any dodgy rumors and to get close to Susie, Jake's lady friend.

The other eager pickleball enthusiasts were scurrying to set up the little nets and fences, just like a scene from *Star Wars* with the little alien creatures working in Tatooine for Jabba the Hut. The tall man didn't look like Jabba, but he had that air of authority. He obviously kept the games running smoothly.

"I've never played either," said a wiry man in gym shorts and a Nike t-shirt. He held his paddle like he just left Wimbledon.

Beatrice's heart sank a little. She was hoping for another newbie that parked their walker next to the bleachers so they could laugh at their missed balls together.

"Ramona, could you show these two the basics?" Non-Jabba called to a salt-and-pepper-haired woman with tortoise shell glasses. She cast a longing look at the couples forming on either side of the little nets, but nevertheless ambled over.

"Hi, my name's Ramona," she said. "The lady that usually teaches the new players is gone today. I'll do my best, but I'm not as knowledgeable as she is."

"I'm Rich," said the man. "We don't mind. We just want to learn the game."

"My name is Beatrice, Ramona. Where's Henry Huggins and Ribsy?" Beatrice pretended to look around.

"Huh?" said the woman with a blank stare.

"It's from the Beverly Cleary children's books. *Ramona the Pest* and her sister, Beatrice. It's an old series for kids."

"I must have missed that one. Never heard of it," Ramona said drily.

"I think I read it to my kids way back when," the man said.

Beatrice gave him a grateful look.

"Let me show you how to set this up." Ramona led them to the other side of a huge, grey curtain divider. A storage area under the stage held more of the pickleball nets and fences. She grabbed a set and dragged it over. "You line these up with the little arrow painted on the floor." Then she proceeded to push metal poles together, much like setting up a tent frame.

The floor had a mishmash of red, white, black, and grey intersecting lines, like telephone wires after a tornado hit. Some were for the three basketball hoops on this half of the gym; the grey ones were exclusively for pickleball.

As Ramona constructed the net, she explained the boundaries. "The grey lines on either side closest to the net are the kitchen. A player can't be on or in the kitchen when a ball is in play. When you serve the ball, you need to be behind these back grey lines."

"Like if you can't stand the heat, stay out of the kitchen," Beatrice nervously twittered.

Ramona rolled her eyes and soldiered on with her instruction. "Here's how you serve." She demonstrated dropping the ball and hitting it with the paddle to the opposite corner. "I recommend starting with it underhand."

Despite the confusion of lines and new vocabulary, Beatrice found herself enjoying the game so much she almost forgot why she came—to find Susie and pump her for information about Jake. A more experienced male player drifted over and became her partner against Rich and Ramona. She served the ball first. It made it over the net, then one bounce. Ramona hit it back, Beatrice waited for the ball to bounce, then she hit it back. It cleared the net but just barely. Rich ran up but couldn't return it,

"Did I hit it in the right place?"

Her partner said, "Not only in the right place but you scored a point. Serve again. Do you remember what to say?"

"I think it's one to zero so I say one-zero."

"You're player one so it's one-zero-one."

A few volleys and then Rich hit it out of bounds. Another point. Much to her surprise she scored six points in rapid succession.

Even Ramona grudgingly said, "Good job! We only play until seven points so more people get to play. You only need one more point."

That jinxed her. She hit the next serve out of bounds, but her partner got the next serve. When he called 6-0-2, she actually understood it meant they had six points, the other team had 0, and he was the second player to serve. He was so good they won the match. All four players met in the middle and clanked their paddles together over the net. Rich didn't look as self-assured as he had when they started. Beatrice thought of Bobby Riggs—male hubris goes before a fall.

"Time to move to the other side of the curtain," he said to her. "You're ready for more of a challenge."

Ramona also was ready for more challenging play so she and Beatrice teamed up on the other side with the regulars. Soon Beatrice was running and swinging like Venus Williams. The solid thwack of the ball against her paddle felt so satisfying.

When she hit the ball barely over the net so it dropped in the kitchen and was difficult for the other team to return, Ramona said, "Good dink." Whatever that was.

After their close game that teetered back and forth with the opposing team finally winning it eight to six, Beatrice saw a blond, solidly built woman sitting on the bleachers by herself with a bouncy head of hair, just as Sandra described Susie. She had a faraway look in her eyes, like they were focused on some distant place, not the rollicking fun on the pickleball courts.

Beatrice told Ramona. "I think I need a break."

She sidled next to the woman and said, "Do you mind if I join you? My legs feel like rubber after all the running."

The blonde nodded and moved over. Up close Beatrice saw her red-rimmed eyes and the dark circles under them. Grey roots showed under the dyed hair. Free of makeup, her face was blotchy, the wrinkles frozen into a mask of sorrow. Her navy t-shirt looked like it had been lying on the bedroom floor until she threw it on, as did the grey capris with the crisscross cut-outs. The only glimmer of brightness was the gold heart-shaped pendant dangling from a delicate chain engraved with the words, *Always in my heart.*

Beatrice introduced herself and said, "This is my first time playing pickleball. It's more fun than I expected."

The woman shrugged. "I suppose if you're in the mood to play." She moved her hand to the gold pendant and clenched it tightly.

"And your name is?" Beatrice looked expectantly at the woman.

"I'm Susie." Her eyes swept over Beatrice, then moved back to the action on the court.

"Do you play here often?" Beatrice continued to draw her out.

"I've been playing here for a few years."

"You must be good." Beatrice said. "I'm grasping the basics, but I still don't get all the rules. Don't step in the kitchen, but you can play a ball that lands in the kitchen. You only get points if it's your team's turn to serve. The ball has to bounce twice before you can volley. It's a lot to remember. Plus knowing which lines on the floor are for pickleball and which are for basketball. Yikes!" Beatrice pretended to smack her head.

"I know, it'd be nice if we had an area just for pickleball. But you'll get used to it."

"So do you want to take a chance on a newbie like me for a partner? We could play together when something opens up."

"I'm not feeling up to it right now. My friend Gail dragged me here. Told me I should get out and socialize instead of moping at home alone. Maybe later."

She waved Beatrice away with a halfhearted gesture, then slumped over like a marionette with broken strings.

A suntanned woman suddenly popped up in the bleachers like the clown in a Jack-in-the-box, concern written all over her face. "We just got home from our cruise in the Mediterranean so I missed the news about Jake. How awful. I know you two were seeing each other. I'm so sorry for your loss." She reached her arms out to touch Susie, aiming for a hug.

Susie cried out. "You have no idea!"

The other woman froze mid-hug.

Susie shrieked. "I knew this was a big mistake. You're all so judgy. I told Gail I didn't belong here." She pushed off from the bleachers, brushing past Beatrice, and ran along the sidelines to the women's locker room.

The woman stared aghast at Susie's retreat. "I didn't know she felt that strongly. They hadn't been going together all that long. Jake wasn't the nicest man around."

Beatrice said, "I'll go talk to her. Maybe I can help."

She followed Susie into the locker room. Doors hung open from the row of unoccupied stalls. Loud sobs came from the closed door at the end. The sound echoed throughout the empty room, filling the air like women wailing in a Greek tragedy.

Beatrice tapped lightly on the door, "Susie, it's Beatrice. Do you want to talk?"

Susie bawled, "No. All those people hated Jake. They don't understand. Go away. Leave me alone."

"I don't know who Jake was. I'm certainly not making any judgments. I'm just here to listen."

Between bouts of weeping Susie whimpered, "You don't know me. Why should you care?"

"You seem like a nice person with a huge burden. I can tell you're suffering. Sometimes talking to an objective listener helps. I don't know any of the other players so I'm not going to repeat what you tell me. I just want to help." Beatrice leaned her head against the door, listening intently, trying to ignore the scent of toilet bowl cleaner.

"I miss Jake so much." The sobbing subsided to sniffles.

Beatrice saw by Susie's feet under the door that she was sitting on the toilet, pulling reams of TP from the roll. She heard her blow her nose.

"Please open the door and come out. No one is around. You can tell me all about him."

The changing area was deserted, and the benches were a perfect place to sit down and talk.

"It's so hard to talk about him." Susie opened the door, clutching a wad of toilet paper. "I still can't believe he's never calling me up again. He always told me hustle on over and pick up a six-pack on the way."

"You have to believe he's in a better place." Beatrice gently led her to a bench and sat down. "Let's sit for a while." She patted the space next to her.

"I guess you're right." With her head drooping Susie sank onto the bench. "He's over the rainbow bridge with Buddy. They're probably playing fetch and swipe the shoe. Jake would laugh when Buddy barked at strangers and scared them. Or when he ran away with Marco's shoe. It made Jake so happy. I didn't even mind when that dog chewed on my hundred-dollar sandal. Like he said, it'll dry off."

The weeping subsided to an occasional hiccup. Beatrice took

advantage of the lull to ask, "What else made Jake happy?"

"My chocolate chip cookies. Spending the weekend in bed." Holding up her hand, Susie enumerated by touching each finger. "Chicken wings and jalapeno poppers from the Pour Sports Bar. Winning at poker. And playing pickleball. He was really good at both games."

"I'm sorry I won't get to see him on the court."

"He liked to talk trash, but it was all part of the fun. We would laugh so hard when he made wisecracks about the nerds." Susie added hastily, "Never to their faces. The jokes were just between us."

"So he had a great sense of humor. Sounds like a fun guy."

"And he treated me real well, especially when it was just the two of us. He'd bring me breakfast in bed when I stayed over. Coffee and Kwik Stop donuts. He could be so sweet." Susie's eyes gleamed as she reminisced. "And he was good to his mom when she was still alive. He always sent her cheese and sausage on Mother's Day."

"Jake must have been big-hearted." Beatrice patted her shoulder. 'You can always tell a man's character by how he treats his mother."

"You don't know the half of it. Once when I was planning to make breakfast for him. I found a big wad of fifties in an empty oatmeal canister. I counted eight thousand dollars. At first he got pissed." Her voice broke into a little hiccup. "Yelled at me. Accused me of snooping. Said I was sticking my nose where it didn't belong. I almost started to cry. But I didn't. Jake hated when I cried."

The grieving woman clutched the necklace to her chest and squeezed her eyes shut.

"Wow. That's a lot of money'" Beatrice exclaimed. "Did he say where it came from?"

After opening her eyes Susie said, "He won it playing poker. But here's the sweet part. He was saving it up for a cruise for his mother. She always wanted to go on a Caribbean cruise. He wanted to surprise her for Christmas. He got mad when I found where he hid it. Said I'd blab to his mom. But he must have forgot. I didn't talk to his mother—never even met her." She shrugged and raised her eyebrows. "He took me out to Frank's Diner to apologize for yelling at me. Even ordered me my favorite strawberry-rhubarb pie for dessert."

"What a sweet gesture! Did he accompany his mother on the trip?"

"She passed before he could contact the cruise line. But Jake used some of the money to take me on vacation to Milwaukee. We went to the Harley Museum and gambled at the Potawatomi Casino. Stayed overnight on the top floor of a huge hotel. The elevators were made of glass so you watch people in the lobby get smaller and smaller as you go up. Ever ride on one of those?"

"No, I have never had the pleasure of that experience."

Susie shivered. "It was a little scary at first, but Jake told me to not be a wuss. We were going to take in a Brewers' game, but he lost too much money at the blackjack table so we just went to the casino bar and drank."

"Sounds like a special trip. You'll always have your fond memories to sustain you."

"I got more than memories. See this?" Susie held up the shiny heart pendant for Beatrice to examine. "It's called cremation jewelry. I got Jake's ashes in this little urn."

CHAPTER EIGHTEEN

Sandra slid the bank statement out of the envelope and studied it once more. She spread it out on her kitchen table, pressing the creases on the folded paper. She felt like evil leeched onto the lines of the paper. Jake's ill-gotten money. He took advantage of someone's pain. Was he selling heroin or fentanyl to desperate addicts, making money from their wretched dependency? If he was a pusher, wouldn't the amount of each deposit differ? These installments showed up at regular intervals. Did somebody owe him a lot of money, too much to pay back all at once? What about blackmail? Maybe Jake knew someone's dirty secrets, secrets so ruinous they'd pay anything to keep them hidden. Too bad Vlad insisted she turn it over to the police before she discovered the truth.

Gaston wandered over to paw at her leg. His quiet whimper informed her he needed to go out, but she ignored him. The fake name on the account proved how corrupt the money was. The pooch grew more demanding: The whimper soon became a whine. When Sandra still didn't rise and head toward the hook that held his leash, he bit the cord belonging to her phone charging station and tugged on it, nearly disconnecting it from the outlet.

"Stop that, you rascal." She stood up and yanked the cord out of his mouth. "I heard you. We'll go for a walk.'

The instant Sandra snapped the leash onto his collar, he swept her toward the door like a tugboat pulling the Queen Mary out to sea.

"Let me get my sweater on. It's chilly out there." Her sweater hung on the hall tree but, before she reached the foyer, her cell phone rang. Arthur's name appeared.

'Hello, lovely lady. Big Band Night at the Senior Center was wonderful. I danced with the most beautiful woman there. All the other gents were jealous." He couldn't hide a hint of bravado in his voice.

"All three of them. And two of them were pushing walkers. I'm sure the ladies were extremely jealous because my man can trip the light fantastic without a cane," she said with a giggle.

"Too bad they turned the music off at seven. I was ready to dance forever with you. Your head resting on my shoulder was pure bliss." He sighed.

"I still have a stereo that works and a Righteous Brothers album. We can put on the oldies and dance in my living room. How about tonight?" Sandra asked.

"I'm sorry. I can't tonight. That's the reason I'm calling. I need to go out of town on business for a few days. I have a few loose strings to tie up in New York. I'll be counting the minutes until I come back."

"I understand. I'll miss you, too, love. Please call me when you get there so I won't worry." Sandra switched the phone to the arm holding Gaston's leash as she reached for her sweater.

"I'll text the minute my plane lands. I'll bring you back something special from the Big Apple. Goodbye, my angel."

After hanging up, Sandra thought for a moment. *When did Norm say Marco would be cleaning out Jake's apartment? He said the landlady gave Marco some flack about it at the bar. What day was it?*

The brisk morning air promised colder weather was on its way. The birch tree leaves were beginning to turn yellow, and the summer annuals bloomed brightly in their last hurrah before dying. The incipient blooms of purple asters and yellow mums warmed her heart, filling her with joy. Sandra might be in the autumn of her life, but she had plenty of time for action before winter set in. Time to exonerate her beloved and enjoy a new life with him.

Gaston sensed the lightness in her step. He trotted happily down the sidewalk, then squatted in the grass. Sandra hoped she wouldn't have to bend down to pick up poop, but he only let out a stream of urine. Quickly he wiped his front paws on the grass like a cat in the litter box and moved on.

Sandra dreaded facing the detective with the purloined bank statement. Purloined like in an Agatha Christie novel, not stolen as in his accusation of obstruction. What if she put it back where she found it and took the cookbook with the evidence to Detective Johnson instead? She could put the grey wig back on and present herself to Marco as Jake's estranged aunt. Marco only saw her at the funeral. She hadn't introduced herself. He'd never know she was on the case. Besides, wouldn't he be happy if she caught the killer of his best friend?

"Gaston, Marco's at the apartment today. We're going undercover again." She stopped so abruptly the leash tightened on his collar while the pooch was still moving. Gaston gave her a puzzled look. "We'll wake Norm up and have him drive us over to Jake's building."

Sandra tugged on the leash as she hauled a reluctant Gaston back to her house. He dragged his paws until she made him heel. She knocked loudly on the door to the basement apartment.

"Norm, wake up. I know you're in there." His motorcycle was parked askew in the driveway, like a child had abandoned his Big Wheel to play hide-and-seek. "Wake up. I need your help."

Gaston barked along with her shouts. The door swung open. A bleary-eyed, unshaven Norm swayed unsteadily, holding on to the frame. He wore a grimy grey t-shirt and crumpled plaid boxers. His hair hung in straggles down to his shoulders, the top of his head shiny in the morning light, giving him a greasy aura.

"What can I do you for?" he mumbled.

"Can you please get dressed and drive me over to Jake's apartment? Didn't you say Marco was clearing it out today?" Sandra talked like an old cassette tape played on fast forward.

Norm blinked for a minute to make sure he understood. "Yep. Marco said his buddies were helping on Saturday and Sunday. He borrowed a truck to haul the stuff he wanted to keep to his place. The rest goes to St Vinnie's."

"I need to get my hands on that old cookbook. Hurry."

Sandra told Norm to drop them off a block away. "Marco can't see us together. We don't want him to suspect anything's up," she said.

"Yeah, I suspect my girlfriend is secretly adding glue to my weapons collection. She denies it but I'm sticking to my guns."

'Come on, Gaston. Let's go before he tells the suspicious nun joke."

She undid her seatbelt as Norm slowed the car. The little dog's nose was pressed against the window, adding to the pattern of his earlier smudges.

Sandra paused, fingers on the door handle, and spoke, "Can you please wait here for us? This shouldn't take long."

When Sandra swung the door open, Gaston hopped out of the car, swiveling his head from side to side to check out the surroundings. He waited patiently on the sidewalk as she clambered behind him. The tattered service dog harness hung snugly on his pudgy frame, matching the shabby brown coat worn by his temporarily grey-haired mistress. They only needed a shopping cart loaded with clothes and a sleeping bag to complete a homeless disguise. Sandra was relying on the sympathetic reactions of the movers with Marco.

Sandra spotted the candy red pickup truck as she approached the apartment building. A boxy-looking bruiser carried a big screen television to the bed of the pickup already piled high with a bedroom set and boxes. She hoped she wasn't too late to retrieve the cookbook. If it was packed in one of the enclosed boxes, she feared no one would bother to look through them at the request of an old lady. She followed the sweaty man through the propped open front door and up the stairs to Jake's former apartment, with Gaston at her heel.

"What next?" the man said as he wiped his brow with the back of his hand. "You ain't taking the recliner, are you?"

"Not this load." Marco answered. "The pickup is almost full. We got the bedroom cleared out."

"Are you ready to drive to your place?" A second man with a large bulbous nose and close-set eyes emerged from the bedroom. "Cindy can keep packing up the kitchen."

"I don't need no more pots and pans and such. That can all go to St. Vinnie's." Marco set an empty Jack Daniel's box on a computer desk. "Just let me finish with Jake's tech shit."

"Kind sir, are you in charge of disposing of the items in this apartment? Jake Bender's apartment?" Sandra asked in her sweetest dear old granny voice.

"Yeah, what's it to you?" Marco stood wide-legged, arms folded over his chest as he eyed her and Gaston suspiciously. Gaston sat quietly on his haunches, then rested his head on his front paws. His bright eyes followed the two movers as they floated behind Marco.

"Jake, the poor dear boy, was my nephew. My sister, Angela, was his mother, bless her soul. We had a falling-out, lost track of each other for years before she passed last year. Then I heard from a cousin that her son, Jake, had also passed. Such a tragedy!" She dabbed at her eyes with a crumpled tissue she pulled from her coat pocket.

"Jake didn't ever talk about no aunt, just his mom. He didn't mention any relative in his will. Left everything to me. You're mistaken if you think there's anything here that you can get your hands on," Marco snarled.

"Oh, no. I don't want any of Jake's worldly goods, I was just hoping he had a picture of his mother that you could part with. I don't have any recent picture of my dear departed sister." She sniffed, then blew her nose.

"Hey, Cindy." Marco called to someone in the kitchen. "Did you come across any photos that could have been Marco's mother?"

A slender brunette in a pink camouflage t-shirt and torn jeans appeared in the doorway. "I found a photo album that must have belonged to his mother. It had pictures of Jake growing up. There were some of him with a woman and a man. I guessed it was his mother and father."

"That would be Angie and Ezra," Sandra clapped her hands. "How wonderful!"

"I didn't know what to do with it so I put it in the kitchen counter with his collection of girly magazines. I figured St. Vinnie's wouldn't take them, but one of you goofballs might want some vintage porn." She gave Sandra a wink. "It's all here." She gestured toward the kitchen.

"Bless your heart, dear girl," Sandra clasped her hands to her chest and smiled. "May I have the album? It would mean so much to me."

Marco scratched his head. "I don't know."

"What are you going to do with an old photo album? You don't know anyone in it besides Jake. Half the pictures are fading anyway. Let his aunt have it." The brunette twirled her ponytail around her finger while Jake was thinking.

"I suppose she can have it." Marco turned back to sorting a tangle of electronic gear into the box. "Get it for her and quit interrupting me. I need to have this joint emptied out by tomorrow night."

The slender woman meandered back to the kitchen with Sandra and Gaston close behind. She flipped through a pile of books and magazines until she found the green album with gold etching. She deposited it in Sandra's arms.

"It's kind of awkward to carry. Do you want some help getting it to your car?"

"No thank you, dear girl. I can manage." Sandra watched as the woman dumped the mishmash of utensils from a drawer into a cardboard box. "Did you happen to come across an old Betty Crocker cookbook? It's red and white. It was a gift I gave Angie for a wedding present. She adored that cookbook—used it all the time. I wrote our name and the date on the flyleaf: *Feb. 10, 1962, from Mr. and Mrs. Eugene Harris.* I'd love to have it as a reminder of happier days."

"I think I tossed it in one of these boxes with some other junk headed for the thrift store."

She chewed on her thumb while she stared at the multitude of open boxes on the floor. Her eyes glazed over. "Darn, I'm not sure which one it's in. I know I didn't put it with the nonperishables. The thrift store won't take them." She opened the nearest box and peered inside.

Gaston started to sniff the boxes, touching his nose to each one. He drifted from box to box before stopping at a large box and barking. He pawed at the box until the woman came over to it.

"Try that one," Sandra urged. "My dog has a very sensitive nose, just like a bloodhound. He's very good at finding missing objects."

"If you say so." The woman lifted the box onto the kitchen table and rummaged through mismatched dish towels and faded washrags. She pulled out a black apron with *King of the Grill* stamped on it. A book about mixing cocktails called *Gone with the Gin*. Finally, she exclaimed. "I think this is it."

She hauled out the red and white cookbook and flipped open the cover. "Sure enough. There's your name and Jake's parents. Mr. and Mrs. Ezra Bender." She handed the book to Sandra while Gaston yipped enthusiastically.

Sandra hugged both books to her chest. "I appreciate your help. You've made an old woman very happy. Thank you so much."

The brunette smiled broadly. "My mother always taught me to live by the Golden Rule. You know, do unto others before they do onto you. Something like that. She brought me up to respect old people."

"Time to go, lovey puppy." She yanked on Gaston's leash thinking, *Let's get out while the coast is clear. Smooth sailing all the way to the police station.*

She hustled the dog past Marco and out the apartment door, pausing only to say loud enough for the woman to hear, "Bless you, sir. Your kindness will be rewarded in heaven."

Marco grunted in response as he examined an old box filled with CD-ROMs. He had to blow the dust off some of them.

The brunette drifted in the living room to watch Sandra and Gaston leave. She gave her head a little shake and commented, "I never saw such a smart poodle."

"Poodle!" Marco stopped sorting and straightened up.

Sandra heard him mutter as she fled down the stairs.

"Wasn't the dog that tripped Jake at pickleball a poodle?"

CHAPTER NINETEEN

"Stay in the car with Uncle Norm." Sandra spoke to Gaston in a voice as firm as a boarding school headmistress. "You're not coming into the police station with me. Detective Johnson wasn't very fond of you when he met you the first time."

Gaston whimpered like a dog abandoned on an ice floe drifting out to sea and flashed his mournful big eyes at her. Sandra almost detected tears welling in them until she blinked hard and erased the illusion. *Damn, that dog is good at manipulation! If he were a human, he'd probably be in Congress, he's so convincing.* His frantic pawing on the back of the passenger seat left her unmoved.

"I said no dog detective today."

Norm reached behind him to give the pooch a reassuring pat. "Come on, little buddy. Mom won't be gone that long. If yer good, when she gets back we'll drive to Starbucks by the mall and get you a Puppuccino."

"And we'll get Uncle Norm a double chocolate chunk brownie, if both of you behave while I'm gone." Sandra shot a warning look at Norm.

"Hey, some mistakes are too much fun to make only once," Norm protested. "Sometimes it's good to be bad. Keeps life exciting."

"Not when you're about to meet a policeman like Detective Johnson. That man looks like he could flip the switch on a guy in the electric chair while he's eating a hot fudge sundae."

Sandra grasped the faded cookbook in her lap so tightly her knuckles turned white. She stared dejectedly at the muddy brown Crawford Municipal Building. The shoebox sized bricks reminded her of wandering into the back room of the shoe warehouse with its solid wall of boxes. Nothing but brown rectangles stacked high. Pink hydrangeas and yellow potentillas frolicked in a circle around the entrance, the only splash of color. The wavy lines below the Crawford city sign looked like a preschooler had dragged her fingers through green and blue paint. The Rock River flowed serenely nearby. She wished she were floating in a canoe down the river instead of trudging into the police station.

Norm glanced at the clock on the dashboard. "Didn't you make an appointment to talk to the cop at one o'clock? It's almost ten after."

"I know. I'm just working up the courage to confront the man again." Sandra let out a heavy sigh.

"When you used to have stage fright, didn't you always imagine the audience sitting in their underwear? Try picturing Detective Johnson in his tighty-whities."

"That's like picturing Fred Flintstone in a Speedo. Yuck! I've got to go. I don't want to provoke the angry bear."

Sandra stood as straight as her eighty-year-old back would let her. Didn't she audition for Harold Minsky's show at the Dunes when she was only sixteen years of age? She remembered how nervous she was, all by herself in Las Vegas, even though she'd worked the circuit of theaters and fairs since she was age fourteen. If a sixteen-year-old girl could dance in front of strangers and shed her clothes, then surely an eighty-something woman could stand up to a grumpy cop. She thrust open the door to the police station and marched boldly inside.

A young officer still sporting a trace of acne greeted her at the desk in the lobby. With his hair combed neatly to the side, he looked like he should be wearing Boy Scout khaki instead of policeman blue. She had push-up bras older than him. Why did everyone look so young when she felt so old?

"I'm Sandra Tooksbury, here to see Detective Johnson."

Her announcement echoed through the cavernous chamber of empty desks. Entering the station at one o'clock on a Monday afternoon was like visiting a mausoleum, down to the faint whiff of decay.

"He's been expecting you. I'll let him know you're here." He buzzed an inner office. "Your one o'clock is here."

Sandra slid her left fingers over the opal pendant, a recent gift from Arthur, and her talisman for this meeting. All her efforts to solve the pickleball murder were for him and their future happiness. As she traced the stone in its gold setting, she let her mind wander to last night when he gave her the velvet box with the lovely necklace. "A fire opal for my fiery love," he had declared as she opened it. Her heart flamed, and she clung to that warmth now. No overbearing detective could chill her passion.

The grizzly-like man lumbered into the lobby, wearing a dark grey suit badly in need of a dry cleaning. Permanent creases made by his ample thighs matched the crumples by his elbows. His well-fed stomach hung over the low-slung trousers. He thrust a ham-sized hand toward her.

"Mrs. Tooksbury, good to see you again," he said without much conviction.

Sandra slid her twiggy hand into his giant redwood fist and shook it firmly. Her glinty blue eyes stared directly into his piercing brown ones without blinking, waiting to see if he would look away first. He did.

"Thank you for seeing me on such short notice," she said. "I found something you'll be very interested in."

His eyes drifted to the well-used cookbook that she hugged tightly to her chest, then arched his brow. His face could have been carved on Mt. Rushmore for all the emotion it showed.

"Please come this way."

The detective pivoted toward a maze of small rooms. His jacket pouched around his back, molded by the shape of his rear end. He led her toward a door bearing his name in brass letters. He opened the door and stepped aside to let her enter. As she passed by, she caught the musky scent of his aftershave. The room looked much like its occupant, disheveled and overwhelming. A huge desk bearing a laptop was submerged under piles of folders and empty Styrofoam cups. He cleared several files off a chair, then indicated she should sit there. Before he settled in the black leather office chair across from her, he patted his unruly hair into a shaggy brown helmet with a beefy hand. Detective Johnson fixed his impassive gaze upon her.

Propping his elbows on the sides of his chair, he rested both hands in his lap before he asked, "Why have you come to see me today?"

"Ever since my boa was found around Jake Bender's neck, I've been living under a cloud of suspicion." Sandra willed herself not to squirm under his intense stare.

"I interviewed you several weeks ago. If it's any consolation, I don't think you're a murderer."

"But you think my fiancé is." Sandra leaned forward in her seat, the accusation hanging in the air between them.

"At this stage in the investigation, we're still trying to sort out the evidence. When we're ready to make an arrest, we'll call a news conference. The *Daily Gazette* will be the first to know, and they'll spread the word. Until that point you should go about your normal business. Let the professionals handle the case. We don't need any amateurs interfering, especially one with a performing dog."

He tilted back and started tapping his thumb on the armrest. His eyes wandered to the large clock on the wall. "Is there anything else you want to say?"

"Yes, you may be interested in something I found Saturday. It adds a new wrinkle to the case." Her eyes gleamed with the knowledge of the unexpected development she held in her lap.

"Please enlighten me with your discovery," he said in a mocking tone.

"I was taking my dog for a walk, and we happened to see a red pickup truck parked outside an apartment building on Cole Street. A couple of guys were loading boxes into the truck bed. I asked if they were moving out. The men told me they were just helping a friend. The stuff belonged to his buddy who died; he had to clear the dead guy's apartment that weekend. They were two hefty fellows, could lift furniture all day probably and never break a sweat. Kind of built like you. Solid. Muscular." Sandra sunk to flattery.

"Jake Bender lived on Cole Street. I assume he was the dead friend." The tapping on the armrest continued.

"Yes, he was. The tattooed fellow that seemed to be in charge told me his friend had been murdered. I knew right away it was Jake. I was about to walk away. Gaston was getting restless, and I didn't want him to cause a ruckus. He can do that, you know."

"I'm well aware of what your dog is capable of." Cynicism colored his voice. "After what happened at CHAW, I'd think you'd avoid anything to do with Jake Bender."

"I didn't know that was where Jake lived. Anyhow the friend brought out a load of books that he planned on taking to the landfill and dumped it on the sidewalk. Gaston pulled me over to the pile. I saw this cookbook on top. I used to have one just like it. I used it so much the binding broke and the pages fell out. I asked if I could have the old *Betty Crocker Cookbook* and the tattooed man said yes. So I took it home. You'll never guess what I found inside."

"I'm sure you're about to tell me." Detective Johnson stifled a yawn.

Sandra opened the red and white book and pulled out the bank statement. She waved it triumphantly before handing it to the bored detective. "I found this bank statement. It has the Cole Street address, but not Jake's name. It's addressed to somebody named Eugene Harris, who happened to be inscribed in this cookbook. 'To Mr. and Mrs. Ezra

Bender from Mr. and Mrs. Eugene Harris.' All the deposits are recent. Not from 1962 like the year this cookbook is dated."

Detective Johnson bolted upright. He studied the paper before him with a growing excitement. Then he whistled and said, "You're right. It appears Jake set up this account using an alias. Why would he do that? Where did he get this kind of money?"

"That's what I wondered when I saw it. You can see why I rushed down here to turn the account information over to you," she said triumphantly.

"Thank you. This much money would be a good motive for murder." Detective Johnson traced his finger along the paper stopping at the forty-thousand-dollar balance. "If we find out who gave it to him, we may find the killer."

"You're very welcome. When you widen the search, you'll see my Arthur is innocent. He had nothing to do with Jake Bender, outside of playing pickleball with him."

"I'll need the cookbook, too. It may help me establish who Eugene Harris was and how Jake came in possession of his identity."

The detective reached over the desk for the cookbook.

Sandra slowly clambered to her feet. She placed the cookbook on the only clear spot on the desk. Her intense blue eyes met his murky brown ones and held his gaze for a few heartbeats before she spoke.

"First, my peacock feather boa is confiscated for evidence. Now my favorite cookbook. When this case is closed, is there a chance I'll get either of them back?"

CHAPTER TWENTY

Norm wondered what the hell he was doing driving to Marco's fall bonfire. First off, bonfires depressed the hell out of him. It reminded him of the bonfires his dad burnt on the farm every fall after raking leaves and clearing away garden leavings. Shrub trimmings piled up in the field behind the barn since spring, and Dad added the dead foliage in fall. Then he poured a little gasoline on the pile and tossed in a match. Whoosh! Flames reached to the sky with a monstrous roar, giving his mom's garden waste a proper burial before winter. His dad had a fatal heart attack while tending a bonfire, leaving his mother and brothers to mourn each fall. Even worse, the last time Norm heard the roar of a fire was in a hamlet in 'Nam. Flamethrowers sprayed the simple grass structure because a sniper's fire allegedly came from it. An old woman wailed as she watched everything she owned go up in smoke. He sure as hell didn't want any reminders of that God-awful time. He avoided bonfires like the plague.

Second, Norm didn't like Marco. The guy was a pipe bomb ready to detonate at the slightest offense. He made the skinny woman cry in the bar at Jake's memorial, injured Vlad with the push in the weight room, and punched out a drunk at Hogs and Honeys the last time Norm joined him for a beer. Anger pulsed through Marco's face like a deadly infection spilling over to the unwary victim. Norm never knew what would cause him to flare up, which is why he never refused to tell him a joke. He didn't relish spitting out a few teeth after his jaw connected with the guy's fist. He didn't have that many to spare.

When Marco texted *Bonfire tonight. Perfect time to get drunk and rid the world of Jake's private stuff*, Norm's first impulse was to beg off and text back. *Sorry, man. Working for a pal tonight.*

But Sandra insisted, "Norm, you got to go. The investigation has stalled since I turned the bank statements over to the cops."

"True. But dealing with Marco is like petting a scorpion."

"Please. Marco knows more about Jake's shady dealings than he lets on. We've got to find out where that money came from. Suck it up for the team. Get him drunk and maybe he'll spill his guts. He likes you.

Do it for me. When Arthur finally proposes I want to walk down the aisle, not visit him in the penitentiary."

Arthur was returning that night from some unfinished business deal and planned to take Sandra to a fancy restaurant to celebrate. Vlad and Beatrice had never met the man. Hell, Norm only met him when he had the little fender bender with his expensive car. Sure, he saw Arthur when he picked up Sandra for one of their many dates, but the guy never stopped to chew the fat. Beatrice and Vlad schemed to crash the celebration at the exclusive restaurant so they could get a closer look at him. The couple convinced him the bonfire was better than spending the night alone.

When Norm rode his Harley to Marco's place at the edge of town, there were already a half dozen cars and a few motorcycles. How was he supposed to get Marco to spill his guts with all these idiots around? In the dark he perceived the outline of an old two-story farmhouse with a yard light on in the back. He parked far away from the others, ready for a quick exit. He rolled to a stop. Using his left foot he lowered the kickstand, then dismounted. Muttering "Aw, shit," he brushed road dirt off his jeans and straightened his belt buckle.

Drunken hoots and laughter broke the stillness of the fall night. A Def Leopard tune blasted from speakers, adding to the cacophony of sound. No smoke so the fire wasn't lit yet. Norm breathed in the cloying scent of overripe wild grapes and fading purple coneflowers. Then he dragged himself in the direction of the partygoers.

"There's my man!" Marco declared when Norm rounded the side of the house. "Just in time for a shot and a beer."

A makeshift bar consisting of a plank resting on two sawhorses held a row of shot glasses. Marco grabbed a can of beer from a cooler, popped the top, and handed it to him.

"Cindy, pour Mr. Funny Bones a shot," he said to the skinny brunette, who obviously had some masochistic tendencies since she continued to hang with Marco.

Norm took a sip of the beer and set it on the plank. "When you gonna start the fire?"

Marco slapped him on the back. "Just waiting for you. We need a good story to start the night."

"Seeing Cindy in her cowboy boots reminds me of a joke about my aunt and uncle at the fair. No offense to you, honey," Norm said to her.

"None taken," she answered, pushing her sleeves up to reveal her bony wrists as she poured him a shot.

"Shut up. Norm's telling a joke," Marco said to the men yammering by the makeshift bar.

Norm began, "Uncle Bud and Aunt Viv went to the state fair and stopped by the breeding bull exhibit. They went up to the first pen and saw a sign attached that said: THIS BULL MATED 50 TIMES LAST YEAR. Aunt Viv nudged Uncle Bud in the ribs, smiled, and said, 'He mated fifty times last year.'

"They walked to a second pen that had a sign that said: THIS BULL MATED 150 TIMES LAST YEAR. Viv gave Bud a healthy jab, grinned, and said, 'Wow! That's more than twice a week! You could learn something from that one.'

"The Grand Champion bull had a sign that said: THIS BULL MATED 365 TIMES LAST YEAR. Aunt Viv got so excited she nearly broke Bud's ribs with her elbow. She yelled, 'That's once a day! You could really learn a lot from this one.' Uncle Bud looked at her and said, 'Go over and ask them if it was with the same old cow.'"

Marco slapped Norm on the back. "Good one to get us started. I'll drink to that."

Marco threw back the tequila and slammed the glass down on the plank. Then he walked over to the pile, picked up a can of lighter fluid, and sprayed it on the stack of broken end tables, chairs with three legs, and dry branches bordering the concrete slab that served as a patio. He threw a match and the pile started to burn.

"Let's start with those boxes of old magazines we found in his storage locker."

He pointed to a few boxes scattered on the concrete. A Mack truck lookalike picked one up, carried it closer to the fire, then tossed magazine after magazine on the blaze. The conflagration flared brightly, sending red embers into the black sky. The smell of paper burning permeated the night air.

"Next, I'm gonna dump that box of newspaper clippings. I don't know why the hell Jake thought they were important."

Marco shook his head as he thrust the box toward the fire. He poured them out. Clippings fluttered into the air like a swarm of bees. One blew toward Norm. He snatched it midair before it hit his face and slipped it into his jeans pocket. The crowd ventured to a new box.

"What the hell is this?" Mack Truck held up black satin woman's panties. "There's a bunch of them in here." He brought out a few more in his other hand. "Jake wasn't no cross-dresser, was he?"

"You perv!" Marco jeered. "What the hell are you talking about? Jake was all man. He wasn't no fairy. Those are his trophies. When he did a bitch, he liked to keep a little remembrance of the good time. Probably even Cindy here has a pair in the mix. But you ain't getting them back, babe." Marco winked at the woman.

Norm could see her face flush even in the dim light.

"We were just friends. Good for a few laughs. I never slept with him. He had Susie for that," she said.

"Yeah, friends with benefits," Marco chortled.

"Look at this one." The Mack Truck guy held up a lacy thong and twirled it around with his hand in the air like a cowboy with a lasso before he flung it into the flames. The drunks cheered. He laughed uproariously. "I wish I coulda seen the broad wearing that one!"

Marco said confidentially to Norm, "Jake always said all women have a rape fantasy. They want to get boned, but they have to pretend they don't want it. Their lips may say no, but their body says yes. He could tell when they got all hot and bothered. Jake wasn't one to take no for an answer. He always had a few broads on the side. He made sure Susie never found out."

Some of the other partiers tore into the boxes. After discovering a box of old *Playboys* and *Penthouses*, the well-worn magazines fueled the flames. Some men salvaged centerfolds and threw them into an empty box, spoils of the event.

An AC/DC fan sporting a shirt from their 1990 tour found a box of *Men's Health Magazines*. "Do any of you ladies want these? They got pictures of some well-hung guys." He shoved a photo of a muscular body builder with a skimpy thong covering bulging genitals in Cindy's face.

"What about you, bar maid?"

Cindy stepped back from the aging rock fan, a look of disgust in her face.

"Get that thing out of her face," Norm said.

"I'm just having a little fun with her," he protested, plopping the magazine on the plank.

"She doesn't think you're very funny," Norm said. "Cut it out."

"OK, Buzz Killer!" The drunk left with a parting shot.

Cindy said, "Thanks for handling that jerk."

Marco said nothing but stared at Norm.

"I don't believe in Jake's theory. I got too much respect for the ladies," Norm said to him.

"I say don't knock it if you haven't tried it," Marco said. He reached behind one of the sawhorses and pulled out a shoe box filled with photographs. "I'm saving these from the bonfire. Some were supposedly important. Haven't had a chance to go through them all."

He pulled Norm a few steps away from the drink stand and spoke in a low voice. "I know Jake was doing a shakedown of some dude. Found out from his mother some guy was scamming old women. The asshole tried to pull a fast one on his mom, but Jake got wind of it. Before he could put a stop to it, the old lady died. He found this picture of the two of them. Doesn't the guy resemble somebody who shows up at CHAW? The dude with the black Thunderbird?"

Norm nearly choked on a swig of beer when he saw the picture. A white-haired lady in tiny crystal-encrusted glasses smiled broadly into the camera, arm in arm with Arthur Ashenbrenner. Arthur was turning his head toward the woman, the shot blurred by his movement, but the immaculately trimmed silver hair, the firm jaw line, and the perfectly shaped ear definitely belonged to Arthur, or his twin brother.

"He looks like the champion pickleball player." Norm didn't add, *who's proposed to my best friend.*

"Don't he just!" Marco sneered. "I tried contacting the guy, but he lets my calls go to voicemail. I'm not sure he's the same asshole that went after Jake's mom, but I aim to find out. He cleaned her out of five thousand bucks. Might not sound like much, but Jake said for an old lady like his mother it's a lot."

"Especially for any person living on measly retirement savings." Norm thought of the times Arthur conveniently forgot his wallet and Sandra bailed him out. How was he going to break the news to her?

"Jake bragged he got his mom's money back and then some. He dug around and found more dirt on the guy. Said his mom wasn't the only victim. There's probably more. The scumbag was using the internet, too. Looked up widows on Facebook and used what he found to worm his way into their life. Jake had a Gmail account under a fake name where he stashed the evidence. Used a library computer so nobody could trace the shit back to him. But he didn't have a chance to tell me all the details before he got himself offed."

"What if that guy was Jake's murderer?' Norm said with alarm creeping into his voice. "Let the police handle it. They got the manpower to arrest the jerk and put him away for a long time."

"If he killed my best friend, I'm going to take him out myself, once I'm sure he's the same guy. I'm going to settle a lot of scores for Jake, not just this one. He'd of done the same for me if I was the one got murdered."

"Turn that picture over to the cops. Tell them what you know. There could be more old ladies that could be hurt by this asshole. Don't you want to stop him from ruining more lives?"

"Are you telling me to kiss ass with the cops? Are you crazy? The cops have it in for me. Harassed me all my life. Pulled me over for phony traffic violations. I ain't helping them. No way!" Marco tucked the picture into his shirt pocket and glared at Norm.

"Maybe I'll tell them." Norm thrust out his chin, balling his hands into fists at his side

"If you snitch it'll be the last thing you do. Nobody stabs me in the back. I don't care if you're the funniest goddamn comedian in the world, nobody betrays me and lives to tell about it." Marco raised his fists to his chest and took a step closer to Norm. "I said nobody!"

"I gotta do the right thing." Norm stared without flinching.

Marco put his face so close to Norm's their noses were almost touching. Norm could smell the beer on his breath and feel the heat as Marco humphed in anger, just like a wounded bull charging a matador. He closed his eyes, waiting for the punch to his chin. Instead, Marco gave him a hard shove to his chest. Norm stumbled backwards but didn't fall. He raised his fists in response. Both glared, waiting to see if the other would make the next move.

Cindy looked with alarm at the two of them frozen in combat. "What's wrong with you guys? You're missing out on all the fun."

The drunks surrounding the bonfire had emptied the boxes and tossed in the cardboard. The fire erupted once again as one of them threw in an armful of old videotapes. The acrid odor of burning plastic filled the air and made Norm choke.

A slurred voice hollered in delight, "Here goes Jake's porn collection. Goodbye, *King Dong* . So long, *The Sperminator*."

More gleeful shouts chimed in as several men dug into the box and pulled out old movies: "Here's the classic *Romeo in Juliet*."

"I found *Dawson's Crack.*"

"Don't forget *Indiana Bones and the Temple of Boobs.*"

After each man read the title, he flung the videotape into the blaze, and the others roared with delight.

The loud raucous laughter broke the stand-off. Marco jerked his head back and shouted, "Hey, I wanted to keep those! I know a guy who can convert them to DVDs."

He whirled around and dashed over to prevent any more loss of good porn.

Norm let out a deep breath, "Whew! That was close!" He went back to the makeshift bar to finish his beer.

Cindy gaped at him for a moment, her forehead knotted with concern. "You better leave. Marco looked pretty pissed. He can do serious damage when he explodes."

"I'm outta here, thanks." Norm turned to walk away. It took all his self-control to keep from breaking into a dead run to his bike.

"Better make yourself scarce for a while. Marco's got a memory like an elephant," she shouted after him.

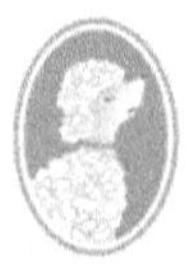

CHAPTER TWENTY-ONE

"When are we going to meet this perfect man?" Vlad asked Sandra earlier that week. "Beatrice would like to make dinner for both of you. Her special lasagna. The recipe makes a lot for just two people."

He was enjoying a Sandra Tooksbury martini, shaken not stirred, James Bond style, late on a Sunday afternoon. He had spent the weekend with his three children.

His injured back had improved to the point he and the kids were able to have lunch at Erin's favorite sandwich shop, then a take a walk along the Story Book Trail in the park. Nicholas read the story to Kaitlyn as they followed the glass covered pages on strategically placed posts. The two younger children delighted in the clever tale about a little girl who wanted to create something magnificent while Erin talked to him about visiting colleges. The beautiful fall day on the nature trail provided family time with very few squabbles. The nightmarish memories of distended dead faces faded when the kids were around.

"I'll mention it again the next time I see him. He's so smitten with me it's like no one else exists. I haven't played mahjongg with the gals since we started dating. He's even dropped out of pickleball to spend more time with me." She sipped her drink and stared at the clear liquid. Then she added, "If only Gaston weren't acting so jealous."

"How is Gaston acting jealous?"

"If we sit together on the couch, Gaston wriggles between us. He jumps up on Arthur when he comes to visit and barks in his face. He even slobbers chewed up treats on his shoes. It's most disconcerting!" She clenched the stem of her martini glass with such force Vlad feared it would splinter.

"Gaston can be a handful at times. I've been on the receiving end of some of his antics." Vlad gazed at the sleeping dog in his sheepskin bed, who had acknowledged his entrance with a little *wuff*, then went back to snooze. "The new dog bed certainly has taken the edge off his anxiety. Maybe I should get one for myself."

"Arthur read these beds can be very calming. I'm glad he made me order one."

She set her glass down and frowned. "Every time I propose a dinner date with you, Arthur remembers he's made a reservation for two at some fancy restaurant. If only he'd remember his wallet when we get there." She sighed. "When we get married our money will be mingled together anyway. I guess I shouldn't complain."

"Whoa, there. What's this about getting married?"

"Arthur hasn't exactly proposed with a ring and all. He did give me this necklace." She held up the opal pendant. "And he talks about all the places we'll go when we are married. He just has a few loose ends to tie up with his consulting jobs."

"I thought he was retired."

"Semi-retired. He moved to Crawford because he was tired of traveling and just wanted to settle down and take life at a slower pace. But he still has one or two big construction projects to finish. He'll have a lot of money coming in then. Especially after he sells his villa in Portofino, Italy."

"Villa in Italy. Wow. Now I really have to meet this man." Vlad leaned forward and said, "I've got an idea. When are you going out with him next?"

"Tomorrow night, in fact. He's coming home from a quick jaunt to L.A. He closed a big business deal. To celebrate he made a reservation at the Chef's Table in Madison. Just us." She smiled sweetly.

"What's Norm up to? I haven't seen him since the funeral."

"He's doing some sleuthing at Marco's. Trying to figure out where Jake's secret stash came from."

"Let's meet tomorrow night. Text me when you leave here. Beatrice and I will meet you at the restaurant. We'll pretend it's just a coincidence."

THE NEXT NIGHT VLAD AND BEATRICE headed to the posh restaurant. Vlad had to dust off his one and only suit. He couldn't button the jacket anymore, and the pants were a bit snug. But he had a new tie— a Father's Day present from the kids—and a freshly pressed shirt. He trimmed his mustache like the old movie actor Clark Gable's pencil look. Very debonair. Beatrice wore a burgundy sheath that she picked up in Amsterdam on their romantic river cruise.

"We look quite the fashionistas," she said as they walked to the car.

"We want to make a good first impression on Arthur, if my plan works."

Vlad spotted Arthur the instant they approached the maître d's stand. His navy tailored jacket fit his broad shoulders like the finest lambskin glove while his thick silver hair was as impeccably groomed as an *Esquire* model's. Vlad felt like a struggling used car salesman in comparison. Arthur's teeth gleamed white like a dental advertisement when he put his head back and laughed at some quip Sandra made.

"What do you mean you don't have our reservation?" Vlad's voice rose with indignation as he addressed the headwaiter. "I called weeks ago. It's our anniversary. I planned a special celebration for my fiancée."

The flushed maître d' fumbled with the handheld device as he scrolled through the screens. "I'm so sorry, sir. We don't have any record of your reservation."

Beatrice twisted her diamond engagement ring as she gazed sadly at the diners seated at the sumptuous linen covered tables. Waitstaff in crisp white shirts and black velvet vests brought trays of artistically arranged food to the lucky few.

"I was so looking forward to this evening. I've never eaten here. I've heard so much about the food."

"Are you certain there's nothing open for tonight?" Vlad asked.

"Nothing until ten."

"That's too late. We both need to work in the morning. You can expect a bad review on Yelp from both of us." He slammed his fist on the stand.

The nearby diners turned to stare at the unfolding scene.

Gaston emitted a little yip from beneath Sandra's table, where he lay quietly, paws folded meekly in front, behaving calmly as his *Service Dog* harness advertised.

Sandra turned in Vlad's direction and waved her napkin at them. "Yoohoo. Vlad, Beatrice." She leaned closer to Arthur and said, "My friends just walked in. I'd like you to meet them."

He watched with a deepening frown as she slowly rose and ambled over to the stand, Gaston at her heels.

"We just ordered our drinks. Perhaps you could join us." Sandra turned to the maître d'. "Would it be possible for our friends to sit with us? We have two extra seats."

The man wiped his brow, gestured to one of the waitstaff, and picked up two menus. He led the way to where Arthur was seated. "We lost this couple's reservation. Since they are friends of yours, we hope you don't mind if they join you."

Arthur's eyes narrowed, and he clenched his jaw. But he quickly switched to a bland expression as he said, "No. Not at all. I've been wanting to meet Sandra's friends."

Vlad and Beatrice ordered drinks as they perused the menus. Vlad widened his eyes when he saw the prices but gamely ordered the house wine while Beatrice said, "Just water, please."

Sandra made the introductions. Vlad and Beatrice shared they both worked at Crawford University.

"I understand from Sandra you're semi-retired," Vlad said.

"I just do a bit of consulting here and there," Arthur said. "No big deal. Soon I'll be completely out of the field. I can devote myself full time to making this lovely lady happy."

"Sandra told us one of your jobs takes you to Italy. To the Italian Riviera. Ever since I watched that series on PBS about the English hotel I've wanted to go there," Beatrice gushed. "It all sounds so exciting. And Sandra will get to see it with you."

"I'm waiting for the finishing touches on the building project to be completed. Then I'll collect my fees. It's complicated. International banking has so many rules and regulations. I won't bore you with all that." He took a sip of his wine and formed a tent with his hands. "Tell me how you two came to meet."

Beatrice giggled, "It began with a misunderstanding about a love poem on the back of a library reserve room request. I thought it was intended for me and that I was Vlad's secret crush."

Vlad's face colored red, and he hastily spoke. "I'm sure Arthur doesn't want to hear about my clumsy blunder."

Arthur smiled. "But, of course, I want to hear this charming story. Romantic mishaps abound in plays and novels. Most amusing."

The cell phone in his pocket buzzed, and he pulled it out. "Please excuse me. I need to take this call from my associate in Italy."

Arthur moved near the restroom sign, out of the flow of traffic. Vlad observed how his demeanor changed as he answered his phone. No longer wearing an amused look, his lips tightened and his eyes shifted furtively from the wait station to their table. Then he turned his back to them.

Beatrice and Sandra whispered back and forth about how handsome Arthur was. Vlad curled his upper lip but refrained from comment. He observed the man hunch his shoulders as he responded to the text. He slipped the phone into his rear trouser pocket and returned to the table. When he sat down the phone dropped out. Gaston tilted his head toward the exposed phone but remained silent. He nudged the phone toward Vlad with his paw.

"Gaston is on his best behavior tonight. Good boy," Vlad said as he reached down to pat the dog and grab the phone. Luckily, Arthur's auto lock hadn't kicked in yet. The screen was still alight. Vlad quickly clicked on the phone icon.

Oblivious to the dog's actions, Arthur smoothed his napkin on his lap and smiled. "I'm sorry for the interruption. Please continue with your fascinating story."

Captivated with Beatrice's recollection of her first encounter with Vlad, Arthur kept his eyes on her face as she grew more animated with the tale.

Although Sandra had heard the story before, she spurred Beatrice on. "Tell him what happened in the bookstore. It's so funny."

"Excuse me. I need to visit the men's room." Vlad rose, concealing the cell phone in his jacket pocket, his finger held firmly on the screen.

His three companions barely noticed him leaving the table.

He fled into an empty stall and scrolled through the recent phone calls. The names of several women leapt out at him. Unless the most recent caller, Shirley Pritchard, was in Italy, Arthur was lying about the phone call being about business. More like monkey business. In addition to Sandra, the name Rita Hanson also appeared several times. What was going on with these women? Then, to his amazement, he saw the name Marco Orlowski. Could it be the same Marco from the incident in the weight room? Jake's best friend? A man wearing a pair of well-made designer shoes stood outside the stall. Vlad couldn't waste any more time scrolling through the calls. After setting Arthur's phone on the toilet tank, he took out his own phone and took a photo of the call log. He'd google the names, do a people search, and see what he could find out.

His three dining companions were all laughing uproariously when Vlad returned to the table. Gaston raised his head and opened his eyes but kept his paws folded serenely. No one glanced his way so Vlad picked up the napkin still crumpled on his chair. He gave it a little shake to conceal Arthur's phone as he slipped it under the table again.

The waiter arrived with Vlad's wine. When he bent down to place it on the table, he noticed the cell phone near Arthur's foot.

"Sir, is that your phone on the floor?" he said.

Arthur quickly snatched it up and stuffed it into his suit coat pocket. "It is mine. Thank you. Must have dropped out when I sat down."

He gave Vlad a suspicious look. Vlad coolly stared back until Arthur dropped his eyes to the menu. The ladies were still tittering about Vlad's comic first encounters with Beatrice.

"Before we order I propose a toast."

The table grew silent.

Arthur lifted his glass and fixed his gaze steadily on Sandra. *"All amore eterno."*

Vlad parroted, *"Amore eterno."*

Until I find out what kind of game you're playing.

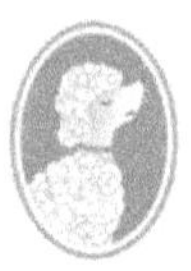

CHAPTER TWENTY-TWO

Vlad broke all speeding laws in his eagerness to get to Beatrice's house after they left the restaurant. Alone in the car with her, he talked like a carny convincing a mark to play a game of chance.

"Gaston saw Arthur drop his phone under the table. He put his paw on it before I was locked out. That's why I went to the men's room in the middle of your story. I was able to look at some of his recent calls. There were several calls to other women besides Sandra. I also saw a call from someone named Marco Orlowski."

Beatrice straightened up, suddenly alert. "Maybe it's the same Marco from CHAW. Do you remember the names of the women?"

"Better than that, I took a photo of the screen. If I'd had more time, I would have gone to the contact list and found their numbers. But someone wanted to use the toilet, and I had to get back to the table before Arthur noticed his phone was missing."

"So that explains your sudden desire to reach down and pet Gaston."

"When we get to your place we'll use your computer to do some sleuthing."

A Harley Davidson bike blocked the entrance to Beatrice's garage.

"What the hell? That's Norm's bike!" Vlad slammed on the brakes, stopping a few feet away from the riderless motorcycle.

"Sandra said he was attending some kind of bonfire event at Marco's. Something must have gone wrong if he ended up here instead of his place." Beatrice clutched her purse a little tighter as Vlad turned off the engine. "Let's find out." She hurried out of the car.

Norm was curled up on the glider on Beatrice's front porch, his leather vest folded under his head for a pillow. Without his ever-present Green Bay Packers cap, the top of his balding head looked vulnerable, like an infant's soft spot. His boots were side by side on the welcome mat. His naked big toe peeked out of the hole in his grey socks. His eyes flew open when he heard their footsteps on the stairs.

"It's about time you showed up. Wait until you hear what I found out about Jake's mother!" Norm blurted out, instantly awake.

"I stole a look at Arthur's phone log. He received a suspicious call at the restaurant," Vlad said.

Beatrice unlocked the front door and said, "Come on in. Let's talk inside."

She held the door open as Norm gathered up his boots and vest and entered the house. Vlad gestured for her to follow Norm. After they were safely inside, he threw the deadbolt and began talking.

"I'm afraid Arthur's trying to deceive Sandra. Some kind of bogus story about unfinished business in Italy. Tonight I discovered that's a lie. There was no call from overseas."

"I learned before Jake's mother died she was involved with some guy who bilked her out of five thousand bucks. Jake was shaking down the guy to get the money back. Marco had a picture of them together. It was kinda fuzzy but from what I saw the guy sure looked like Arthur Ashenbrenner."

The cat wandered in from her bedroom at the sound of their voices and rubbed against Beatrice's leg.

She picked him up and cuddled him in her arms as she reflected, "If Jake was avenging his mother, that would explain the hostility between the two. There was more behind it than just a rivalry between pickleball players."

The cat squirmed out of her arms and ran behind the couch as Beatrice sat down. Norm settled in beside her.

Vlad noticed where the cat went and stationed himself on the recliner, keeping a cautious watch on Max's hiding place "And if Jake was blackmailing him, that would be a good motive for murder," Vlad said triumphantly. "What else did Marco say?"

"He said something about settling old scores for Jake, now that he was gone." Norm scratched the back of his head in contemplation. "I kinda thought he meant there were more people that Jake was blackmailing. I told him to take that picture to the cops. He nearly punched my lights out. Said he hated the cops and would handle it himself. Threatened me if I snitched. Then he got distracted by the drunks throwing crap into the bonfire, and I made a quick exit."

"If he goes after Arthur that means Sandra could be in danger." Beatrice sat upright on the couch. "We need to warn her!"

"Who's going to tell her that Arthur is a liar and a swindler? That will break her heart. What if we're wrong? We can't say anything until we get more proof that Arthur is a charlatan." Vlad drummed his fingers on the armrest of the chair. "Beatrice, you and I are going to start with a google search of those names on the computer and see what we find. And Norm," Vlad paused and studied Norm for a second. "You can check on Sandra."

"I'm on it, Doc. I'm going to watch her like I'm a Doberman on duty. If Marco comes near her when she's with Arthur, I'll be there to protect her. He doesn't scare me." Norm pulled his boots back on and stood up. "I'm heading to the house now."

"Who's going to protect her from Arthur?" Beatrice said in a small voice. "He's the bigger threat."

"That's our job on the computer. Let's get our act in gear."

Vlad extended a hand to help her up.

Ten lines of recent calls from the past two days were a start. Vlad scrutinized the unfamiliar names. Whoever Shirley Pritchard is, she called Arthur twice today and once yesterday. Sandra called three times. Rita Hansen called yesterday, and so did Marco. There's a call from the bank that was missed, and a call to the restaurant. All local. No international calls so Arthur was most certainly lying when he said he was taking a call from Italy.

Beatrice fired up the computer. "Let's start with a search using Shirley Pritchard."

She entered the name in the search bar and got three hits. The first was an obituary. Shirley Ann McFarland Pritchard, age seventy-four, passed away in August of last year at a hospice center. The second hit found a thirty-something woman on LinkedIn working at a marketing firm in Boulder, Colorado. The third Shirley Pritchard appeared to be retired, age seventy-nine, living in Appleton, Wisconsin. No picture. The Yellowbook search gave an address—116 Hudson Avenue—but only the first six digits of a phone number. For ninety-five cents the search engine would come up with the phone number. For nine dollars and ninety-five cents it would search all public records and find the names of relatives.

Similarly, the first two hits for Rita Hansen brought up obituaries—one in Ann Arbor Michigan, the second in Manchester, Tennessee.

"Two dead Ritas," Vlad said. "Rita Marie Hansen passed away in Ann Arbor and Rita Richmond Hansen in Tennessee. There's a young blond Rita Hansen in Sweden who posted photos of herself in mini-skirts and a bikini on Instagram, and a Rita Bertha Hansen who lives in St. Paul, Minnesota. LinkedIn says she's retired from some realty appraisal firm. No bikini pictures, just a professional headshot of a sixtyish woman."

"Let's start with the Wisconsin Shirley. I'll cough up the nine ninety-five and see what we can find out." Beatrice entered her credit card number and got not only a phone number and names of family members, including her husband, Carl, deceased, but Shirley's traffic violations—failure to yield right of way, speeding, and parking near a fire hydrant.

"Maybe we can use the traffic violations to get our foot in the door since they're fairly recent." Vlad paced back and forth as he spoke. "We could pretend to offer her a deal on a driver's safety course for seniors."

"How would that help us find out how she's connected to Arthur?" Beatrice asked.

"Once we get her on the phone, we could say we got her name from another satisfied senior driver, Arthur Ashenbrenner. We can find out how well she knows him."

"What if she doesn't answer her phone? She might think we're scammers." Beatrice looked skeptical. "I never answer if I don't recognize the phone number."

"You're right." Vlad stopped walking and snapped his fingers. "I'll drive up to Appleton tomorrow. It's not that far."

"We can check out Marco just by calling CHAW," Beatrice said. "I can ask to leave him a message at the desk. He usually works out early in the morning. Even if he's not there, they'll confirm his name."

"You're cleverer than Miss Marple." He pulled her to her feet and gave her a quick hug. 'You call CHAW tomorrow morning. I'll call Chuck right now and tell him my back is acting up—get him to cover my lecture in return for me taking his classes while he's on sabbatical. Then I'll head to Appleton bright and early."

VLAD'S STOMACH CHURNED AND RUMBLED so loudly the cat raised his head to look around Beatrice's bedroom for the source of the disturbance. When he only saw Vlad, Max stretched out his paw and flexed his claws in warning. After tossing and turning a few more times, Vlad gave up trying to find a comfortable position. Scattered thoughts moved through his mind like clouds on a windy day. To avoid waking

Beatrice with his fidgeting, Vlad surrendered his spot to the cat and moved to the couch. He dozed off and on, waking up before his alarm went off.

A large double espresso from the coffee bar at the Kwik Stop cured his fatigue. He rehearsed his scenario on the two-hour drive to Appleton. A clipboard lay on the passenger seat beside him. His pocket protector and ballpoint pen completed the professional driving instructor ruse.

He found the address with his GPS and drove up to a well-kept Cape Cod in a quiet neighborhood. After straightening his tie and throwing back his shoulders, he grabbed his clipboard and walked to the front door in his best Magnum P.I. impression.

The woman answered the doorbell on the first ring. Her white hair was pulled back neatly into a bun, and her rounded shoulders and ample hips were shaped like a Mrs. Butterworth's syrup bottle. She opened the door just far enough to see his face before she cautiously said, "What is it you want?"

"Hello, madam. I'm from the Better Road Wise Driving School. I'm here to make you a special offer. Did you know taking a drivers safety course just for seniors can lower your car insurance rates?" He sounded like a TV infomercial.

"I have good car insurance, thank you. I've never been in an accident. Thank you." She started to close the door.

Vlad waved the print-out from the Wisconsin Public Records clipped to his board. "Yes, but I see you've had some traffic violations in the past year. In addition to a fine, you've lost a few points on your driver's license. Wouldn't you like to get some of them back?"

"The traffic judge said if I drive without any new violations, my points come back after three years. I've been very careful with my driving." She jutted her chin out defiantly. "No more tickets."

'If you sign up for our specially designed course, we can speed up the process. If you give me a few moments of your time, I can explain it to you better. Perhaps I could come inside?" Vlad smiled with all the charm of a vacuum cleaner salesman.

"I guess you could come in for a minute. We do have a neighborhood watch so don't try any funny business." She glanced up and down the street before slowly stepping aside to let him in.

"You can sit there." She gestured to a brown and gold plaid couch. She perched on a matching gold armchair like a sparrow about to take flight. "What about this drivers safety course?"

"Our course has been approved by both AARP and Triple A. We'll help you refresh your driving skills. You'll learn some defensive driving techniques to help you deal with aggressive drivers. And you learn strategies you can use on the road every day." Vlad used his infomercial voice again.

"I've been driving for forty some years. I think I can handle aggressive drivers," the woman sniffed. "I just had a few minor slipups."

"According to our records, you had one moving traffic violation for speeding and some illegal parking tickets. A friend of yours took the course. He was so satisfied he gave us your name."

"None of my friends mentioned a driving course," she sniffed. "I'm sure I'd remember if they did."

"It was a gentleman. I believe his name was Arthur Ashenbrenner."

Vlad closely observed her reaction to Arthur's name. She gave him a blank stare.

"You must be mistaken. I don't know anyone named Arthur Ashburner, whatever." Shirley Pritchard shook her head. "Never heard of him."

"He was in my Behind the Wheel group. A handsome man, silver hair. Quite the athlete for a man in his seventies. A pickleball superstar. Always impeccably dressed."

"I'm dating a gentleman that answers to that description. He loves pickleball, too. But his name isn't Arthur. It's Andrew. Andrew Atkins. We're engaged, in fact."

"Congratulations!" Vlad enthused. "Are nuptials in the near future?"

"Oh yes. We're going to get married. He's going to take me to Europe for our honeymoon. And he couldn't have taken a driving course with you recently."

"Because?" Vlad raised one eyebrow.

"He's been gone for several months, finishing up a consulting project in Los Angeles. He's been traveling between there and Italy. He's still much in demand for his engineering knowhow. He wants to retire but the firm won't let him. But now they may not have much choice."

I've heard this bullshit before, Vlad wanted to say. Instead, he asked, "Why is that?"

"He's in a hospital in Los Angeles. He got hit by a car. I've been worried sick. I wanted to fly out there when I heard the news, but he wouldn't let me. Didn't want me to visit him all banged up like that. He's so considerate of my feelings."

I'll bet he didn't want you to visit, Vlad thought, but he managed to say, "I'm so sorry. Will he be laid up for a while?"

"He said rehab will be a few weeks. The doctor wants to transfer him to a rehab center, but he needs two thousand dollars up front. Most of his money is tied up in a bank in Italy so I wired him the cash. What does a few thousand matter?" Shirley shrugged. "He has a considerable sum that will be his when all the regulatory rigamarole is taken care of. We'll pool our money when we get married. Plenty to pay for a honeymoon and a new life together."

"Perhaps I've got the name wrong. Do you have a picture of your Andrew?"

"He's very camera shy. Never wanted his photo taken. But last year we went to Vegas. We were at a restaurant, and one of those traveling photographers took our picture. Andrew shooed him away, but when he went to the men's room. I paid the photographer and had him mail the picture to me. I keep it in the drawer in my nightstand so Andrew never saw it." Her eyes shone as she smiled dreamily. "I take it out and lay it on his pillow while he's away. Would you like to see? He's very good-looking."

"Could I please? I hate to impose, but now I'm curious. Two handsome men with silver hair! What a coincidence."

Shirley scurried out of the room. She returned clutching a photo in a gilded frame to her chest. She thrust it in Vlad's face with a flourish. Seated next to her in a luxurious red padded booth was a handsome, silver-haired man in a dark silk shirt. "This is my Andrew. It was taken about a year ago."

Vlad's eyes widened, and his mouth dropped open. Arthur Ashenbrenner frowned at the camera. His arm was draped over Shirley Pritchard in her glittery midnight blue dress. A bottle of champagne broadcast an air of romance.

He exclaimed, "That's him! That's Arthur Ashenbrenner!" He caught himself before he blurted out, "The asshole liar!" He made his face go expressionless as he said in a controlled voice, "I assure you, Mrs. Pritchard, that's the same fellow who calls himself Arthur Ashenbrenner. Passes himself off as a building consultant with ties to Italy. Has some issues with money. He's in Crawford, Wisconsin, as we speak."

Shirley stared at the photo, then hugged it with both hands crossing her heart. Her face deepened into a dark red flush. She spewed her venom at Vlad.

"Get out, you hateful scammer. Whatever your game is, it won't work with me. Andrew is the sweetest, loveliest man I know. He's not here to defend himself. I'm not even going to tell him about your vicious lies while he's recovering from his injuries. Now get out before I call the police."

The angry woman wielded the gilded frame like a club as she charged Vlad. He hastily rose to his feet. Holding his hands up in surrender, he retreated backwards to her front door.

Before she slammed it in his face, he said, "Consulting the police is a good idea. My name is Vlad Chomsky from Crawford, Wisconsin. Please contact Detective Johnson at the police department. He'd be very interested to see your photo."

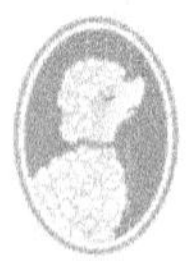

CHAPTER TWENTY-THREE

Norm discovered Arthur's shiny black Thunderbird parked in the driveway when he arrived home. It took all his willpower to keep from retrieving his Milwaukee Brewers' autographed Louisville Slugger from its place of honor on the television stand and smashing the hood of the car, then breaking through Sandra's door and using Arthur's head as a baseball. He'd hit him out of the park and out of her life.

After pulling up alongside the sports car with the driver's side window rolled down, he hacked up a loogie and spit it onto the seat. Small satisfaction on a job well done.

I had that little cat nap at Beezy's so I'll keep watch from the Adirondack chair for the rest of the night, in case Marco gets it in his head to go out looking for Arthur and finds his car here. Norm went into his house for his plush Packers throw and settled in under the maple tree, hidden from view of the driver's side of the car but in full view of Sandra's door.

The streetlight shining behind the tree cast an eerie shadow over the driveway reminiscent of the art in the old superhero comic books. He felt like Batman keeping watch over Gotham City. The baseball bat popped into his mind again. Having a weapon wasn't a bad idea, especially after the menacing look in Marco's eyes. The flames had reflected in them like a demon in Hell. Norm cast the throw aside, hustled into his apartment, and grabbed the bat. Taking the steps two at a time, bat in his right hand, his confidence surged with the feel of the bat's weight, ready for anything the night pitched at him.

Norm's eyelids grew heavy. *I just have to rest them for a second.* The noise of the rumbling engine woke him with a start. His head jerked forward and his eyes flew open in time to watch Arthur carefully back his Thunderbird out of the driveway.

I think I'll check on Sandra before I turn in. Norm wiped the sleep from his eyes and stumbled to his feet. Still gripping the bat, he staggered toward the house. The dim streetlight guided his way across the lumpy lawn. He used the bat's handle to knock on Sandra's door.

When she peeked through the crack and saw him, she said, "It's two in the morning. Isn't it a little late for a baseball game?"

"It's a long story. Mind if I come in?"

"Not at all. I was about to change into my nighty and go to bed, but I want to hear what happened at Marco's." Sandra flung the door open and ushered him into the silent room, still in her wrinkled purple pants suit and stocking feet. "I fell asleep on the couch watching reruns of Bluebloods with Arthur. His arm started to cramp from holding me upright. Luckily, the show came to its conclusion before it went totally numb."

"Why didn't he stay the night? You've been seeing him long enough for a sleepover."

"I suggested he stay, but he insisted he had a busy day tomorrow and needed an early start. He's so considerate of my feelings. A true gentleman."

Norm glanced around. "Where's Gaston?"

"I had to shut him in the bedroom. He refused to let Arthur sit on the couch with me. Kept growling," she said in a frustrated voice. "I don't know what got into him. He was so well-behaved at the restaurant. He was even nice to Vlad for a change."

"Why don't you let the poor little guy out? We can sit in the living room, and I'll tell you what happened at the bonfire."

Gaston bounded into the living room and hopped on the couch next to Norm. He gave his face a big lick and wiggled excitedly. Norm put his arm around him.

"That's a good boy. You got lots of kisses for Uncle Norm."

Gaston happily crawled into his lap and settled in, refusing to look at Sandra.

She perched on the love seat and said, "What about Marco?"

"You were right about him. He's got an idea of what Jake was up to, but he thinks he can handle it himself. I told him to turn what he found over to the cops, but he hates the police. We almost came to blows over the whole thing. He threatened me if I squealed to the cops. So I felt safer with a bat at home."

Norm felt guilty about leaving out the picture of Jake's mom and her male friend, but he agreed with Vlad. No sense in upsetting Sandra until they were sure Arthur was a conman. To distract her, he asked, "How about your meeting at the fancy restaurant? Did Beatrice and Vlad join you two lovebirds?"

Sandra's face shone with happiness as she recalled the events of the evening. "We had such a good time. Beatrice told some funny stories about how she and Vlad met. Arthur explained his project in Italy and how we want to travel there. Even took a phone call from there while we waited for our food. Gaston sat quietly by my feet. Everything went off without a hitch. On the way home Arthur commented what nice friends I had. He suggested we get together again sometime."

"Maybe we should all go out to eat some night. I feel bad that Arthur and I got off on the wrong foot with the car dustup." Norm looked sheepish.

"I'm sure he's forgotten all about it, dearie. He's just so busy right now. He even skipped playing pickleball for a while. But now he's been going back to CHAW. Invited me to watch some big game, some playoff with another fitness club on Saturday." Sandra shrugged. "The whole Jake investigation seems to have stalled. Haven't heard from that horrible detective since I dropped off that phony bank statement at the police station."

"From what I saw at the bonfire, Jake Bender was a piece of shit. He cheated on his girlfriend. Bragged about his exploits. Watched porn films. All the idiots who hung around with him thought he was great. I don't get it."

"Stupidity is as destructive as evil if you judge by its results. It causes a lot more damage in the world because there's more of it," Sandra said.

"When you're dead you don't know you're dead, but you cause pain for others. It's the same for stupid people. And I hung around plenty of them last night."

"Enough philosophizing. I'm exhausted. Time for bed." Sandra yawned and got up from her loveseat. She shuffled toward the door to let Norm out.

He gently pushed Gaston over to the pink pillow on the couch before he stood up. He reached into his pants pocket where he had shoved the key to his basement apartment. He felt the newspaper clipping he'd placed in that pocket earlier and fished it out. He unfolded the yellowing paper from *The Las Vegas Review Journal*. A young Jake Bender's face stared back at him with a trace of a sardonic smile and cunning eyes. Underneath his photo a one-word caption proclaimed ACQUITTED!

Norm stared at the paper incredulously. "What the hell! Ya gotta see this newspaper article from 1993!"

Norm's voice shook with excitement. "It's Jake Bender. He was charged with homicide. But he got off.”

Sandra rushed to his side and began reading aloud. “Wisconsin man accused of staging girlfriend’s suicide found not guilty in Nevada courtroom. Jacob Bender was arrested in 1992 for the death of Melissa Zuehlke, 30, whose body was found in their Las Vegas home on July 18, 1992.

“Investigators said Bender reported that Zuehlke had taken her own life, due to an overdose of valium while soaking in the bathtub. Further investigation showed the bathtub drowning appeared to be staged. Conflicting evidence suggested she had been placed in the tub after her death. A medical examiner who conducted an autopsy disagreed and stated that a small amount of water was found in her lungs, indicating she was alive when submerged. The toxicology report revealed that level of valium was not necessarily lethal, but her death was complicated by a heart condition. Repeated calls to the residence due to domestic violence cast suspicion on Bender, but the lack of hard evidence was repeatedly cited by the defense attorney, Craig Winter.

“After a two-week trial a jury in Clark County court determined that Bender was not guilty of first-degree intentional homicide. He was released from jail Wednesday night.”

“Zuehlke! I know that name,” said Sandra, her face wrinkled with intense concentration. “Where did I hear it before? I heard it somewhere recently.”

“Was it at the Senior Center? You know a lot of people there,” suggested Norm. “Think hard. It could be a clue to the killer.”

“You’re asking a lot from an old lady at two o’clock in the morning.”

“Was it one of Arthur’s friends? Maybe some of the people at pickleball?”

Sandra’s face suddenly brightened. “That’s it. It was at pickleball. There was an older gentleman there who introduced himself to me. Franklin Zuehlke. He teamed up with Arthur when they took on Jake and Susie. He was very old. Walked so slowly across the gym I was afraid he’d keel over.”

“He doesn’t sound like a promising suspect. From what you’ve told me, Jake was in great condition. Could an old guy who can barely walk really strangle him with your boa?”

“Never underestimate an old man playing pickleball. That’s what he said. Old people are often disregarded. Written off. Remember on the river cruise how you thought Clarence was decrepit and impotent. None of you took him seriously except for me."

"That's only because he pulled out his little blue pills, and you were hot to trot," Norm scoffed.

"That's not true. When I looked beneath the façade, I saw a powerful man. He turned out to be the mastermind of an international jewel theft ring. Skilled in the art of deception. How many years had he eluded capture until he met Gaston and me? We solved the case for Interpol."

Norm almost said, *hoodwinked by another smooth liar*, but wisely only stated, "You saved my ass that time."

"Why can't an old man be just as capable of murder as someone younger? There's no expiration date for vengeance."

"Nah. You're barking up the wrong tree. No way an old guy could pull it off."

"I just remembered something else!" All hint of fatigue melted away as she continued talking excitedly. "I met his wife. Her name was Nancy. She's in the Memory Care unit at the nursing home. Suffers severe dementia. Poor sweet lady! Allison asked me to bring Gaston to see her in her room. Thought he'd cheer her up. But it didn't work. She was too agitated."

"Gaston didn't give her a little nip, did he? He can be cantankerous at times."

"No, he was a lovebug. Gave her hand a friendly lick. But she was upset about her daughter."

Sandra stood up and paced around the living room. Gaston hopped off the pink pillow and followed closely at her heels.

She continued, "The poor addled woman said she'd gone away and was in trouble. I thought she was talking about a teenager, but it could have been someone older. It's hard to tell with dementia. The past is more real than the present. I'm trying to remember what she called the girl."

"Don't stop. You're on a roll," said Norm, catching her excitement.

Even Gaston gave an encouraging *yip*.

"Started with an 'M' I think," Sandra tapped the side of her cheek as she struggled to recall. "Was it Mary? Michelle? No, it was Melissa! I'm sure of it."

"Just like in the article." Norm waved the clipping.

"No wonder she was so upset. The poor girl was found dead in Las Vegas. So far from home. And she was at the mercy of that monster, Jake Bender." Sandra blinked away tears.

"The old fellow has a lot on his plate. I feel sorry for him," Norm clucked sympathetically. "The pain of losing a child never goes away, as we learned from Shar Fredrick." He was referring to the murder they had helped to solve in the summer. "He's lost his wife in a way, also. She's certainly not the woman he married. But is it enough for murder?"

"I'm too tired to think about this anymore tonight." Sandra stretched and yawned.

Gaston took that as a signal to trot off to the bedroom ahead of her. She could barely get the next words out. "See Vlad and Beatrice tomorrow. Figure out where to go next."

Norm said, "Have a good night. Sweet dreams."

As he let himself out, he thought, *If Vlad locates the women connected to the names in Arthur's phone, it may be the last peaceful dream you have for a long, long time.*

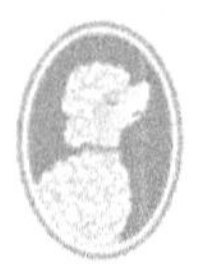

CHAPTER TWENTY-FOUR

Vlad was still thinking about what he'd learned from Shirley Pritchard as he trudged up the walkway to Beatrice's house. Arthur Ashenbrenner had an alias—Andrew Atkins. Were either of them his real name? He certainly was adept at lying. The stories he concocted had a ring of truth to them. He presented his fraudulent schemes so cleverly his victims never suspected he was a con. Pulling off a romantic scam on gullible elderly ladies was one thing, but murder was a whole different ball of wax. Or rather a pickleball full of wax.

Once inside Beatrice pulled him next to her on the couch and listened intently as he described his conversation with the elderly widow.

"She refused to believe me when I told her Arthur was living two hours away in Crawford under an assumed name. She threw me out of her house, threatened to call the cops on me."

"You poor man." Beatrice laid a comforting hand on his leg. "At least you tried to convince her of the truth."

"Hell, I begged her to do it." Vlad's face was grim. "Maybe we should call the police. I'd like Detective Johnson to see the picture of Andrew Atkins. That scam artist may be slippery as hell but he's no match for that pit bull cop. Once Johnson set his sights on Arthur, he's a goner."

"Your plan worked. You got Shirley to talk. Now we *know* Arthur is a scoundrel. Disgraceful! Scamming older women. I can't believe Sandra fell for his act." Beatrice shook her head in disbelief.

"His love bombs are pretty powerful—knows just what to say to make a lady believe his nonsense. Promises her a romantic future. Honeymoon trips to Europe." Vlad frowned. "Plus he's very handsome, if you go for blindingly white teeth and perfectly sculpted hair."

Beatrice tightened her hands into tiny fists. "Arthur makes me so furious. Shirley Pritchard will be so devastated when she finds out the truth. We have to tell Sandra. We can't let her continue to be duped by him."

"We need to be careful. A few kind words can make someone's day, but only one word can ruin their life." Vlad spoke the next words slowly. "I value her friendship too much to dump this on her. Sandra is so in love with Arthur. She'll probably deny anything we tell her, just like Shirley Pritchard did. If only we had some proof, like that photo of him with another woman."

"What do we do next?"

"We either keep digging for more proof or we turn over what we found to Detective Johnson. He'll have more resources. Maybe Arthur's fingerprints are on file in their database. The police have easier access to phone records."

Beatrice shook her fist in the air. "What if Arthur uses a burner? He's too slick to leave behind any records of his double dealing."

"My clever darling!" Vlad grabbed her hands in his and stroked them gently. "You're right. His cell phone calls are probably hard to trace. We can try the other woman in his call list—exhaust all possibilities before we give up. Maybe Rita Hansen will be more cooperative. This time I'll spring for the nine dollars and ninety-five cents to get her information."

"We don't have a moment to waste. Let's get started." Beatrice jerked her hands away and stood up. "The sooner we uncover the truth, the better for Sandra."

Vlad slowly rose and asked, "Have you heard from Norm? Hopefully, he had a quiet night keeping watch over Sandra. If anything popped, he'd be beating on your door."

Vrrrooom. The roar of a motorcycle shook the windows like a hurricane bearing down on a grass hut. The motor sputtered to a halt.

Vlad and Beatrice exchanged knowing looks. They said in unison, "Speak of the devil!"

Boots clumped on Beatrice's porch followed by the loud pounding on her door. The thunderous noise woke Max from his favorite napping spot behind the couch on the heat duct. Curiosity drew him out. He yawned and stretched his front paws, extending and contracting his claws. He plunked down on his haunches to survey the action while Vlad warily eyed those claws.

"I better let Norm in before he knocks the door off its hinges," Beatrice said as she hurried to the foyer.

An impatient Norm bulldozed past her clutching an old newspaper clipping in his fist. He waved it about so wildly he nearly knocked over the vase of flowers ensconced on the hall table.

Beatrice rushed to steady the bouquet as he shouted, "Look what

I rescued from the bonfire. It's from the Las Vegas newspaper. An article about Jake Bender. He was accused of homicide, but he got acquitted."

"You must be joking! Let me see," Vlad reached for the article.

Beatrice huddled next to him as he read it out loud.

"Accused of homicide. Another scoundrel. Worse than Arthur."

"It says he was acquitted. Doesn't that mean he's not guilty?" Beatrice asked.

"All it means is there wasn't enough evidence to convict him. Guilty or not, a young woman was deprived of her life," Vlad answered through gritted teeth.

"Or Jake made her life so miserable that she committed suicide."

Beatrice picked up the cat and nuzzled him. Max pushed his head against her chin and purred in a comforting vibration.

"Poor girl. She must have felt so alone."

Norm flapped his arms excitedly. "There's more. Sandra thinks she knows the woman's parents. Her mother is in a nursing home, suffering from Alzheimer's. But she met the father at pickleball. Name's Franklin. He's some ninety-year-old still batting the ball around."

"Oh my God! I played against him." Beatrice exclaimed, involuntarily squeezing the cat.

Max squirmed out of her grasp and ran back behind the couch.

"He knew I was a newbie. My first real game with the regulars. He hit every ball in my direction. My partner tried to help me, but I never even got to serve. The old fellow was merciless. He hit a dink over the net. The ball dropped so quickly it was impossible to return. He's that good, for an old guy."

"I wonder if Jake realized he played pickleball with his dead girlfriend's father?" Vlad said thoughtfully.

"Would Jake Bender even care?" Norm's voice was filled with scorn. "He was a total jerk."

"An eye for an eye, like the proverb says. Just because Franklin wears glasses doesn't mean he's blind. He knew exactly who Jake Bender was. You'd never forget someone accused of killing your child." Beatrice insisted. "Maybe he finally got revenge."

"I told Sandra and I'm saying it again." Norm said vehemently. "No ninety-year-old guy is capable of strangling a younger man like that, no matter how much he'd like to."

"I saw Jake in the weight room; I agree. He was just too strong. I don't care how good the old guy is at pickleball. He's no match for Jake

Bender. I saw the boa pulled around the victim's neck. I couldn't have done it." Vlad shuddered when he spoke the last part.

"Old age is no place for cowards. Look at Sandra for a prime example," Beatrice argued. "Franklin could have seen his opportunity when Jake was vulnerable and took it."

Vlad put his hand up like a cop directing traffic. "Stop. We're getting sidetracked. Today we're going to investigate the other woman from Arthur's phone."

"Okay. Let's get going."

Beatrice fired up the computer. Once again she googled Rita Hansen and scrolled past the obituaries. "We can rule out the Ritas that have departed."

"Not even a slick operator like Arthur could scam a dead woman," Norm said.

Next, Beatrice came to Rita Hansen in St. Paul, Minnesota. Her LinkedIn profile revealed a woman very experienced in real estate appraisals who once owned a successful firm. Skilled at contract negotiations, she was "uniquely positioned to understand and advise the real estate industry" with 500+ connections. No activity posted.

Norm studied the headshot of the older woman with grey cropped hair and a faint haughty smile. "I wouldn't mess with Rita."

"She owned her own business. You don't get that far ahead unless you're very smart and forceful," Beatrice said.

"One of us could pose as a real estate agent looking for advice. I can't think of another ruse for convincing her to talk to us." Vlad tapped his finger on the computer desk as he spoke.

"Let's see if she's on Facebook. We may get a better idea for a plan from her posts." Beatrice read aloud Rita's post from that day: "Is God unfair in not choosing to save everyone? Fair would send people to hell. You don't want fair. You want mercy."

"Sounds like she's got religion. We could dress up and pretend to be Jehovah's Witnesses. I think I have an old *Watchtower* laying around my apartment," Norm offered.

"No, I've got a better idea. Look at this next post; it's a video of a tortoise shell cat with a little pink nose. She wrote: *I found this sweet little baby in the high school parking lot after my grandson's concert. She's way too friendly to be a stray. I can't help but wonder if someone is missing her. She's very skinny, has a scrape on her mouth and looks like one of her claws has been ripped out. I set her up in the garage with food, blankets and a litter box. My cat, Saber, is suspicious about what's going on in there. DM me if she's yours,'* Beatrice said excitedly. "We can say it might be our cat. That's how we'll get out foot in the door."

Vlad stood up. "You should send her the message. She'll be less suspicious of a woman. Tell her you'll come to her house on Saturday to check the cat out. Get her phone number and address."

A few minutes later Beatrice said triumphantly, "I got it. She answered right away. She still has the cat, and I set up a meeting for Saturday morning."

Vlad bent down and planted a kiss on her smiling lips. "Good work, my own little Kinsey Millhone. We'll get a hotel somewhere in St. Paul for Friday night so we meet with Rita Hansen bright and early Saturday morning."

"How ya gonna bring up Arthur Ashenbrenner with her?" asked Norm. "He ain't exactly a popular topic of conversation."

"Look at her hobbies list. Besides gardening, eating, watching movies, and crafting, she wrote pickleball. I'll wear my hot pink *It's a Good Day to Play Pickleball* t-shirt. We'll have an instant bond."

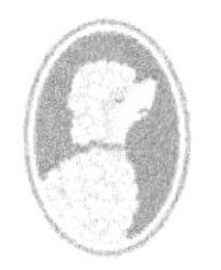

CHAPTER TWENTY-FIVE

Sandra ignored the stink eye from the CHAW receptionist. The woman started to say no dogs when she saw the top of Gaston's head but stopped mid-sentence when her eyes lit upon the Service Dog harness. Her mouth snapped shut, then she muttered, "Some service dog!"

Gaston obediently sat on his haunches and gazed at the CHAW lady in big- eyed puppy innocence.

"Scan your member card," she said in icy tones.

"Oh, dearie. I'm not a member. I'm here to watch the pickleball tournament." She flashed her most charming smile.

"That'll be four dollars. Give it to the man at the table." She swiveled her head in the direction of the gym.

A long queue had formed in front of a smiling man with curly salt and pepper hair who greeted everyone with a hearty, "Welcome to our first pickleball tournament." Sandra was surprised to see so many people out to watch pickleball on a Saturday morning. *Such a loud buzz from these fans standing in line, you'd think it was a Bruce Springsteen concert.*

Sandra's metallic pointy shoes were starting to pinch her toes a bit. The little heels threw her lower back out of alignment. She knew she should have worn something more sensible, but the heels augmented the satin jacket with the jeweled leopard design on the back. She wanted to look her best for Arthur's big day. She was fluffing her red hair into wispy bangs when she heard a voice behind her exclaim,

"Grandma Sandy, is that you?"

Sandra whirled around to see a wide-eyed Kristin standing in front of an improvised concession stand. The young custodian paused in the act of sweeping kernels of popcorn from the floor into a long-handled dustpan. The shock of recognition on the girl's face made Sandra feel a bit ashamed for deceiving her.

"Y-yes, my dear girl. It's me. I-I am so…happy to see you," Sandra mumbled. Although from the expression on her face, she clearly wasn't very happy.

"Your hair! You dyed it red. And your jacket is glitzy. You look different from when I saw you last." Kristin's mouth dropped open as though King Charles had just appeared in the hallway wearing sweats with a pickleball racquet in his hand.

Sandra dissembled nervously. "I splurged on a makeover at the beauty salon yesterday. Do you like it?" She turned her head from side to side to show different views of her hairdo.

"It's hard to believe you're the same person." Incredulity crept into Kristin's voice.

"They gave me a facial, too. I feel like a new woman."

"You're wearing new clothes, too. Not like anything I've seen in the thrift stores."

"Oh, this old jacket?" Sandra said offhandedly. "I bought this at Fredrick's of Hollywood long before it went out of business."

"I never heard of Fredrick's of Hollywood, but it sounds expensive. I thought you were living on a fixed income. At least that's how you made it seem when we met at St. Vinnie's," she said in an accusatory tone.

"I wasn't always retired, dearie. I have a good instinct for fashion. Some clothes never go out of style."

Kristin stared at Gaston. "And you have a service dog. She wasn't with you at the funeral."

"Gaston is a 'he.' Sometimes I take a chance and leave him at home. Dogs don't do well at funeral homes. At least this one doesn't." Sandra reached down and patted the dog's head. "But today he's a good boy."

Kristin's eyes narrowed as she scrutinized Gaston. "I've seen him before. The day he tripped Jake Bender in the gym and ran away with the pickleball."

Then she turned her gaze on Sandra from her fancy shoes to the top of her poofy hair." You were there that day, too. Your hair was red back then. Not grey like at the funeral."

"Um. Well, I believe I was. But I was wearing a red wig. My real hair is grey as can be. Sometimes I like to recapture my lost youth. I'm just a silly vain old woman, I guess." Sandra gave her an embarrassed smile, then looked down at her feet.

"I don't know what you're playing at, but I think you're anything but silly." Kristin's eyes grew hard, and her face closed into an impassive mask. "You had me suckered into believing you were a lonely old lady. I'm not sure why you were pretending to be something you're not. I'm sure you had your reasons. Now I better get this cleaned up."

She turned back to the popcorn mess.

"I did, my dear. I'm sorry." Sandra said in a small, sad voice. "I hope I can explain it to you someday."

Kristin refused to look up. People had skipped past Sandra so she got back in line. She told herself, *I'm a detective. Sometimes I have to use subterfuge to solve a case. The ends justify the means.* Somehow she didn't feel much better.

When Sandra drew nearer the money collector, she noticed the incipient bald spot forming at the back of his head. Another aging athlete sheltering on the pickleball court.

"Why aren't you playing today? You look like you could swing a mean racquet," she said.

He pointed to a black brace on his leg. "Unfortunately, I blew out my knee last week. Now all I'm good for is taking your money. No charge for the dog," he joked.

Sandra slid four singles over the table, and the man stamped a red basketball on her hand.

He said sheepishly, "We had to borrow a stamp from the youth program. Hopefully, we'll make enough profit today to buy our own custom-made pickleball stamp. More tournaments are on the horizon."

The bleachers were already filled with enthusiastic pickleball fans. Their lively chatter echoed throughout the cavernous gym. Sandra scanned the sea of faces, hoping for a glimpse of Arthur. She recognized Franklin sitting amid a group wearing blue CHAW t-shirts. Red, yellow, and green shirted groups were clustered together surrounding the CHAW players, but no Arthur.

"He promised to meet me here when I arrived," she muttered nervously to Gaston. "I hope the team has forgotten what happened the last time we came to watch Arthur play pickleball."

Gaston also surveyed the crowd in the gym. Although he stayed close to his mistress, his little head never stopped moving. He sniffed the stale air, taking in the cacophony of odors—antiperspirant, ladies cloying perfume, sporty aftershave, and the lingering smell of athlete's sweat. His extra alertness made Sandra feel uneasy.

"You need to be on your very best behavior," she had warned him in the car before Norm dropped them off. "It's Arthur's big game. He's been training a long time for this moment."

"You better be good, Gaston," Norm teased. "Or Mom will take you shopping at the flea market."

"I've got chicken jerky treats in my handbag for a good boy." Sandra patted her crossbody purse.

"And enzyme oral hygiene chews if you're bad."

Norm winked at the pooch on Sandra's lap. He slowed to a stop at the passenger unloading zone, and the two detectives hopped out.

Since then the uncharacteristic way Gaston stood glued to her side felt unnatural, like he was a robot dog. She almost wished he'd nip at a stranger's ankle just so he'd act more like his normal self. Even a quick tug on his leash would reassure her everything was all right.

Sandra slowly headed for the CHAW people. The conversation with Kristin had thrown her off her game. She tried to let go of the guilty feeling that she'd been dishonest with the girl. Once the case was solved, she'd make it up to her somehow.

Surely Arthur would soon appear. The announcer's voice was heard on the overhead speakers.

"Testing-one-two. Please take your seats, ladies and gentlemen. The tournament is about to begin. The best players of the southeastern Wisconsin region compete in the first Crawford Pickleball Shootout. You're going to see a lot of action this morning in men and women's doubles.

Franklin noticed her approach and waved her over. He moved a gym bag to the floor to make room for her.

"It's the Dancing Queen and her performing poodle. Arthur asked me to save you a spot." He scooched over and patted the now vacant space. "There's quite a crowd here today." He rubbed his hands together gleefully. "It's going to be great."

"Where is Arthur? I thought he'd meet me at the door."

"He's warming up in the locker room. He and Kent are discussing their game plan. It's more than just skill. Strategy is important, too," Franklin explained.

"Kent is his partner, not you? I thought you two were inseparable."

"Nah. I'm good enough for the fun league but not for hardcore play. You need to be fast on your feet. I'm sadly lacking in speed. This is official. Big time. They're playing for eleven points today, not seven."

"I appreciate you watching for me and saving me a seat." Sandra smiled gratefully. "There's so many people. I was getting nervous."

"Is your pooch going to behave today? I'm surprised you brought him." Franklin glanced at Gaston.

"Gaston is my service dog. I never know when a spell might come over me. He gives me advance warning so I can take my medication in time." She patted the dog reassuringly. "I rarely go anywhere without him."

A few of the blue shirted CHAW players watched Gaston like they suspected his service dog harness had explosives tucked inside. The blond woman, Susie, glared at Gaston through narrowed eyelids. Her mouth was drawn tightly down in a disapproving frown. If looks could kill Gaston would be lying stretched out under the bleachers, paws up with a dagger through his heart. The pooch instantly settled at Sandra's feet next to the gym bag, his head resting on his paws, but his eyes never stopped moving.

A cheer erupted from the group around her as Arthur came out from the locker room, racquet in hand. His partner trailed behind him. Kent looked solid and robust, not as rangy as Arthur, but definitely a force to be reckoned with. Arthur bounced on his feet a few times and took some warm-up swings. Both he and Kent had pristine blue shirts and matching sweatbands. If thick hair was one of the criteria for making the tournament, both men were shoo-ins. Kent's wavy brown hair had not a hint of grey. The two men graced their teammates with toothsome grins.

Then Arthur noticed Sandra. His grin grew wider as he sauntered over to her side. His smile faded for a second when he noticed Gaston behind the gym bag, but he quickly recovered his pleasant expression.

"My lovely lady. Here at last. Please give me a good luck smooch." Arthur planted a brief kiss on the side of her cheek. "I didn't know you were bringing the dog. You seemed undecided last evening."

"I was afraid all the excitement might bring on an attack. I might need Gaston's help."

The announcer continued. "The first match in the men's doubles is Arthur Ashenbrenner and Kent Jacobs in the near court with Tom Harvey and Chuck Grassel in the far court. All four players are tremendous athletes. Arthur is a super dangerous player—undefeated in the Madison YMCA men's singles."

Arthur and Kent tapped their racquets together with a macho grunt, then took their positions behind the farthest grey line. The two men settled into a threatening stance, ready to lunge at whatever shot was lobbed their way. Arthur's fierce facial expression signaled an intensity that belied his earlier smiles. A flex of his racquet, a bounce on his toes, he was energized to win.

Before the play could commence, a small boy entered the gym carrying a hot dog. His mom held the door open for him as he toddled past. The child licked catsup off the end of the bun. As he tilted the hot dog upwards, the wiener dropped out of the bun. Gaston watched it fall, then bounded toward the child, streaking across the gym floor like a comet across the sky, leash trailing behind.

"Gaston! Come back here!" Sandra shouted.

The dog ignored her. He scooped up the frankfurter in his jaws and disappeared into the hall.

"That damn dog! I knew he'd cause trouble." Arthur muttered.

Sandra jumped to her feet as quickly as her creaky knees would let her and followed the dog's path out of the gym. "Sorry, so sorry."

She mumbled on her way past the fans in the first row of the bleachers. The crowd watched her leave before turning their attention back to the game.

"Tom Harvey is serving first," the announcer said as she exited the gym.

Sandra caught a glimpse of Gaston's tail on the stairs going to the second floor. A weight room sign on a large arrow pointed up. She scurried down the hallway toward the stairwell, hoping to catch the pooch on the landing. Surely he'd stop to gobble the hot dog there.

Her heart was pounding when she stepped on the bottom step. She looked up. No Gaston on the landing. She had to use the railing to steady herself as she went up the first set of stairs. She tottered across the landing on her pointy shoes and grasped the railing desperately on the next flight. Hauling herself upward, she soon stood on the second floor. Still no Gaston.

"You naughty rascal. When I catch up with you, you're in the kennel for the rest of the day," she shouted. Her words echoed throughout the empty hallway.

Sandra kicked off her shoes, then carried both of them in one hand. She walked down the deserted hall in her stocking feet. "If I wreck my last pair of panty hose, you're going to be very sorry, dog."

On her left side was the darkened weight room. The hulking machines loomed silent and unmoving. Everyone must be downstairs watching the tournament. She tried the first door. It was open. She peeked her head inside and gave a loud "Yoohoo!" No one answered.

The next equipment room also had no light and no movement.

As Sandra continued down the hall, she went past room after deserted room. On the right, one room had freestanding punch bags for kickboxing, dark and eerie like headless people. The next room had pulleys hanging from a raised bar like medieval torture instruments.

"What are those things used for?" she whispered, then shuddered.

The last room on the right had a plaque: *Mind and Body Studio.* Yoga mats were stacked high in the corner next to some padded cylinders that looked like giant blue tootsie rolls. An exit sign glowed over a nearby open door to a second stairway.

"I know you're there, Gaston. It's the end of the trail for you." Sandra was out of breath and ready to throttle that dog.

Gaston was licking his chops on the landing before another set of stairs. He devoured every bit of the wiener and barked happily when he saw her.

"You're a bad boy. You promised to be good." Sandra scolded him, hands on her hips. "Look at you! You scarfed up that little boy's hot dog. You ran away from Mom. I'm very, very angry with you."

Sandra bent over to pick up his leash. Her back gave a little twinge when she straightened up.

"Let's get back to the gym."

But Gaston refused to move. Instead, he scratched his front paws on the metal hand railing and whined.

"We're not going down those stairs," Sandra said firmly. "Let's go back the way we came."

She peered over the railing. The stairwell was dimly lit. The steps descended downward into darkness. The brown block wall had no cheerful posters, no artwork. Just depressing brick, stark and unwelcoming. Cracked floor tiles, peeling safety strips.

"Let's go."

Sandra tugged firmly on the leash. Gaston pulled away; his scratching grew more frantic. His loud whines reverberated throughout the small space. She could feel pressure building behind her eyes.

She was tired of fighting the stubborn pooch.

"All right. You win. We'll go your way."

The stairs were crusted with dirt so she slipped the uncomfortable shoes back on, vowing to donate them to St. Vinnie's. She felt a bit dizzy at the top of the stairs and reached her free hand out to grasp the cold metal. An unpleasant musty odor assaulted her nostrils. At least Gaston heeled obediently at her side.

When Sandra arrived shakily at the first landing, she saw him. His arms and legs akimbo like a skydiver who jumped from a plane without his parachute. He lay sprawled at the bottom.

Gaston pulled her downward. She had no will to resist. She let him lead her toward the body, clad in gym shorts and a sleeveless tank. Dark matted hair. Bulging arm muscles. Tree trunk thighs. The man's skin exhibited an unearthly pallor. Blanching. Her investigator's handbook said it starts to occur thirty minutes after death.

As they grew near she saw the eagle tattoo on his arm, a banner clutched in its talons. This eagle's flight was over. It would never move again. She recognized his perpetual sneer even in death, the cold uncaring eyes now sunk deeply into his socket.

"Marco!" she gasped.

Gaston plopped next to the dead man and stared. Sandra moved as close as she dared without disturbing what now was a crime scene.

She muttered, "I'm too damn old to bend down and feel for a pulse."

Besides, the impossible angle of his head told her no living human's neck arched that way. She nudged his arm with the pointy toe of her shoe. It was heavy and stiff. Rigor mortis was starting to set in. As she leaned over for a closer look, she smelled the faint odor of wintergreen, like he'd been sucking on a breath mint. His mouth gaped open. She didn't see a green lozenge. But the scent persisted.

Sandra was reaching to lift Marco's head, shift it to the left so she could see if the blood was starting to pool in a purplish discoloration at the back of his neck, maybe find the source of the smell, when Gaston barked. Twice. And the spell was broken.

"Death always arrives too early or too late," she commented to Gaston.

He didn't answer.

"We need to tell someone."

She thought of the smiling man at the door, the kind man who took her money. She pulled on Gaston's leash.

"We better go to the front desk."

This time the dog meekly followed.

CHAPTER TWENTY-SIX

Rita Hansen opened the door on the first ring of the buzzer. She was a sturdy, steely-haired woman of sixty years of age with commanding brown eyes, high cheekbones, and a forceful jaw. Deep vertical creases between her eyes suggested a lifetime of intense squinting at spreadsheets. A crisp white shirt, sleeves rolled up to tackle Saturday morning chores, and well-fitting designer jeans telegraphed she was a force to be reckoned with.

"You must be Beatrice," she said, extending her hand in a firm shake. "I'm Rita. Please come in."

The woman led Beatrice past an elegant living room furnished with valuable Arts and Crafts furnishings and a Persian rug into a comfortable family room. "I appreciate your punctuality. I still operate on business time. It's hard to adjust to retirement after thirty years as a boss."

"I am so glad my friend Diane O'Connor shared your post with the picture of the lost cat. The kitty looks exactly like my Cocoa. She got away from me two weeks ago. I've been searching high and low for her ever since."

Beatrice crossed her fingers. She hoped the person she had carefully chosen from Rita's Facebook friends list wasn't coming over for coffee in a few minutes.

"I went to high school with Diane. She lives in Wisconsin so we don't get together very much, just keep in touch on Facebook. How do you know her?"

Beatrice hesitated for a moment before she spoke. "We…uh…met at the Wisconsin AAUW leadership retreat and hit it off. We've been Facebook friends ever since."

"You live in Wisconsin, too?"

"Just across the river." Beatrice hastily added. "May I see the cat? I miss little Cocoa so much. She's such a sweetheart."

"Of course. Come this way to the garage. My cat, Saber, doesn't get along with other cats so I was afraid to bring her inside. He would probably swipe at her with his claws. Chase her right back into the garage."

As if on cue, an enormous yellow and orange striped cat hopped down from his perch on a giant cat tower and planted himself directly in Beatrice's path. His yellow eyes narrowed as he surveyed her with a flick back and forth of his tail. His guttural meow sounded less than friendly, more like a panther's growl. He drew closer, sniffed at her jegging-clad leg, then hissed menacingly. Sharp fangs gleamed when he pulled back his lips. He hunkered down like he was ready to pounce. Beatrice jumped back in alarm.

"Saber, as in saber-toothed, certainly seems fitting," Beatrice twittered.

"Maybe he smells the scent of another cat on your clothes. He's very alpha around other kitties," Rita said. "Don't worry. I just trimmed his claws so he can't scratch you."

Beatrice wanted to ask if she had also filed down the sharp fangs but she merely said, "My other cat is slightly alpha, too. He gets along with darling Cocoa, though. Who wouldn't? She's such a sweetheart."

She sidled past Saber, staying close to Rita as the woman filled her in on the stray cat.

"Cocoa misses you terribly. She's all over me when I feed her and clean her litter box. When I shut the door I can hardly stand to hear her meow. So pitiful."

Rita opened the door to the garage and flicked on the light. The fluffy cat blinked her amber eyes at the sudden brightness and scampered over to check out the new visitor. Beatrice admired her beauty: a mosaic of brown, orange, and cream patches ending in a wide black stripe down the middle of her forehead, nose, and chest. Arching her back, she rubbed against Beatrice's ankles and purred loudly. When she picked the little cat up she felt the vibration throughout the kitty's whole body. She stroked the cat's silky fur. The little tortie rubbed her wet nose on Beatrice's chin, purring even louder.

"My little Cocoa. Sweet as hot chocolate and marshmallows. That's how she got her name."

"She's certainly happy to see you," Rita said with a smile.

Beatrice buried her face in the little cat's fur and inhaled. The tortie still had the scent of the outdoors about her plus a hint of gasoline. Although she had intended to say the cat wasn't hers, when the kitty kneaded her paws on her chest she changed her mind. Max was about to have a little companion. She couldn't abandon the small cat in the dreary garage.

"Thank you so much for finding her. I was offering a reward for her return. I have fifty dollars in my inside pocket."

Beatrice shifted the cat to her shoulder and unzipped her fleece jacket, revealing her hot pink pickleball shirt.

"That won't be necessary. Seeing you two reunited is reward enough." Rita waved her off before Beatrice reached for the cash.

"I'd like to repay your kindness. May I take you out for coffee?" Beatrice persisted, unwilling to lose this chance to investigate.

"I have a better idea. I just made a fresh pot. Why don't you have a cup with me before you get back on the road?"

"I'd love it. It's a long drive home." Beatrice jumped at the offer, like a winner on *The Price is Right*. "Perhaps we'd better leave Cocoa where she is until I'm ready to go?" She brushed her lips across the top of the cat's head before she set her down.

The tortie followed closely at Beatrice's heels up the steps to the kitchen, mewing noisily. Rita nudged the cat gently away with her foot.

"You'll soon be back safe at home, kitty," she said. "You don't want to tangle with Saber today."

As proof of her warning, the yellow and orange cat perched on the kitchen counter like a vulture, closely monitoring the two women. "I call him my guard cat. I pity any intruder who messes with my Saber."

Beatrice cautiously moved past the cat's watchful eyes and sat down at the table as far away from him as possible.

"Cream or sugar?" Rita said as she placed a cup of coffee in front of Beatrice and slid the creamer and sugar bowl toward her. She settled into the chair across from her and asked, "I can't help noticing your shirt. So where do you play pickleball?"

"We have a local athletic club—the Center for Health and Wellness—where we gather to play." Beatrice poured some cream into the cup and slowly stirred it. "I'm a beginner. I've been seeing a man who loves pickleball. He's encouraged me to try it."

"I play four times a week at the Y. We have a huge group of pickleball aficionados. It's a great game for retired folks. Fast and fun and not too hard on the body." Rita sipped her coffee and smiled. "Perfect exercise for me."

"My gentleman friend is older and quite a good player. He could almost be a professional, but he said that would take all the fun out of playing. How about you? How did you get started?"

"I sold my home appraisal business three years ago. After thirty-five years of inspecting houses and managing people, I got tired. My husband had passed away, and I confess I was slightly depressed." Rita folded her hands on the table and stared at them.

"Oh, no." Beatrice reached across the table and gently patted her hand. "I'm so sorry for your loss."

"Thank you." The woman looked up with a sad smile. "I realized I needed a change. My daughter encouraged me to take up a hobby. I tried a cooking class, then making pottery. Then I stumbled upon pickleball. It was just what I needed."

"Good for you." Beatrice smiled encouragingly.

"I met a nice group of people who talked about things beside property values. It was wonderful."

Beatrice took another sip of her coffee. "I have a flexible schedule at work so I learned to play pickleball. Arthur's so happy. He's shooting for us to play mixed doubles eventually in tournament play."

"Arthur? Did you say your friend's name is Arthur?" Rita's cup was almost to her lips but she set it down to gape at Beatrice. "What a coincidence! I played with a man named Arthur, too. A top-notch player."

"You're kidding! Another Arthur?" Beatrice squeaked..

"I even dated him for a while. Arthur Atkins. But he turned out to be a scoundrel." Scorn crept into Rita's voice.

"For goodness' sake! What on earth happened?"

"It started with little things. We'd go to a restaurant, and he'd forget his wallet. So I'd pay. No big deal at first."

'Oh my God! Arthur forgot his wallet last Saturday when *we* went out." Beatrice gasped.

"He was semi-retired. Worked as an engineering consultant. Traveled a lot. He told me his money was tied up in foreign banks. He started to borrow money from me. Just until his check from Croatia came through, he said." Rita's grip on her mug tightened briefly before she set it down.

"My Arthur says he's semi-retired, too. Only *he's* working on a project in Italy."

Rita dropped her eyes, sadly gazing at her mug. "It gets worse. I'm embarrassed to say, I lent him a substantial sum."

"Oh, no. How awful!" Beatrice murmured sympathetically. "You wouldn't happen to have a picture of the man?"

"He was very camera shy. Disappeared whenever anyone pointed a cell phone in his direction. But he went with me to my fortieth class reunion. A photographer took pictures while we were dining. Arthur is in one of mine."

"May I see your picture? My Arthur is very handsome. Always well-dressed. Thick head of hair. His smile is so charming."

"Sounds just like the man I dated. I paid fifty dollars for a small album, a memento of the night. Please wait right here while I get it."

Rita pushed away from the table and scurried off. Saber followed her with his eyes, then turned his gaze back to Beatrice. Once again he flicked his tail back and forth.

She soon returned with a red photo book labeled *Class of 1980.* She quickly flipped to a section with guests seated at tables. She pointed to a man sitting next to her. It was Arthur Ashenbrenner.

Beatrice gulped, clutching her hands to her chest. "Oh my God! It's the same man. He's running the same scam on me."

Rita commented drily, "Forewarned is forearmed. I wish someone sounded the alarm when we started dating."

"May I take this album with me? I'm going to confront the man. He can't get away with his lies."

"Good luck. I've been calling him, asking for my money back. But he's ghosting me. Disappeared from the face of the earth." Rita smiled wryly. "Probably never see him again."

"Why don't you go to the police?"

"I have a reputation to uphold as a shrewd businesswoman. Once Arthur's case hits the news, people will know what a fool I was. I couldn't stand the humiliation. Besides fifty thousand dollars seems like a small price to pay to get him out of my life."

"Fifty thousand!" Beatrice exclaimed. "Sandra….um, I mean…I can't afford to lose fifty thousand dollars."

"Please take the book. Use it however you think best." Rita slid the album into a plastic grocery bag and handed it to her. "Do you want some help with Cocoa? I can lend you a cat carrier."

"No, thank you. I drove with a friend. He's waiting for me in the car. We'll manage just fine."

When Rita opened the door to the garage a second time, the little cat scurried over to Beatrice, rubbing desperately against her legs while mewing so loudly her cries reverberated throughout the garage. Beatrice gathered her up in her arms. Immediately the tortie pushed her head under her chin. Her rough tongue licked Beatrice's neck.

"You poor baby," she crooned. "I'm taking you back home. You're safe with Mama."

Vlad's mouth dropped open when Beatrice came to the car clasping the tortoiseshell cat to her chest and dangling a shopping bag from her wrist.

"What the hell?"

He stared at the little cat trembling on her lap. The more the poor cat shivered, the louder she purred.

"We've adopted a new pet. And I have evidence to show Sandra." Beatrice held up the bag with the photo book. "Proof that Arthur is a scammer."

After a last glance at Rita's house, Beatrice noticed Saber positioned in the bay window, keeping her under surveillance even as they drove away.

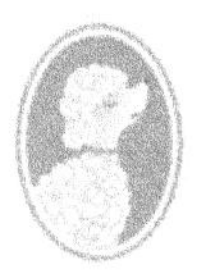

CHAPTER TWENTY-SEVEN

"Turn into this strip mall," Beatrice said, making her voice heard above the cat's earsplitting meows. "I see a PetSmart store next to Old Navy."

Vlad clenched the steering wheel so tightly his knuckles turned white. A thin sheen of perspiration glistened on his forehead as he tried to tune out the cat's cries. His head throbbed like the seven dwarves were extracting brain cells from his skull with little axes. Cocoa clung to Beatrice's shoulder like on a log adrift in whitewater rapids, her claws digging in through the warm-up jacket, yowling all the while. The ten miles to the freeway from Rita Hansen's house were the longest ten miles of his life.

"We need to get some kitty paraphernalia for your apartment," Beatrice said as he swung into the closest parking spot.

"My apartment! I thought she was going to join Max at your house. I don't have room for a cat in my small place," Vlad protested. "You have all the cat stuff already."

"Look at this scared little girl," Beatrice said as she stroked the tortoiseshell's silky fur with a gentle touch. "How long do you think she'd last with Max bullying her? He chased you into my broom closet, and you're a grown man."

Vlad's face flushed red at the unpleasant memory of being stalked by the black and white terror. "OK, I'll take her. But it's only temporary. We can gradually introduce them to each other. Train them to get along. Maybe we should look for a cat whisperer for Max, like on that animal TV show."

Beatrice disengaged the claws from her shoulder and set Cocoa on the seat, quickly exiting the car. The little cat mewed frantically, scrambling to the back seat, then to the front, terrified of being alone.

"We'll make it fast. Just the basics. A food dish, water bowl, litter box, wet and dry food." Beatrice led the way to the cat food aisle. Serene tabbies—unlike any cat Vlad knew—gazed down at them Zen-like from the various bags of dry food. Kitten Food, Adult 1-6, Hairball Control, Adult Indoor, Urinary Tract, Perfect Weight, Light, and that was just from one manufacturer!

"Who knew there were so many kinds of cat food?" Vlad shook his head in amazement. "How do you know what type to get her?"

"We'll start with the young adult type." Beatrice put a small bag into the cart. "Once you take her to be checked out by the vet, he may have some recommendations." Then she added some cans of chicken and fish." "She'll let you know what she prefers when she turns her nose up at the food you put out."

"Can we get her some kitty downers? If she won't take them, I could use a few," Vlad said.

Beatrice laughed and shook her head.

One hundred fifty dollars later, Vlad emerged from the store, arms loaded with every conceivable thing a cat could need, including a catnip mouse, a scratching post, and a tweeting bird on a string tied to a wand.

At the last minute Beatrice added a cat carrier explaining, "We'll put her in this for the drive home. She's safer if she's confined. I'd hate to have her jump in your face and cause an accident. Besides, you're going to need one when you take her to the vet."

Beatrice folded her warm-up jacket and spread it over the bottom of the carrier. Then she picked up the cat, pushed her inside, and deftly closed the door.

"Now we're off for home. I'm not looking forward to presenting our evidence to Sandra. She's head over heels for this jerk."

"Speaking of Sandra, I received three phone calls from her while we were in the store. They just showed up on my missed call list," Vlad said as he checked his phone.

Beatrice glanced at her mobile. "She tried to call me, too. Something major must have occurred for her to try both our phones."

Vlad leaned back in the car seat and stared out the window at the bustling shoppers, drumming his fingers on the steering wheel. "Let's not rush to return her calls. We need to consider how we want to confront her with what we've discovered. She'll be devastated when she finds out her soul mate is a philanderer."

He started the ignition and drove back into the traffic heading for the freeway.

"A martini might be a good place to start," Beatrice suggested. "Get her mellow and relaxed before we lower the boom,"

"Will we see fireworks or waterworks? I don't know how she's going to react."

Beatrice craned her neck to survey the cat carrier on the back seat. "Cocoa has finally settled down. Poor little thing is probably exhausted. I'll find something on public radio, and we can enjoy some peaceful listening on the drive home."

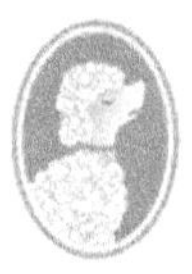

CHAPTER TWENTY-EIGHT

The hulking detective bristled with anger when he saw Sandra and Gaston seated in the CHAW director's office. "You again! I should have guessed. Whenever there's trouble, that dog shows up like a bad penny."

He stormed across the room and planted himself in the swivel chair facing her. His scowl was so fierce, Sandra feared his eyebrows were permanently stuck in one black line across his forehead.

Sandra sat quietly with hands folded on her lap, ankles crossed, and eyes cast downward while Gaston snoozed at her feet. When Detective Johnson stopped speaking, she fixed a calm, wide-eyed gaze on his reddening face. Her bright blue eyes sparked as they met his stormy glare.

"Gaston led me straight to the body," she said. "I realize you disparage his ability to solve crimes, but there's no denying he has a nose like a bloodhound." No sense mentioning the whole wiener incident— just a minor distraction from Gaston's remarkable achievement in finding Marco's body.

The detective inhaled deeply and closed his eyes. When he opened them he pulled out a small notebook and pen from the breast pocket of his disheveled suit coat and gazed at her with an intense concentration. "Please tell me all the events leading up to the discovery of the body."

"The pickleball match was about to start when Gaston suddenly tore across the gym. I knew right away something was up. He must have had one of his psychic visions. I can't explain it, but Gaston senses when there's trouble."

"Because he's usually the cause of it," the detective muttered under his breath as he scribbled in the notebook.

Sandra waited until the pen stopped moving before she spoke again. "Of course, I immediately followed him. I hated to leave because my fiancé was about to play the first game in the tournament. He's a pickleball superstar. He and his partner won the match, and I missed it." She sighed with a regretful expression. "But I felt compelled to stick with

Gaston."

"Go on, please. You were chasing after the dog. Then what happened?"

"I caught a glimpse of his tail as he ran up the stairs. So I kept hot on his heels. I couldn't move very fast because I had on these awful shoes." She lifted her feet to show the detective. "Sometimes a woman sacrifices comfort for style. Foolish vanity. But I didn't know my detective skills would be needed."

"Detective skills!" The man snorted, then bit his lip. He looked ready to poke her with the pointy end of the pen, but instead jabbed the paper so hard he made a hole.

"I took off my shoes and made it up the stairs. I had to catch my breath for a minute. I'm over eighty years old. I know it's hard to believe because I take good care of myself. I practice dance moves every day. But two flights of stairs are a lot at my age. I didn't see Gaston when I got to the top."

"Where was the dog?"

"I couldn't find him. I searched the weight room first. No one was there. Everyone was downstairs watching the tournament. The entire floor was deserted. I tiptoed down the hall, past a lot of dark rooms. I was creeped out until I caught up with Gaston."

"What happened next?"

"He insisted we go down the back stairs. I didn't want to. I argued with him. Pulled on his leash. He refused to budge. But he can be so stubborn. Finally, I gave up and put my shoes back on because the steps were so filthy. We went down the stairs. Slowly because only the emergency lights were on. I didn't want to trip and fall."

"You didn't see anyone else around?"

"No one. Just me and Gaston. I peeked over the edge of the stairwell and saw the body in the basement. He was lying all twisted at the bottom of the stairs. Then I knew why Gaston had insisted we go that way. He sensed there was foul play."

"What did you do next?"

"When we finally got to the bottom, I took a closer look. But I could tell the man was dead. I was careful not to touch anything because I knew it was a crime scene. I didn't want to disturb the evidence. I recognized the victim. He was at Jake Bender's apartment the day I found the cookbook. He let me take it from the trash."

"Are you sure the upstairs hallway was deserted when you were chasing after your dog?" Detective Johnson raised a quizzical eyebrow.

"Positive. I didn't see a soul. But I know the victim hadn't been dead long." She spoke with confidence.

"Pray tell, how did you come to this conclusion?" Sarcasm crept into the detective's voice.

"I bought the *Private Investigator's Handbook, Large Print Edition*. I studied it thoroughly. I can't depend solely on Gaston. I need to educate myself so I can be a good partner. It told me rigor mortis sets in after two hours. I'd put the time of death at seven-thirty, eight o'clock, this morning."

"You bought the *Private Investigator's Handbook*. That qualifies you to make an observation about the time of death?" he said with barely controlled anger,

"If I'd been able to more closely examine the body, I could have checked if livor mortis had set in. His skin already had the whitish discoloration caused by the diversion of the blood flow. Where the blood pools at the lowest points—my handbook calls it lividity—would have told me how long he'd been dead by the size of the blueish purple patches."

"Now I've heard it all. Some little old lady after reading an investigator's handbook figures she can determine the time of death in a murder investigation." Detective Johnson gripped the pencil so hard it broke in two pieces.

"I was respectful of the crime scene. I didn't touch the body. I merely said *I could have*."

"Do you realize the killer also *could have* been lurking in the stairwell? I could be investigating two murders." The man glowered so fiercely Sandra had to look away from his disapproving scowl.

"Gaston would have protected me." She reached down to pat the poodle, who opened his eyes and yipped sleepily before settling back down.

"Stop right there. I can't listen to any more of this. I should charge you with obstruction of justice. Tampering with evidence. Interfering with an ongoing investigation, at the least. You could face up to five years in a federal prison, a hefty fine, or both. What happens to your brilliant detective dog if you go to prison?" He thrust the broken pencil stub at Gaston's head.

"You don't have to take that threatening tone with me, Detective. I was only trying to help with the investigation. How long would Marco's body have lain there if Gaston hadn't interfered, as you call it?"

"Marco. So you know the name of the victim? What else have you been withholding from me? I should run you in right now." Detective Johnson leaned forward as though he was ready to brandish a pair of handcuffs and lock her up.

"'Eighty-year-old Woman Arrested.' The *Daily Gazette* will love that headline. I bet even national news will pick up that story. Incompetent police department jails private citizen when murder investigation stalls. You'll be the laughingstock of the country." She tapped her chin thoughtfully. "Maybe I'll get an interview on *Sixty Minutes.*"

"You wouldn't…. I ought to…" The detective sputtered. "I'm ordering you to stop what you're doing. Let the police handle this. A cold-blooded killer is prowling the fitness center. I'm going to ask a judge for a temporary restraining order if you persist in turning up where you're not wanted."

"Fine. Gaston and I will quit the case. Maybe you'll realize we'd catch the killer sooner if we worked together. There's a saying in Africa: *When spider webs unite, they can tie up a lion.* Good luck catching the lion on your own."

CHAPTER TWENTY-NINE

"That asinine detective is as stubborn as your uncle Bud's Old Bessie!"

Sandra was still sputtering as Norm drove away from the drop off/pick up point at CHAW. The pickleball tournament was abruptly aborted. All the spectators and players had been isolated in the gym until the team of policemen recorded names and statements, a procedure that was certain to take hours. Sandra sent Arthur a text explaining she'd see him at home, then called Norm to come and get her and Gaston.

"Did he step on your foot and flick you in the face with his tail like Bessie when Uncle Bud tried to milk her?"

"'" No, but he refused to even consider sharing evidence in this latest murder!" Sandra harumphed. "After Gaston discovered the body and I pinpointed the time of death for him. The ingrate! He'll be wasting valuable time with his medical examiner while we could be hot on the trail of the killer right now. Right, Gaston?"

Gaston let out an agreeable yip, then promptly settled down on the old fleece blanket in the backseat. Soon his doggy snores filled the air.

Norm slowly shook his head. "I can't believe Marco is dead. He was so ornery he made the Devil cry. Too ornery to go down easily."

"Somehow he was lured to the back stairwell at CHAW and pushed to his death. If only we could discover who he met there."

"What time did you figure he died?"

"By the condition of rigor mortis, I calculated around seven-thirty or eight o'clock."

"Just when CHAW is setting up for the pickleball tournament." Norm gripped the steering wheel excitedly. "It could be one of the players."

"Or one of the officials or even a spectator." Sandra added, equally excited. "I know you don't agree with me, but Franklin was there early enough to save me a primo spot."

"Not that bull about the old guy getting revenge for his daughter."

"People are older far longer than they are young. Plotting revenge could take a lifetime. Hiding anger hardens into revenge, and Franklin may have been biding his time until now. With all the commotion today organizing for the tournament, it would've been easy to slip upstairs and commit mayhem."

"Revenge explains Jake's murder, but why kill Marco?"

"There has to be a connection. It's up to us to find out. You know where Marco's place is. Let's go there before the cops start investigating."

"Are you crazy?" Norm took his eyes off the road for an instant to stare at her. "What happens if we get caught?"

Sandra jerked her head toward the snoozing Gaston in the back seat. "You forget we have a watchdog with us. We'll post Gaston as a lookout and park the car where we can make a quick getaway."

"I don't like this. We better check with Vlad and Beezy before we do anything rash."

"I already tried several times, the minute the detective finished with me. Unfortunately, my call went right to voicemail. On both phones. They must be out of town."

Sandra didn't notice the guilty look on Norm's face as he muttered, "Yep. Probably went out of town for the weekend."

Sandra thrust her index finger in the air. "First, we need to take a slight detour to my house. There's something I need to get."

Sandra ordered Gaston to stay as she dashed into the house. He whined halfheartedly and fell back asleep. Norm tapped the steering wheel impatiently as he waited.

"You're no help, little buddy," he said to the snoring pooch. "Can't you bark some sense into her?"

Sandra came out of her apartment wearing the shapeless brown coat and her black orthopedic shoes, carrying a large metallic gold makeup kit. Norm knotted his brow in a puzzled look as he watched her slide in and plunk the bag firmly on her lap.

"Are you planning to freshen up your makeup when we get to Marco's?"

"Oh, no! This is my detective kit." Sandra wore a confident smile as she patted the bag. *The Private Investigator's Handbook* suggested putting together some useful tools for investigations. I went to ACE Hardware and picked up a few items."

"Tell me you don't have a gun in there." Norm studied her warily for a few moments.

"No, dearie." She laughed. "I don't have a license for concealed carry yet. But I did enroll in a course that starts in October."

"You what?" he exclaimed.

"I decided to take this detective gig to the next level. It started with creating a detective kit. I can't allow Gaston to do all the heavy lifting."

After a short drive to the outskirts of town, Norm bounced the old Buick over several ruts in the gravel driveway leading up to Marco's house. His Green Bay Packers cap slid farther back on his head with each bump. Sandra was jostled so much from the potholes that her teeth rattled. She grasped the gold bag tightly so the contents wouldn't spill out on the floor. Even Gaston woke up from the back seat with a sharp *ruff*. Hopefully, the shock absorbers wouldn't fall off after this harsh treatment. She wasn't so sure about her false eyelashes. One seemed to be hanging precariously from her left eye so she plucked off both of them.

As Norm eased the old car to a stop, she noticed the lawn next to the driveway was trampled down like a herd of wildebeests had stampeded past. Patches of white paint clung to grey clapboard in tired wisps. Empty tequila fifths and brown beer bottles lined the steps to the sagging plywood back porch.

Norm circled around to the back before he finally parked behind a cluster of linden trees, the car's nose pointed toward the highway. "I think we're pretty well-hidden from the road here," he stated as he killed the engine. "It's an ideal spot for a quick getaway."

Sandra stationed Gaston at the head of the drive, removing his Service Dog harness and tossing it into the back seat. The pooch ran around in a few circles, overjoyed at losing the tattered disguise.

"Stay, boy!" she ordered. "Bark real loud if you see a car heading this way."

Gaston made a motion to follow, but a second stern "stay" stopped him in his tracks. He gave a complaining whine but perched obediently at the side of the road. His sad puppy eyes bored a hole in their retreating backs.

The curtainless windows of the weathered farmhouse made Sandra think, *abandon all hope you who enter here,* as they crept up to the porch. Norm held her arm carefully as they plodded over clumps of dirt. He opened the creaky screen door, and they slowly picked their way past empty beer cases and packing boxes filled with electronic gear and household items.

"Leftovers from cleaning out Jake's apartment," Sandra noted. "Looks like they never made it to St. Vinnie's."

Norm tried the back door. It was locked. "This door looks pretty solid. I'm not sure I can bust in." He gave a tenuous push against the thick wooden door, curls of black paint peeling off.

Sandra bent down to peer closely at the tarnished lock, her tousled red hair bobbing as she looked up and down several times. "No worries. That's why I brought my detective kit."

She set the kit on a nearby packing box and extracted a can of WD40. She fitted the thin straw into the lock's mechanism and gave it a squirt. Before replacing it in the bag, she closed her eyes.

Scrunching up her face, she said, "I'm envisioning the lock's mechanism. The set of key pins and driver pins have to align with the shearline before the lock turns and opens. Should be around five or six of the driver pins attached to springs stacked close as sardines."

"How the hell do you know that?" Norm blurted out.

"Chapter Sixteen in the handbook—how to pick a lock." She pulled out a thin L-shaped device. "This is a tension wrench. I insert it into the keyway with a little light pressure." With her left hand she stuck the wrench into the lock and gently torqued it to the right and then to the left. "The plug turned a little more to the right so this is the direction the key turns."

Norm whistled. "I can't believe you're doing this. Can't you get in trouble for having lock picking equipment?"

"It's not illegal to own it, only to use it to commit a burglary."

With her right hand she pulled out a small pick with a sharpened hook on the end. "Here's where my skill at sewing sequins on costumes serves me well. You need a steady hand for this."

She gently slid the pick into the keyway, bending down close to the lock to hear the mechanism click. Maneuvering the pick to lightly touch the pins, she felt the first one resist. She kept pressure on the lock with the tension wrench as she picked her way slowly and carefully through the six pins inside, setting each one as she felt some resistance. Suddenly there was a loud click. The lock disengaged and opened with some additional pressure from the tension wrench. The door swung open as Sandra pushed slightly more forcefully,

"Voila!" Sandra gave a little bow and waved her hand to enter.

She dropped the tools back into the bag and snatched it off the box, leading the way into Marco's kitchen.

"How did you learn how to do that?"

"I practiced on your door when you were gone. Then I tried it on Vlad's. I even broke into the Jackson's apartment when they were at work. Easy-peasy once you get the hang of it." She blew on her fingernails and rubbed them on her shirt. "All in the handbook."

They found themselves in Marco's kitchen. His table was covered with half opened mail, empty fast-food containers, and cans of beer.

"I'll sort through this mess while you check out the next room. See if we can find any proof that he and Jake were up to something illegal. But before you touch anything, put on these." Sandra brandished a pair of latex gloves from her gold bag. "We don't want to leave any fingerprints behind."

Norm grabbed the gloves and sped into the next room. Sandra sat down on a kitchen chair and took a deep breath. Her hands had been steady as she picked the lock but now she felt like she could barely lift them. She wrinkled her nose at the disgusting pile of junk but straightened her shoulders and picked up the first envelope. Marco's cell phone bill. Nothing interesting there. Literature from the National Rifle Association. A bill from the funeral home. Political junk mail asking for donations. Nothing.

Norm shouted from the next room. "I think I found something inside his gun case."

He dashed into the room waving a six by nine manila envelope. He pulled a stack of fifty-dollar bills from inside. Before they could count it, Gaston began to bark.

"What's it say on the envelope?" Sandra pointed to the scrawl barely decipherable on its front.

Norm squinted as he read, *"First installment. The well is running dry.* What the hell does that mean?"

"We don't have time to find out. Shove the money back. Mix it in with this pile of mail for the police to find."

Norm slid the envelope on the bottom of the pile. He snatched the detective kit from the floor by Sandra's feet and pulled her to a standing position. "We better haul ass!"

Gaston's barking grew more frantic as Norm guided Sandra back through the trash on the porch and over the uneven ground. When they reached the car, they could see the police cruiser in the distance.

Norm thrust Sandra and the bag into the front seat as Gaston hopped onto her lap. He bolted to the driver's side and slammed the door shut, the key still in the ignition, his hands shaking so much he could barely turn it. They sped down the road in the opposite direction feeling like Bonnie and Clyde.

"Blackmail! It has to be blackmail. Marco and Jake were in on it together!" Sandra exclaimed once her heart stopped pounding and she could speak again.

Norm wished he hadn't seen the picture in the envelope. The one Marco showed him at the bonfire with Jake's mother and Arthur.

The police would discover the connection soon enough.

.

CHAPTER THIRTY

When Norm spotted the gleaming black Thunderbird parked in Sandra's driveway, his first impulse was to pull a U-turn and drive far away. Anything to distract Sandra from going home.

"Anybody hungry for a cheeseburger and fries? Breaking and entering sure works up an appetite." He slowed as he signaled to turn.

Gaston gave an agreeable yip and stood on his hind legs, paws pressed against the side window, his nose pointed in the direction of the nearest McDonald's.

"Wait, dearie!" Sandra exclaimed. "I see Arthur's car in my drive. Pull in quickly."

"The cops must be finished with the interviews at CHAW," Norm said.

"I must find out what happened after I left. The police will have finished collecting names and addresses." She sighed. "Poor Arthur. This was going to be his day of triumph. He was sure he and Kent would take home the trophy for the Men's Doubles."

Arthur was slumped on the front steps, still in his blue pickleball team shirt and athletic shorts. His head rested on fists propped up on his knees, silver hair cascading over his downcast eyes. As Norm eased the Buick behind his sports car, Arthur raised his downturned eyes to stare blankly as they parked. He managed a half-hearted "hi" as they approached.

"Oh, dear. He looks like he just lost his best friend," Sandra muttered.

She greeted him with her most sympathetic smile and asked, "What happened? Are you all right?"

She settled on the steps beside him and reached for his hand. "Tell me all about it."

Before Arthur could begin, Norm said, "I'm going to take Gaston for a walk around the block. Give ya some time alone."

He reached in the back seat for the leash and shepherded the poodle down the street as best he could handle. The dog plopped down at the end of the driveway and refused to budge until Norm coaxed,

"I know where she keeps the Pork Chomps."

Then Gaston trotted away.

"There was another murder at CHAW," he began. "That tattooed man, Marco's his name. Big, muscle-bound guy. They said he was a friend of Jake's. Somebody found his body this morning."

"That 'somebody' was me," Sandra murmured. "Gaston and I stumbled upon him in the stairwell."

"Was it terrible for you, my darling?" Arthur gripped her hand.

Sandra widened her eyes. "No, not really. It was just so… unexpected."

"Especially on the day of the tournament. We were in such a good mood. Kent and I aced our first game. We were on a roll. Never even made it to the elimination round when they closed off the gym. Cops started taking names as people filtered out. Only not me. I wasn't so lucky. That damn detective gave me the third degree."

"I'm sorry. He seems to hold a grudge against you."

"All because of that little spat with Jake Bender. Hell, I barely even knew the guy. He was just some loudmouthed braggart who thought he was God's gift to pickleball." He brushed his hair out of his eyes and locked onto her gaze. "You saw how he was that day. Spouting off to everyone. I didn't know him long enough to loathe him. He was just an annoyance."

'What did Detective Johnson want to know?"

"What time I arrived at CHAW. Where did I go first. Was there anybody who could corroborate my whereabouts, the same old shit. Everybody in the men's locker room could testify they saw me arrive."

"What time was that?" Sandra hoped it was close to nine o'clock.

"I guess around eight. Kent and I met beforehand to discuss our game plan and size up our first opponents. We did a few stretches to get warmed up."

"You called me at seven to make sure I was awake. You said you were heading over to CHAW right away. Are you sure you met with Kent at eight?"

"Of course I'm sure. You're starting to sound like that detective," Arthur said bitterly. He jerked his hand away. "I know what time it was because I checked on my Fitbit to see how many steps I had before playing the match."

"I don't mean to grill you." Sandra gently rubbed his thigh in soothing circles. "I'm merely worried about proving your innocence. The police will look for consistency in your testimony. The more you rehearse, the better you sound."

Arthur stood up abruptly. "I'm not speaking to that cop again without my lawyer present. All my answers will be no comment unless he charges me with something. I'd like to see him try." He began pacing in front of the steps. "That's not the worst part of the afternoon. After my session with Dudley Do-Right, I got ready to drive home. When I looked in my gym bag for my keys, I noticed my wallet was missing. Can you believe that? Somebody had the guts to steal my wallet while the place was crawling with cops."

"Not your ostrich leather billfold!" Sandra rose to face him and held out her arms. "My poor dear man!"

Arthur leaned into her embrace. "Yes, my beautiful one-of-a-kind wallet. All my cash—several hundred dollars. Credit cards, driver's license, health insurance ID.—everything. Now I'll have to call each place to get a replacement. It will take weeks for them to arrive in the mail. In the meantime I'm broke." He rested his head on the top of hers as he spoke, his voice cracking with emotion. "I'm t-t-totally destitute. Every cent I just got from the bank was in that wallet. No identification to even access my checking account since I'm new in town."

"Don't worry." Sandra hugged him closer. "I can help. I'll lend you some money. How much do you need?"

Arthur stepped back, both his hands firmly gripping her arms. "You'd do that for me, darling?"

He gazed deeply into her eyes, as she nodded yes.

"I can't believe what a treasure you are. You're such a kind, loving lady with a generous, giving heart. The day I found you was the luckiest day of my life."

Sandra smiled sweetly. "We can go to the bank right now. I'll withdraw some money from the ATM machine. How much do you think you'll need?"

"Just enough to tide me over for a few days. I think one thousand dollars should do it."

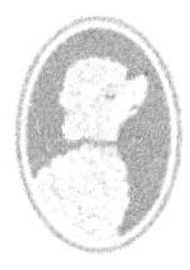

CHAPTER THIRTY-ONE

Vlad stole a sideways glance at Beatrice thumbing through Rita Hansen's class reunion book. Listening to the Saturday morning format of quiz shows and call-in conversations produced the desired calming effect. A talk show doctor came on the air next, dispensing advice for various ailments. Vlad didn't even mind that his credit card took a hit because of a small cat and Beatrice's big heart. He reached over and touched her hand, then caressed her fingers lightly with his thumb. She gave his hand a gentle squeeze in return, dispelling all his anxieties about Sandra. He almost forgot the image of Jake's stiff body, his face frozen in death. If only they could journey down this highway forever with the doctor on the radio resolving all his questions about eczema and hemorrhoids.

The ringing of his cell phone broke his reverie. He pressed the green phone icon on his steering wheel, and Norm's voice came booming from the audio, replacing the reassuring opinions of the doctor.

"When are ya getting back to town? All hell's broke loose here. Marco's been murdered. Pushed down the stairwell at CHAW. Gaston found his body. The cops shut down pickleball. Kept everybody in the gym except Sandra. Cuz she was with Gaston."

"What are you talking about? Slow down. You're not making much sense." Vlad turned up the volume on the audio to be sure he heard correctly. "You said Marco was murdered?"

Norm gave them a brief account of what happened to Sandra at the pickleball tournament. "That beast of a detective read her the riot act when she told him Gaston discovered the body."

"Poor Sandra. Was she freaked out over seeing a corpse?" Vlad asked, recalling Jake's bloated face.

"Nah. She tried to establish the time of death by assessing the condition of Marco's body. Said she learned how to figure it out from her private detective handbook. Her attitude gave that detective conniption fits."

"Yikes!' Beatrice gulped. "I wouldn't like to poke that particular bear."

"Then she made me drive her out to Marco's place. She brought her private detective kit that looks like a makeup bag. She had her lock picking tools inside. Did you know she taught herself how to pick a lock? All from the handbook."

"You're kidding!" Vlad exclaimed.

"I wish I was because she made me break in and enter with her. Said she practiced breaking into our digs."

"Son of a gun! I knew I had more than two Lindt chocolates in the candy bowl.' Vlad harrumphed. "Now I know why they kept disappearing."

"There's more. I know how Jake got all that money in the fake account. He was blackmailing Arthur! I found a shitload of money hidden in Marco's gun case in a small manila envelope. That picture of Jake Bender's mom cozying up with Arthur was tucked in, too."

Vlad's voice went two octaves higher. "What did you do with it? Tell me you didn't steal it!"

"Hell no. I left it for the cops to find. Arthur's ass is grass when they find it."

"Rita Hansen produced more proof that he's a first-class scoundrel. She brought him to a class reunion and had her picture taken with him." Beatrice picked up the class reunion book and grasped it tightly. "He used a different name. Just like Shirley Pritchard. Same snow job. Conned her out of fifty thousand."

Norm whistled. "That's major fraud. What ya gonna do with that info?"

"We were going to show Sandra the picture and give her Rita's phone number. But now I'm thinking we should turn everything over to the police. Marco's name was on Arthur's recent call list, too."

"Yeah, go to the cops," Norm said. "Put another nail in his coffin. But do it quick. He's with Sandra as we speak. No telling what he's up to."

"If he's capable of killing a blackmailer, it's not too farfetched to think he'd harm an old lady. Especially if his cash cow runs dry." Beatrice looked at Vlad with alarm. "Maybe Jake's mother didn't die of any natural causes."

"Damn. You could be right. We're heading straight to the police station."

DETECTIVE JOHNSON SLOUCHED IN HIS SWIVEL CHAIR, shuffling

through the stack of papers heaped before him. His ratty brown suit coat hung over the back of the chair. He undid the top button of his wrinkled white shirt, and his tie hung loosely around his neck like he'd been on an all-night bender. The frown of displeasure at being interrupted deepened into a scowl when he recognized Vlad and Beatrice. His lips curled into a snarl.

"What the hell are you two doing here?" Detective Johnson growled, "It's been a bitch of a day. Unless you've found another body to report, get out of here."

They straggled into the room, Vlad leading the way. He hovered near the crowded desk and cleared his throat a few times. Beatrice wielded the class reunion book like a shield in front of her. She nudged Vlad with her elbow to begin.

"We discovered some information about Arthur Ashenbrenner we want to share with you," Vlad nervously began. "He's been scamming elderly women, defrauding them of money, by faking romantic intentions."

"Just how did you come by this information?" The detective smirked. "Torture him into confessing by playing 'It's a Small World' nonstop?"

Vlad took a deep breath and continued, "I got a look at his calls when he dropped his phone and found some suspicious names. Women besides Sandra. So we did a people search and contacted them."

"You did what? More of your damn amateur sleuthing!" The detective rose from his chair, slammed both his hands on the desk, and leaned forward to glare at Vlad. "You didn't feel the need to bring this information to my attention until now? We found a second body today under highly suspicious circumstances."

Vlad struggled to meet his angry eyes. "No! Not another victim!" he exclaimed with an Oscar-winning performance. "We didn't hear a word. We were in St. Paul until now. Following up on one of the names I found."

Beatrice jumped in. "Who was the victim?"

"A friend of Jake Bender's. Marco Orlowski. If you can shed some light on this investigation, I want to hear about it immediately." He thumped his fist on the desk.

Beatrice opened the book to the page with Arthur and Rita's photo and slid it toward him. "The woman in the picture is Rita Hansen from St. Paul. She had a relationship with Arthur, only he called himself

Arthur Atkins. He scammed her out of fifty thousand dollars."

"Do the St. Paul police know about this?"

"She didn't file a complaint. Didn't want anyone to know what a fool she'd been. I wrote her phone number on that slip of paper with the photo. I'm sure she would help with the investigation," Beatrice said.

The detective studied the sheet of paper for a moment, then looked up. "There's two names on the paper."

"The second is Shirley Pritchard, another lady who's been scammed," Beatrice said. "He is still working on getting money from her. She refuses to believe he's a liar."

Vlad wrung his hands as he spoke. "We're afraid he's moved on to our friend Sandra."

"You should have brought this to our attention right away," Detective Johnson sputtered. "We have the proper tools to investigate. I ought to charge you with—"

A policeman burst into the office, flourishing a manilla envelope stuffed full of cash in a sealed evidence bag. "Boss, you won't believe what we just found at the victim's house."

Vlad and Beatrice exchanged a knowing look. An envelope, just like Norm said.

The uniform strode across the room and plopped the envelope on top of the pile of papers. "Look inside. There's more than money."

Detective Johnson reached into a pocket of the jacket hanging behind him and pulled on a pair of latex gloves. "Let's see what you got here." He eagerly reached for the bag.

Vlad gaped expectantly as the man grabbed the manilla envelope. He and Beatrice shuffled a little closer to get a better look, peering over the desk as the man's fingers touched the top. He fumbled with the clasp, then dumped out the contents, whistling at the outpouring of cash. Vlad could see a corner of the photo of Arthur and Jake's mother. He swooped in to verify Norm's description of the two.

The detective jerked his head up as he noticed Vlad's movement.

"You two get the hell out of here," he commanded. "This is an official murder investigation. You've done enough damage with your snooping. You'll be hearing more from me."

CHAPTER THIRTY-TWO

Sandra dabbed her lips with a tissue after carefully applying her lipstick. She formed a sexy pout and gazed at her image through half-closed "come hither" eyes. Not bad for someone eighty years young. Enough pussyfooting around. She was about to lose control with Arthur, and she didn't just think she'd like it. She *knew*.

The translucent lace insets revealed tantalizing cleavage on her new pale pink dress. Similar insets on the sides made her waist appear slimmer. Best of all, the back zipper easily came undone. Just needed the slightest touch. She was ready.

Her MedicAlert pendant was resting in the charging cradle. The green light indicated it was fully charged. Sandra automatically reached to slip it back over her head, but then she thought, *Arthur will be here with me all night. Why would I need a medical alert device when I have him to call 9-1-1? The pendant won't be necessary tonight of all nights.*

She had to chase Gaston off the dress where she had laid it on the bed while taking a shower. Annoying dog! Not like he didn't have plenty of other comfy spots to snooze. "Get off my new dress," she shrieked.

His back claws snagged the lace on the side when he jumped down. Luckily, she was able to smooth it out. She slipped it on, turning side to side in the mirror. It draped alluringly in all the right spots. Arthur would be helpless to resist when he saw her in it.

"You're a naughty puppy," she scolded. "You're spending the night with Uncle Norm."

"N-n-n-n." Gaston whined pathetically when he heard the words naughty puppy, but Sandra's mind was made up. No dog was going to ruin this evening. She had been waiting two months for this moment. Two months and two thousand dollars. Arthur promised to pay her next week when he got paid from his consulting work and his new check card was reissued. His stolen wallet had certainly slowed him down with all the hassles of getting his identification straightened out.

Norm answered on the first ring. When she explained she needed a favor from him that night, his voice sounded strangely hesitant.

"Yer sure ya don't want Gaston around in case there's an

emergency?"

"No. Arthur will be here, and he's capable of handling things."

She swore Norm muttered, "That's what I'm afraid of."

But when she said, "Please speak up. I didn't catch that."

He said, "I'm afraid I have a Moose Lodge meeting tonight."

"Oh dear. I'll have to ask Vlad, but he has that new cat. Poor thing is scared of Gaston."

"Never mind," Norm sighed. "I'll skip the meeting. What time do you need me?"

After she hung up she puzzled over Norm's behavior the last day or two. Ever since they broke into Marco's house he'd been acting bizarre. So had Vlad and Beatrice. They popped in without calling first, surprising her and Arthur at unusual times. When they saw Arthur they made some hurried excuse to leave. Their dislike of him was so apparent, even he noticed the coolness. He suggested they spend more time at his place to avoid such awkward encounters. She thought, *Time heals all wounds. Once my friends get to know Arthur like I do, they'll see what a great guy he is.*

"We really need to talk," Norm said when he picked up Gaston. "Vlad and Beatrice found out something very important about Arthur. I'll call them, and they'll be right over with the news."

"I'm sorry, dearie. I don't have time to discuss Arthur. He'll be here any minute. Besides, I know all there is to know about him. See the beautiful opal necklace he gave me." She pointed to the oval pendant on the gold chain. "Any day there will be a ring to seal the deal. He promised once the mess from the stolen wallet is cleared up."

Gaston trotted up to Norm with a yippy greeting. "Good boy," he said. "Such a good little buddy," and scratched his upturned belly until the poodle whimpered with delight.

But when Sandra handed Norm the leash, some treats, and a can of dog food, Gaston scurried away. He tried to crawl under the credenza but Norm was too fast and grabbed him before he disappeared.

"I don't know what's wrong with this pooch," Sandra said. "He's been out of sorts all day. Look what he did to my new dress." She pointed to the barely visible snag. "I'm convinced he's jealous of Arthur. He acts up whenever we go on a date."

"Maybe he's trying to tell you something," Norm said as he snapped the leash onto Gaston's collar.

"I've spoiled him too much. Overindulged his every whim.

Arthur agreed with me; Gaston needs some discipline. I'm thinking of taking him back to obedience school for a refresher."

Norm headed for the door, treats and dog food tucked under his arm. "Give Mom a kiss good-bye. We'll see her tomorrow."

Gaston jumped on Sandra's thigh but she only let him lick her hand, explaining, "I spent too much time making myself look good for tonight to ruin my makeup with a doggy kiss."

"You've succeeded. Arthur's a lucky man." Norm said.

He parted with a mumble, "Way more than he deserves."

Gaston tossed one accusatory look at her before he plodded out the door.

THE BRISK KNOCK ON THE DOOR MADE Sandra's heart beat a little faster. When she opened it Arthur stood there, smiling broadly with a single red rose.

"Gather the rose of love whilst yet is time," he said.

"What a lovely thought!" Sandra planted a kiss on his cheek as she inhaled the flower's delicate fragrance. "Let me get a bud vase for it."

She rummaged in the hall closet for a small crystal vase,; thankful she had not donated all of them to the thrift store. When she returned to the living room, Arthur had settled comfortably on the sofa, one arm carelessly flung over the back. The top button of his powder blue polo shirt was undone, revealing a hint of his masculine chest. His hair shone like silk in the glow of the table lamp. Sandra barely controlled the urge to fling herself in his arms. All in good time.

She placed the vase in a prominent spot on the credenza and picked up the cocktail shaker, fully loaded with the ingredients for a Sandra Tooksbury dry martini, including her top-quality gin.

"I'll fix us a drink," she said as she shook the silver container with earthquake force.

When she poured the contents into the martini glass, she bent close to his face, giving him a good look at her cleavage peeking through the lace. Then she poured one for herself and snuggled companionably next to him, her head nestled on his shoulder. He tightened his arm around her, drawing her closer.

"You look ravishing tonight, my love. Is that a new dress? I've never seen you in it before."

"Actually, it is new. I wanted to wear something exceptional for tonight. It's our two-month anniversary."

"Two glorious months with the love of my life. This calls for a special toast." Arthur raised his glass. "*Amore mio! Il tuo per sempre.*"

Sandra touched her glass to his with a ping. "Ditto to whatever you said." She took a sip. "I planned a special dinner tonight. I have beef stroganoff warming in the slow cooker. A tossed salad is waiting in the fridge. Dessert will be a surprise."

In addition to pilfering a few Lindt's chocolates after breaking into Vlad's apartment, she'd helped herself to his tube of mango Lovelicious hidden in the nightstand. She figured since his engagement to Beatrice, he won't need that anymore.

"Ah-ha! I smelled the aroma of your delicious food the second I stepped in. But you're missing something."

Sandra surveyed her living room. His beautiful rose on the credenza. A few candles strategically placed for when the lights go off. "Unchained Melody" playing softly in the background. Her best Fredrick's of Hollywood plunge bra and lace-up front panties.

"What did I miss?" Sandra kicked off her high heels and sank on the couch beside him. "I planned everything for our romantic evening."

"There's no Gaston. Where is the little imp? Hiding under the love seat for a sneak attack when I walk past?" His mouth turned down into a sour expression when he said the pooch's name.

"He's spending the night with Uncle Norm. I wanted it to be just the two of us. I've been thinking about you all day." She lowered her eyelids and half-opened her lips in a steamy pout, sliding her hand to the exposed part of his chest. "To touch you like this."

Then she shifted her hand behind his neck and pulled him to her in a gentle caress. Their lips met. She inhaled deeply, filling her nostrils with his spicy cologne and tasting his minty mouthwash as they kissed passionately. Arthur's arms tightened around her as her heart beat faster. She felt her control slipping away as her other hand moved to his thigh. Love at long last!

The loud pounding at the door broke the spell. Startled, Arthur broke off their embrace and lurched away. He sat bolt upright and straightened the front of his shirt.

In a tight voice he muttered, "You'd better see who it is before they break the door down." He reached for his martini.

"It's probably Norm. Gaston wasn't cooperating when he came to pick him up. Maybe he ran out of dog treats to make him behave."

She stood up. The pink lace dress had ridden up to her thighs, exposing the tops of her nylons and garters. She yanked it down, smoothed it over her hips, and slid her feet into her shoes. The pounding grew louder. She sashayed to the door, shouting, "Hang on. I'm coming as fast as I can. Show a little restraint."

Sandra flung open the door and barked, "Now what do you want?"

Her eyes widened in astonishment at the sight of Detective Johnson holding an official-looking piece of paper flanked by two uniformed officers. His face was grim as an executioner's as he announced, "I'm looking for Arthur Ashenbrenner. His car is in your driveway. Is he here?"

Sandra flushed red as she stuttered, "Y-y-es, he's here." She glanced over to the couch where Arthur sat frozen as an ice sculpture at Winterfest.

His handsome face drained of all color as he stammered, "What do you want?"

The detective torpedoed his way into the room, leaving Sandra and the two officers following in his wake. His voice boomed, "Arthur Ashenbrenner, I have three warrants for your arrest. Rita Hansen has filed a complaint with the St. Paul, Minnesota, police for financial fraud in the amount of fifty thousand dollars. We have a warrant for Arthur Atkins, alias Arthur Ashenbrenner, from them also for identity fraud."

Sandra's fingers grew numb, and her knees began to buckle. She grabbed the edge of the credenza to keep from collapsing. "Arthur, what does this mean?" She turned her wild-eyed stare toward him. "Who's this woman—Rita Hansen?"

Arthur took a moment to compose himself before he answered calmly, "No one important. Just a former lady friend, a disgruntled business partner. She made some bad investments and wants me to cover them." The color returned to his face as he stood eye to eye with the detective. "You said three warrants. What's the third?"

"I'm arresting you on suspicion of homicide in the death of Jacob Bender." Detective Johnson produced a set of handcuffs and ordered, "Please hold out your hands."

"Homicide!" Sandra gasped. "You must be mistaken. Arthur would never harm anyone."

The detective slapped them on Arthur's wrists as he said, "You have the right to remain silent. Anything you say can be used against you in a court of law. You have the right to….”

As the detective droned on repeating his Miranda rights, Sandra stared at Arthur in disbelief. Thoughts swirled in her head with twister force. *Arthur, a murderer! Snatching up my beautiful peacock boa and tightening it around Jake Bender's neck. Can't be. He's so sweet and loving. Swindling some gullible woman out of fifty thousand. But I'm his soul mate.*

Arthur cried out defiantly, “I didn't kill Jake Bender. If anything, I'm the victim.” He turned to Sandra with pleading eyes. “Please believe me, darling. I didn't do it. He was blackmailing me. I can prove it.”

Sandra stood stunned. Lifting her eyes to meet his was like lifting heavy weights. Her lips moved to form words of trust and compassion but no sound came out. All utterances died as she struggled to remain standing. She closed her eyes, hoping this was all a bad dream, but when she opened them Arthur in handcuffs was still there.

“You'll have your day in court,” Detective Johnson promised. “We're taking you down to the station for booking. You can call your lawyer from there.”

“My lawyer! He'll want a retainer.” Arthur's eyes remained focused on Sandra, his expression shape-shifting from defiance to affection. “I know you'll help me with this, my love. For our life together. Please give my lawyer whatever he needs.”

All the puzzle pieces fell into place. His frequent absences, the lost wallet, the exaggerated compliments, the opal necklace, the love tokens, the isolation from her friends, Gaston's intense dislike for him. She saw the complete picture: Arthur was a controlling scoundrel. The words finally came.

“Go to hell!”

Arthur gaped in astonishment. “But darling, you don't understand.”

“I understand you're a complete asshole. I fell for your lies.”

Detective Johnson spoke gently to her as the uniforms led Arthur away. “We will appreciate your cooperation in our investigation. When you feel you're ready, please come down to the station and give us your statement. Your eyewitness testimony will strengthen our case, especially if you've become a victim of fraud.”

Sandra stared sadly at the lonely rose in the crystal vase as she answered, “I'll certainly help all I can.” She sighed. “Life is so uncertain. Today I got a rose. Tomorrow I'll deal with the thorns.”

CHAPTER THIRTY-THREE

"There's no fool like an old fool in love," said Sandra.

Sandra ignored the plate of pancakes Norm placed on the TV tray before her. She poured some cream in her coffee and watched the clouds swirl in the cup without lifting it to her lips. The oversized clock read one o'clock in the afternoon. She was still in her satin pink bathrobe and fuzzy slippers. Gaston rose on his hind legs, resting his front paws on her lap, and licked her hand. She lifted it to pet his head, then let it drop back into her lap. The pooch wagged his tail and licked it some more, but her hand lay still.

It had been three days since the police led Arthur out of her life. Three days of listening to Vlad and Beatrice relate step by step how they untangled the web of his deceit. Norm admitted he saw the picture of Jake Bender's mother and Arthur with the wad of cash. Her heart was ripped to pieces like tax returns through a shredder. Whenever she thought about putting her life back together, the pieces slipped through her fingers.

On the second day of mourning for the lost relationship, her friend Juanita called. "I'm so sorry to hear about your new man getting arrested. I know how happy he made you feel."

In a teary voice Sandra said, "Thanks, it was quite a shock to hear all the charges."

"I thought you should know. Rosalie sneaked a peek at the file when everyone was out of the station. Two women filed financial fraud complaints, but there may be others."

"At least I'm not the only fool."

"But that's not all. The detective looked into Arthur's and Jake's bank records. They matched Arthur's withdrawals to Jake's deposits in some fake account. The amount was the same so they figured Jake was extorting money from Arthur, especially after seeing the picture of Mrs. Bender and Arthur in an envelope with a shitload of cash. So there's the motive."

"Norm told me about the p-picture." Her voice cracked. "I h-heard that, too."

"But here's something you haven't heard. According to the bruising on his neck, whoever throttled Jake was left-handed."

"Arthur's right-handed! I've seen him use his right hand all the time."

"Right. However, there's an eyewitness from CHAW who puts him entering the men's locker room at precisely the time of the murder. Arthur had the opportunity. The police are hoping the witness is so credible that the right- and left-hand discrepancy is moot."

"Thank Rosalie for me. But I'm off the case. I'm not a detective anymore. I can't even detect when someone's playing me."

"Oh, honey! Your loneliness clouded your good judgment. You are a damn good detective. Look how you caught that international jewel thief."

In a small sad voice Sandra said, "You've mistaken me for Gaston," and hung up.

By the third day Norm took control of the situation by making her breakfast, her favorite blueberry pancakes with real maple syrup, none of the corn syrup junk.

"Ya weren't the only woman taken in by Arthur," Norm said soothingly. "Look at the others Vlad found. He prob'ly only scratched the surface. The cops will find more dames parted from their money."

An expression of concern clouded Norm's face. Sandra hadn't put on her makeup or bothered getting dressed or even taken Gaston for his morning walk. Instead, she sat crumpled on the sofa watching old detective shows with actors that were now six feet under, their ghostly faces flickering across the screen.

She sighed. "I suppose you're right."

"Ya know, the cops just arrested Henry Winkler for investment fraud." Norm paused to watch her reaction. "It was a big Fonzie scheme."

None. Not even a twinge of her usual smile or eye-rolling.

"I got a psychic joke for ya. Might give ya ideas for yer new act with Gaston." His voice rose on a hopeful note.

At the mention of his name, the poodle emitted a little yip, then sat on his haunches. His eyes never left Sandra's face.

"This guy visited Madame Esmerelda. The famous psychic and healer. During the show Esmerelda glides over to him, puts her hand on his shoulder, and says, 'You WILL walk.' He says softly, 'But I'm fine. My legs already work.' She gestures dramatically and says even louder,

'YOU…Will…WALK!'

"The guy decides to play along, gets up, and walks in a small circle. The audience goes nuts. After the show he walks out and shakes his head, figuring this Madame Esmerelda is a just a big fake. Then he discovers his car got stolen."

Gaston barked his approval. A hint of a smile appeared on Sandra's face. She took a sip of her coffee. Then she picked up the fork and stabbed the pancake, breaking off a chunk with a big berry and slowly chewing it.

"Don't tell me you have more bad jokes."

"I got a couple more. Like the ice cream company that got away with committing fraud. Their assets were already frozen."

"Enough already!'' She slammed the fork down. "I'm not going to wallow here in self-pity if it means I have to suffer through more of your awful jokes trying to cheer me up."

"That's my girl! My jokes are a fate worse than death. I'm going to keep on telling them until you move off the couch."

"I can take a hint. I'll get dressed."

An hour later Sandra came out of her bedroom with her eyes made up and her showgirl red lipstick generously applied. Hair fluffed out with a rhinestone barrette was keeping her bangs out of her face. Although she wore her fuchsia tunic with the splashy flower pants, her feet were clad in sensible multicolor sneakers.

"Ya look like a woman on a mission," Norm grinned. "What are ya up to?"

"There's one person in this whole Jake Bender investigation that I wronged. I feel ashamed of myself for lying to that poor girl at the fitness center. I owe her the whole truth and a big apology. Could you please drop me at CHAW for a little while?"

"Sure thing. I need to run to the hardware store for some drill bits. I want to fix that loose step by the back door before the snow flies. I'll run a few errands and pick you up after."

Gaston ran to where his leash and Service Dog harness were hung. He gave it a huge yank, and it tumbled to the floor. Then he dragged it over to where Sandra stood and dropped it at her feet.

"I wasn't planning on taking you in with me, lovey puppy."

"Why don't ya take the little fella with ya? He's been cooped up all morning. Besides, he might get inspired by all the exercise equipment."

"The woman at the front desk always wears a sour lemon face when she sees him." Sandra bent down to slide the harness over his head. "Let's give her something to complain about."

Just as Sandra predicted, the friendly smile on the receptionist turned into a hostile frown at the sight of Gaston. If she screwed up her eyes any tighter, she'd need plastic surgery to smooth her forehead out. In a tone that would freeze a polar bear, she sniffed, "May I help you?"

"Is Kristin working today? I have a little something for her." Sandra held up a brightly colored gift bag containing some fancy wrapped chocolates. "She was so helpful the last time we were here."

The woman clicked a few keys and studied the building schedule on her computer screen. "The yoga class just left the studio on the second floor. She should be up there cleaning it before the after-work group meets."

Sandra flashed her the sweetest smile she could fake. "Thank you, dearie. I so appreciate your help."

She remembered the last time she scurried down the long hall to the main stairs, in a frantic attempt to catch up with Gaston. She stopped abruptly when they reached the steps, grasped his leash a little tighter, and squeezed the handles of the gift bag in her sweaty fist. A wave of anxiety swept over her. *How could I have been so wrong about everything?*

"Gaston, we have to make things right with Kristin today."

He must have agreed because he trotted obediently up the stairs.

The early afternoon was a slow time on the second floor. The noon fitness crowd departed, and the weight room had only one sole enthusiast with earbuds, grunting in time to inaudible music.

A gaggle of older ladies ambled out of the kickboxing studio, chatting happily. A fine sheen glistened on their faces. A few acknowledged Sandra with a cheery hello and "cute pooch" as they passed by. Perspiration mingled with the flowery scent of body lotion and expensive perfume wafted in the air. Gaston gave a friendly yip to their retreating backsides.

The yoga studio loomed ahead. Kristin's cleaning cart was parked outside the door. Sandra walked slowly on little cat feet, like Sandburg's poem. She hid for a moment behind the mop and broom handle watching Kristin as she spritzed the yoga mats and swiped them down. Her ponytail swished from side to side as she flung the mats from one pile to another, spraying and wiping without breaking into a sweat.

She hummed a wordless tune with a country and western rhythm.

"Ahem," Sandra cleared her throat and stepped into the room. Gaston followed on scraggly dog feet, nose down, snuffling along the tile floor like he was on a rabbit hunt. Sandra paused on the threshhold, unsure if she was welcome to venture any farther into the young custodian's domain. "Hello, Kristin."

The young woman straightened up at the sound of Sandra's voice. "Oh, it's you again," she said scornfully. "What do you want?"

"I was wondering if we could talk for a minute."

"I'm kind of busy here. When I'm done in the studio, I have to set up the punching bags next door for the kickboxing class." Kristin bent down to spray the next mat, vigorously rubbing it with the towel. "Make it fast." She didn't look up.

Sandra wound the gift bag handle tightly around her finger. "I'd like to apologize for misleading you earlier. I'm so sorry I wasn't more forthright."

"You mean you're sorry you lied to me about missing your granddaughter." No disguising the venom in her voice. "And how I reminded you of her. I bet you don't even have a granddaughter."

"You're right. I don't." Sandra hung her head. "I was investigating Jake Bender's murder. Trying to exonerate my fiancé, Arthur Ashenbrenner. I hoped you knew something that could lead me to the killer."

The young woman gave a bitter laugh. "Boy, did you get that wrong! Your so-called fiancé strangled Jake with your fancy boa. Not that the bastard didn't deserve it. I heard Ashenbrenner's been charged with homicide. I may even be a witness when he comes to trial."

"I-I- was shocked to find out he victimized me along with a lot of other women. I can't believe he's a murderer." Sandra went on in a small voice, "But I was wrong to deceive you. I hope you can forgive me."

"Forget it. I've come to expect people to act shitty toward me." Kristin sat back on her haunches, lowering the spray bottle and cloth. "Even my own mother moved away and left me."

"I know, dearie. You've had a difficult time of it. I brought you a little something to make amends."

Sandra held out the gift bag and stepped closer to Kristin. Gaston whined and hung behind, still nosing about the room.

"Listen to my dog. He's saying he's sorry, too."

"I'll bet he's sorry. I saw how sorry he was when he ran away with that wiener in his piehole." She picked up the bottle and rotated the mat single-handed, refusing to meet Sandra's eyes.

"Please take this. I'm just a foolish old woman trying to set things right."

She moved next to the girl and placed the bag down on the pile of mats. A familiar odor lingered in the close air of the studio. Sandra struggled to recall where she had encountered that smell before. She inhaled deeply, running through her recent visits to the care center and Jake's apartment. The aroma resembled chewing gum, or breath mints. She took another inhalation. The strong odor of wintergreen assaulted Sandra's nostrils. Gaston stopped sniffing and barked sharply twice. Then she realized what the scent was. The cleaning solution Kristin swabbed on the mats to disinfect them. The same odor on Marco's body.

"It was you!" Sandra pointed a shaking finger at the girl. "You killed Marco. You sprayed his face with that chemical."

Kristin hastened to her feet. "You're crazy, old woman. Why would I want to kill Marco?"

"He was best friends with Jake. And Jake sexually assaulted you. Harassed you constantly. Trapped you in empty rooms. Maybe Marco took up where Jake left off."

Kristin took a step toward Sandra, brandishing the spray bottle in her right hand like a blowtorch. "He caught me alone in the upper stairwell. Lunged for my boobs. I sprayed him in the face, then pushed him over the railing." She aimed the nozzle at Sandra. "Maybe I need to give you a little taste of this to shut you up."

Before the young woman came any closer, Sandra backed away. Gaston emitted a low growl deep in his throat, his bright eyes focused on the hand holding the bottle.

Sandra blurted, "You're the one. You strangled Jake. It wasn't Arthur. It was you. You were working that morning. You had motive and opportunity."

"Jake Bender tried to rape me for the last time. I was cleaning the men's locker room first thing. I was a little slow finishing up. Then *he* snuck up on me. First one in when CHAW opened. On the prowl. He found me. Stripped off his clothes and grabbed at mine. But he wasn't expecting me to fight back." She lifted the sprayer. "This baby works better than pepper spray. I got him right in the eyes. While he was blinded, I grabbed your boa from my cleaning cart and flung it around his neck. Put my foot at the base of his spine and pulled back hard."

"You could have claimed self-defense."

"No one would believe me. I told you." She spoke in a hard voice. "I shoved him under the shower, washed off the spray, and stuck the pickleball in his mouth. Nice touch, wasn't it?'

Sandra nodded her head. "So the police would think it was another player."

Kristin thrust her gloved hand toward Sandra and waved it. "Best of all, I wear gloves when I clean. No prints."

She dropped the towel. "Now I have to take care of you. Maybe a plastic garbage bag over your head. Dying won't take long. Move you into an empty room for someone to find. Old people die all the time. Probably won't even do an autopsy."

"Detective Johnson will never be fooled by you. He knows we're on the case."

"Yeah, a delusional old lady. And her mangy poodle. Ha!"

Before she could take another step closer, Gaston hurtled himself at her feet. Kristin tried to spray him in the eyes, but he dodged the stream of solution and circled around her barking frantically. She twisted her body to attack him again, spritzing and missing. Gaston darted and pivoted, leading her in a clumsy dance.

Sandra grasped her Medi-Alert pendant and pressed hard.

A sweet voice rang out, "Hello, Sandra. This is Susan. How may I help?"

"I'm being attacked at CHAW. Jake Bender's killer. In the yoga studio, second floor. Please send for help."

"What the hell do you think you're doing?" Kristin turned her attention to Sandra. She dropped the bottle and shouted at the alert device. "Don't listen to her. She's off her rocker."

Susan cried, "The EMTs are on their way. I'm dialing the police next. Hang on, Sandra."

"You got it all wrong. I'm the one being attacked by her vicious dog."

Kristin made a grab for the pendant. "Give me that."

Gaston leapt from behind, hit her square behind her legs, and knocked her down. He dashed over to Sandra to guard her, teeth bared, with a snarl as threatening as any Doberman. The murderer scrambled to her feet but the floor was so slippery she plummeted to her knees. She desperately crawled toward the sleuths.

"Don't rat me out," she begged. "I rid the world of two scumbags. I should get a medal."

"It wasn't for you to judge, to take matters in your own hands. That's why we have a justice system. You have to let the police do their jobs."

Outside the window sirens blared. Footsteps thundered down the hallway. Two burly EMTs burst into the room, followed by a patrolman. They surveyed the trio, Gaston still growling at the fallen woman.

"Where's the killer?" the cop asked.

Sandra pointed to Kristin, by now using a supply cabinet to pull herself up. Her jeans were soaked with the cleaning fluid. "It's her. She killed Marco in the stairwell. I recognized the smell from his body. Wintergreen. She sprayed him in the face and pushed him to his death."

'I didn't do it. She's a lunatic," Kristin protested.

An EMT said, "Is that the vicious dog? He's a service dog. Doesn't look very ferocious."

Sandra boasted, "He's a famous dog detective. He helped solve the poisoned pie murder. Ask Detective Johnson."

"I don't need to ask him. He's right behind you."

Sandra turned. Detective Johnson pushed the cleaning cart aside and entered the room. With fists on his hips, he glowered at the mess.

"Ask me what?" he thundered.

Gaston barked at the policeman and wagged his tail so hard his rear end shook.

"Detective Johnson, I'm so happy to see you!" Sandra pointed an accusing finger at Kristin. "This woman just confessed to the two murders at CHAW. Check out the solution in the bottle. It will match the chemicals on Marco's body."

"Did you learn forensics in your detective handbook, too?" he said wryly.

He jerked his thumb at Kristin and ordered the patrolman. "Cuff her and take her down to the station for booking. I'll handle the witness here."

For the second time in three days, Sandra heard the Miranda Rights delivered to an accused killer. With an arched eyebrow, she faced Detective Johnson with a sardonic smile. "I'll be happy to lend you my Private Detective Handbook."

CHAPTER THIRTY-FOUR

When the realization hit Sandra that her next overnight stay was almost the county morgue, she grew weak-kneed. Adrenaline flowed throughout the aftermath of Kristin's arrest. Detective Johnson's matter-of-fact interview in the CHAW office kept her grounded and professional in her account of the young woman's actions and confession. However, when Norm opened the passenger side door for her, she collapsed into the seat. Gaston climbed on her lap and licked her face. Only then did tears start to flow.

"Kristin threatened to kill me.' she sobbed. "Put a plastic bag over my head. Make it look like natural causes. I can't believe she'd do something so evil. If not for Gaston…"

Norm reached over from the driver's side and covered her cold hand with his warm one. He gently rubbed the surface, trying to bring some warmth into her icy fingers. "There. There. Gaston protected ya, just like I knew he would. Yer safe now. Besides, ya prob'ly had a few tricks from the detective handbook up yer sleeve. That girl had no idea who she was tangling with."

"It's true." She wiped her eyes and blew her nose. "I did have a few self-defense moves I've been dying to try. Like stomping on the attacker's instep. A knee to the groin. Or a thumb in the eye. But she never got close enough, thanks to Gaston."

"Whaddaya say we cruise to Collins' Dairy for a hot fudge sundae? Ice cream to soothe the soul. I'll get vanilla and let Gaston lick the dish."

Gaston yipped in agreement.

It was a beautiful day for an arraignment. Feathery white clouds tickled the bright blue sky. Vlad and Beatrice took the afternoon off from work to escort Sandra to Arthur's proceedings. Norm and Gaston trekked along the Interurban Bike Trail without the Service Dog disguise. They all agreed to meet at the Rose Grotto for supper.

The county courtroom was filled with onlookers as an unrepentant Arthur was ushered in, accompanied by his smartly dressed female lawyer. In his navy tailored suit with a red tie, he looked ready to take the debate stage in a presidential primary. Shoulders back and chin held high, the only sign of weakness was a slight twitch in his eye as he faced the judge. He answered in a clear "not guilty" when asked how he pleaded to the charges of financial and identity fraud.

"What are the arguments regarding bail?" the judge asked, fixing Arthur's poised young lawyer with a jaded stare.

She answered in a ringing voice, "I recommend Mr. Ashenbrenner be remanded on his own recognizance. He has a clean record. He's never been charged with any crimes before this."

The district attorney lunged to his feet. "Mr. Ashenbrenner is clearly a flight risk, your honor," he declared firmly. "The defendant has no family in the venue, no job or other local contacts that would compel him to stay around." He turned to glare at Arthur for a moment before addressing the judge. "He assumed several aliases with bank accounts in those names. The defendant has a history of disappearing when his victims attempted to reclaim money owed to them. There's no guarantee he'll appear for the trial."

The judge studied the paperwork before him, then answered. "I agree. I'm setting cash bail at two hundred thousand dollars." He slammed the gavel down. "The defendant may commit no crimes. He shall have no contact with the victims. Additionally, he must turn in his passport. Should the defendant violate one or more terms of his recognizance, he will be arrested."

Much to Vlad's surprise, Shirley Pritchard stepped forward. "I'll post his bail. We're engaged to be married. I'll vouch for his appearance in court."

Arthur flashed a toothy smile at her before he solemnly faced the judge, who spoke again to the clerk on his left. "Bailiff, file the paperwork for this man. If cash bail is posted, the defendant is free until trial, as long as he complies with the other conditions of my order."

As Arthur swept out of the courtroom, he gave a triumphant smirk as he passed Sandra, Vlad, and Beatrice. Shirley Pritchard narrowed her eyes into a glare that would kill at ten feet if only she remembered to charge her death ray glasses. Vlad broke out in a cold sweat when he recalled how she menacingly wielded the heavy picture frame when they last met. He hoped Arthur realized she was not a woman to trifle with.

Sandra rose and grabbed the purple blazer neatly folded on the seat beside her. No drab brown today. She slipped it on and smiled at her companions.

"That was easier to witness than I thought it would be. I hope I'm called to testify. I saved all his emails and love notes. Shirley Pritchard is in for a rude awakening at the trial when she finds out her fiancé is a liar and a con artist."

Vlad glanced at his watch. "We still have an hour before we meet Norm. What would you like to do?"

"Let's drive down to Riverview Park and walk over to the island. I could use some fresh air. I'm going to call Norm and have him bring Gaston to meet us there."

A FEW MALLARD DUCKS LINGERED on the edge of the river. Large signs warned park visitors not to feed them so they would migrate south. Apparently, the ducks hadn't read the sign. A curtain of gold-green leaves from the willow trees rippled in the September breeze. As they crossed over the footbridge leading to a small island, Sandra paused to gaze at the shimmering reflection of the trees in the water. Gaston also stopped. He hadn't left her side the whole time they meandered through the park, not even to tease the ducks.

"How's your new cat doing?" Sandra asked Vlad.

"She's so happy to see me when I come home, but I'm gone so much. I feel guilty."

Beatrice added, "She is so affectionate and a little needy."

"I introduced her to the kids. Love at first sight." Vlad chuckled. "They're begging Maria to let them bring her to the house. I think they're wearing her down. Erin showed her a picture of Cocoa on her phone. Even my uncooperative ex had to admit she's adorable."

"Kids can be pretty persuasive when they all gang up on a parent." Beatrice smiled. "They have your number for sure."

"Are ya sleeping better, Doc?" Norm asked. "Having a cat in the place prob'ly don't help."

Vlad looked into the distance before answering, "It's not the cat. It's me. I've seen too much evil. I can't deal with the memories of the dead." He vigorously shook his head. "I don't want to talk about it. Please don't spoil the day."

"Where do bad rainbows go?" Norm popped in.

"I haven't a clue," Vlad replied.

"Prisms. It's a light sentence and gives them time to reflect."

Gaston barked as the others groaned. "Did ya like that one, little buddy?" Norm patted the dog's head. "You appreciate Uncle Norm's sense of humor."

The gang of sleuths reached the gazebo at the center of the island. The rose bushes surrounding it still had a few late blooms. Bees buzzed loudly as they swarmed from blossom to blossom in the warm September sun. Throughout the summer newlyweds pledged their undying love to each other under the gleaming copper tiles of the octagon roof. Today the island was deserted except for them.

As they settled onto the wooden park benches to warm their faces in the sun, a companionable silence settled over the group. Gaston hunkered down at Sandra's feet and crossed his front paws in a pose so Zen that Vlad half expected him to produce a dog version of "o-o-om."

"I was wrong about karma," Sandra broke the stillness. "Nothing happens by chance. You create your own fate by your actions. Life is like a boomerang. What you give, you get back. Jake Bender acted hatefully; he got hate back."

"Arthur will get his comeuppance, too," Beatrice said, patting her hand.

"One can only hope." She let out a huge sigh. "Yesterday I wrote Kristin that I forgave her."

"You what?' Vlad said incredulously. "She tried to kill you."

"I wronged her first with my deception. I won't give in to hate, like she did. I refuse to dwell on her evil words. I choose love and grace. I let go of all the dark thoughts and self-recriminations. Karma will take care of what is meant to be."

Beatrice smiled kindly. "I admire your spirit of forgiveness."

"Time to move on." Sandra waved her hands in the air like a revival preacher. "Hallelujah! No more pickleball games. No more nearly dead butt cheeks from sitting on cold metal bleachers. The only kitchen I want to see is the one preparing Gaston's and my steak dinners." She lowered her voice to a confidential tone. "You know Detective Johnson admitted he owes us one for solving his murder case."

"When that cop said he had a beef, I'm not sure he was talking about making you dinner," Norm said with a wink.

Sandra flashed him a steely look as she opened her mouth to argue.

Vlad interrupted before she could speak. "Never mind what the detective said. How about a burger at the Rose Grotto? My treat."

When he heard the word "burger," Gaston scrambled to his feet and started barking.

"There's your answer, Doc," Norm laughed. "The famous dog detective has spoken. Let's go."

ACKNOWLEDGMENTS

After finishing a book there are many people to thank so I apologize if I have forgotten anyone. First, I'd like to thank my readers. If you've enjoyed this book enough to read the acknowledgments, your enthusiasm is much appreciated. Many of my local followers asked, "When is your next book coming out?" They gave me motivation to cross the finish line.

Thanks to Karen Hodges Miller, Editor Extraordinaire, for her wisdom and patience, especially when technology grabs me by the throat and leaves me whimpering. Karen is always there to fix things, like those mysterious black dots multiplying at the end of several chapters.

Thanks to the talented authors of both my writers' groups. To my Zoom Group, Sherri A. Lynn, Wendy Loos, Jack Saarela, and Karen, our facilitator: Your sharp eyes and thoughtful comments were a lifeline when characters and subplots got muddled. Of course, my hometown group has been with me from the start. Four books and two unpublished manuscripts later, I'm still writing, due to your support: Fran Milburn, Paul Marose, Bruce Benz, Kay Ferguson, and John Ashenbrenner, who let me borrow his last name for the scam artist, Arthur.

Thank you. Vivian Fransen, for your proofreading talent. My terrible typing needs your help.

Eric Labacz, you always capture the humor and quirkiness with your wonderful covers. I appreciate your artistic genius.

My daughter, Megan, a very talented editor and producer of podcasts, took time from wedding planning and pregnancy to read my book. Her suggestions for sharpening my prose were spot-on.

Joyce and Robert Herald, you will find echoes of your darling dog, Emma, in Gaston—only the good parts. Thank you for spending time with us in Arizona and letting me study your pooch.

Most of all, I thank my loving, supportive husband for his great coffee early in the morning, his even better Manhattans after a hard day, and especially his patience when my "just a minute while I finish this thought" turns into two hours.

ABOUT THE AUTHOR

Janice Detrie enjoys writing Gaston the Poodle mysteries—this is her fourth! A retired literacy coordinator, she loves reading a variety of books, especially a good cozy mystery. Most days she can be found seated at her computer, writing or procrastinating about writing. Her hobbies include making jewelry, Zumba-ing, shopping at thrift stores, and anything that gets her away from housework. She has two children and three grandchildren including a new grandbaby. Janice lives with her husband in Watertown, Wisconsin, which bears a strong resemblance to the fictional Crawford.

You can find her on BookBub, Amazon, Facebook, and Goodreads. To read her blogs and see an interview, visit her website at janicedetrie.com.